Praise for Thomas Kies

Random Road
The First Geneva Chase Crime Reporter Mystery

A *Library Journal* Book of the Month

"Kies's debut mystery introduces a reporter with a compelling voice, a damaged woman who recounts her own bittersweet story as she hunts down clues. This suspenseful story will appeal to readers who enjoy hard-nosed investigative reporters such as Brad Parks's Carter Ross."

—*Library Journal*, Starred Review

"Kies tells a taut, fast-paced tale, imbuing each character with memorable, compelling traits that help readers connect with them."

—*Booklist*

"Kies's fiction debut lays the groundwork for an entertaining series."

—*Kirkus Reviews*

"Noir for the modern day, *Random Road* is an impressive debut that offers a mystery that will keep readers guessing until the final pages."

—*Mystery and Suspense Magazine*

Darkness Lane
The Second Geneva Chase Crime Reporter Mystery

"Multiple murders and shocking twists are key components in Geneva's ultimate uncovering of the truth. The flawed but dedicated heroine anchors Kies's second mystery with a compassion that compels readers to root for both justice and redemption."
—*Kirkus Reviews*

"Kies neatly balances breathless action with Geneva Chase's introspection and sleuthing savvy."
—*Publishers Weekly*

"There's a solid thriller here—the key is sex trafficking—but the real pleasure is watching Geneva work. Cheer her on as she wrestles with that vodka bottle and trembles with fear as she confronts the monster behind the child-slavery ring. She's also pretty good at standing up to a newspaper publisher about to screw the help into the ground."
—*Booklist*

Graveyard Bay
The Third Geneva Chase Crime Reporter Mystery

"Journalism may be changing, but investigative reporters like Geneva Chase will always find the truth. *Graveyard Bay* is a tense, razor-sharp hunt for some genuinely terrifying criminals, set in a vivid and believable New England winter."
—Joseph Finder, *New York Times* bestselling author of *Judgment*

"When it comes to gritty real-life plots, believable characters, and on-point descriptions of both people and place, Thomas Kies can't be beat."

—*New York Journal of Books*

Shadow Hill
The Fourth Geneva Chase Crime Reporter Mystery

"Kies follows a traditional path of multiple interviews peppered with Geneva's everyday problems; his crisp character portraits keep it all interesting. Kies's fourth is sleek and engaging. If you miss Kinsey Millhone, you might give Geneva a whirl."

—*Kirkus Reviews*

"Complex characters and brisk plotting make this a winner. Readers will look forward to Geneva's further adventures."

—*Publishers Weekly*

Also by Thomas Kies

The Geneva Chase Crime Reporter Mysteries
Random Road
Darkness Lane
Graveyard Bay
Shadow Hill

WHISPER ROOM

WHISPER ROOM

A GENEVA CHASE CRIME REPORTER MYSTERY

THOMAS KIES

Poisoned Pen
PRESS

Published by Poisoned Pen Press, an imprint of Sourcebooks
P.O. Box 4410, Naperville, Illinois 60567-4410
(630) 961-3900
sourcebooks.com

Library of Congress Cataloging-in-Publication Data

Names: Kies, Thomas, author.
Title: Whisper room : a Geneva Chase crime reporter mystery / Thomas Kies.
Description: Naperville, Illinois : Poisoned Pen Press, [2022] | Series:
  Geneva Chase crime reporter mysteries ; book 5
Identifiers: LCCN 2021042361 (print) | LCCN 2021042362
(ebook) | (trade paperback) | (epub)
Subjects: GSAFD: Mystery fiction.
Classification: LCC PS3611.I3993 W48 2022 (print) | LCC PS3611.I3993
  (ebook) | DDC 813/.6--dc23
LC record available at https://lccn.loc.gov/2021042361
LC ebook record available at https://lccn.loc.gov/2021042362

Printed and bound in the United States of America.
VP 10 9 8 7 6 5 4 3 2 1

Chapter One

We waited for the deafening thunder of flash grenades, the sickening barrage of gunshots, and the possible outcome that both hostage and hostage-taker were dead. I don't know about the others in our small crowd of reporters, but I'd seen and heard it before. My name is Geneva Chase, and I've been a crime journalist for nearly twenty years, working for four newspapers, three magazines, and a half dozen websites. More often than not, when a man with a gun holds someone hostage in a standoff with police, it ends badly.

Nerves get frayed, fatigue sets in, mistakes are made, testosterone takes over. People die.

On that particular night, fear and expectation hung in the air, mixing with the heavy fog that wrapped around us like a wet towel. It was the kind of damp that makes your clothes cling to your skin.

I elbowed my way through the pack of reporters, television crews, and curious neighbors until I got to the police barriers blocking the cul-de-sac.

The cops had separated the curious crowd from the potentially dangerous scene with yellow-and-white plastic sawhorses and mustard-colored police tape. Beyond that, vague shapes were hiding in the mist. I could see the usually quiet country road was blocked off by dozens of police cruisers and EMS vehicles. Blue and white flashing lights intermittently lit up the dark-gray murk surrounding us.

The only sounds I heard were low murmuring voices from some of the TV journalists as they talked into their microphones or cell phones, reporting live on social media channels. Collectively, we were all as quiet as possible in anticipation of the carnage that might lay ahead.

Being slightly claustrophobic, the combination of the fog and being pressed so tightly against other people made my chest tighten. Drawing in deep breaths, I peered through the misty curtain, wondering how it was all unfolding.

The worst one of these I'd seen was when a husband held his wife and three children hostage back when I was in Boston. The standoff lasted for six hours. Finally, the cops decided that the husband had become too unhinged to negotiate with and they rushed the family's house. There were flash-bang grenades, followed by a flurry of gunfire. Both the husband and wife were killed as was one of the children. Three cops were wounded.

It was determined that the husband had shot his wife and then killed himself.

The child that was killed? "Friendly fire."

Honestly, it would have saved a lot of time and lives if the husband had just shot himself first.

Barely visible, farther up the road, was the fuzzy outline of the massive SWAT armored vehicle. I couldn't see them, but I knew there was a small army of men in black uniforms, night-vision goggles, and high-powered rifles skulking in the darkness.

The cop standing in front of me on the other side of the barrier was wearing the standard uniform for the Sheffield Police

Department. Officer Paul Bartolo was a beat cop I knew well from my crime reporter days with the *Sheffield Post*.

Startled to see me, he leaned over the barrier. His voice was barely more than a whisper. "Miss Chase, I heard you weren't with the newspaper anymore."

"I'm working freelance these days. The editor from the *Post* called and asked if I'd cover this one for her."

After working on some major metro newspapers, I eventually ended up at the *Sheffield Post*, my hometown newspaper. It was my last stop. I had a drinking problem and it cost me every other job I'd had. The only news outlet in the world that would give me one last chance was the *Sheffield Post*, and I came damned close to blowing that as well.

Even worse, last Christmas I'd downed a couple of drinks while on the job and made a mistake that almost got me killed. I've been sober since then. Nearly three and a half months.

Hardest thing I've ever done.

I'd left the newspaper almost four months ago. Most of my income now came from a company called Lodestar Analytics, primarily doing corporate and political background checks. Boring as hell but the pay was good.

And once in a while, the company's owner, Nathaniel Rubin, throws me a bone and I get to play detective. Only it doesn't say I'm a detective on my business card. Instead, it says I'm a research analyst. It makes me feel a little like a sexy scientist.

Officer Bartolo craned his neck and peered into the fog behind him. Like the rest of us, he was waiting for it all to go to hell. He was in his fifties, about five-seven, a little shorter than me, and was carrying an extra twenty pounds that spilled over his duty belt. I whispered, "What can you tell me about what's going on?"

He shook his head. "Not much, Miss Chase. All I know is that it's a hostage situation. You probably know more than I do."

All I really knew was what the *Post* editor, Laura Ostrowski, had told me about a half hour ago while I was eating dinner with my sixteen-year-old ward, Caroline Bell. In midbite of eggplant Parmesan, my cell phone buzzed.

Seeing the caller ID, I answered. "Laura?"

"Genie. Can you fill in on the crime beat tonight?"

"Where's Colby Jones?"

She sounded like she was teetering on her last nerve. "Probably piss drunk in some bar."

Back in the day, when Colby and I were both at the *Boston Globe*, he could drink me under the table, and that's saying something. He'd ended up at the *Sheffield Post* just like I had a few years earlier. No one else in the world would hire him.

I mused that the *Post* could probably host its own AA chapter.

"Sure. What's the deal?"

"Do you know who Elliot Carlson is?"

I certainly did. He was the smarmy six o'clock news anchor for our local NBC affiliate. Carlson was in his late forties, a television pretty boy, and a self-centered, smug son of a bitch with a deep voice and a commanding stage presence. About a year ago, we were both at the trial of Laura Fleming, a reality television star who'd been arrested for physically attacking an Uber driver, knocking out three teeth and leaving deep scratches on the man's neck.

A week into the trial, it become a media circus for the showboating defense attorney and the overly aggressive prosecutor looking to make a name for himself.

Usually a desk jockey, Elliot Carlson was there in person because that kind of freak show boosted ratings. When Fleming copped to a plea deal and the trial wrapped up, I started to walk out of the courtroom when, in his loud announcer's voice, Elliot proclaimed, "Tell all my friends at the *Pennysaver* that I send my best."

For someone working at a daily newspaper, having that paper called a *Pennysaver* was an insult akin to someone calling your mama fat. A *Pennysaver* is a free mailer that's mostly advertisements for lawn-mowing, snowplowing, or selling used cars. There's no news content in a *Pennysaver*.

I stopped where I was and in my own loud voice, I answered, "I would, but you've got no friends, asshole."

Weak, I know. But it was all I could come up with.

And since that was last year, I can pretty much guarantee I was buzzed at the time. I hated sitting on those hard wooden courtroom benches without having a couple of vodka and tonics beforehand.

I answered Laura's question. "Yeah, I know who Elliot Carlson is."

"It just came over the scanner. His wife called the cops. He's got a gun, and he's barricaded them both in their house, and he's holding her hostage."

I gasped. "Holy crap. Give me the address."

———

So, when Officer Bartolo couldn't give me any information, I played my ace in the hole to get out in front of the other reporters covering this story. And trust me, when a news celebrity, even a low-level one like Carlson, gets into this kind of trouble, it attracts a lot of attention from media.

We love to eat our own.

I texted the assistant chief of the Sheffield Police Department, Mike Dillon. Mike and I have a history. The love of my life, Kevin Bell, died about two years ago, and Mike's wife left him about the same time. For a little while, we found solace in each other's arms. He thought we were lovers. I thought we were friends with infrequent benefits.

When I wouldn't make a commitment, he ended our

relationship, such as it was, and took up with a much younger woman. She was pretty, bright, and owned a successful real estate company. Those were all bullet points on the plus side.

But I suspected that she knew her biological clock was ticking and wanted children. Mike already had a son, so making babies wasn't on his bucket list.

Mike and I had remained friends, and I suspected he might harbor a glimmer of guilt for breaking up with me.

I wouldn't hesitate to use that.

Even though I knew Mike was on the scene, and I knew it was wrong, I texted him: What's going on?

As I visualized him contending with a life-and-death situation as well as keeping a leash on the SWAT team, the text I sent felt selfish. I harbored no illusions that he would text back any time soon. So I was shocked when almost immediately, he responded. He's under arrest. Coming out to make a statement to the press. Talk later?

That made me smile. I texted back: You bet.

I heard an odd murmur behind me as others somehow got the word that the hostage situation had come to a successful conclusion.

One of the reporters said, "It's over, thank God."

Another talked into her phone, "Elliot Carlson has been taken into custody."

One of them, a reporter from the *Bridgeport News*, who was standing right next to me, stage-whispered, "Well, this turned out to be a bust."

In one aspect, he was right. If it bleeds, it leads.

There had been no bloodshed.

But in another, Elliot Carlson, big shot anchorman taking his wife hostage was a novelty item. One we could chew over for days. The readers would love it.

Chapter Two

When I saw Mike emerge from the fog and stride up to the police barrier in his uniform, my heart gave a faint, but noticeable, flutter. He's a good-looking guy, tall with ruggedly handsome facial features, a slightly receding hairline, and dark-brown, predatory eyes, a little like a wolf's. Yeah, I still had feelings for him.

He was accompanied by Captain Dick Belsky, who headed up the city's SWAT team. Belsky is in his fifties and prematurely gray, with deep ravines around his eyes and mouth that betrayed the high stress of a cop's life.

Both Mike and Belsky were still wearing their black bullet-proof vests, except instead of wearing the traditional cop uniform that Mike had on, Belsky was in a black combat jumpsuit.

Mike came up to the barrier, and the crowd went silent. When Mike spoke, he didn't need a microphone; his voice was clear and filled with authority. "At seven fifteen, we received a phone call from Michelle Carlson, who said she was locked in an upstairs bathroom, hiding from her husband, Elliot Carlson, who had a rifle and was threatening to kill both her and himself.

"The police negotiation team successfully persuaded Mr.

Carlson to put down his weapon and come out of the house at eight thirty-two. No shots were fired. Needless to say, this has been a traumatic event, but I want to emphasize that Mrs. Carlson is safe. In an abundance of caution, she's being checked by emergency medical personnel. Now, I'm going to refer any questions you may have to Captain Belsky, who headed up the negotiation team responsible for the safe ending to what could have been a violent evening. Thank you."

As others were peppering the SWAT team officer with questions, Mike turned and texted: Want to get a pic of the crime scene?

I almost giggled. Once again, I answered: R U kidding?

You can't tell anyone I let you do this.

I swear.

Then to my absolute delight, he turned back around and held up the police tape, gesturing for me to follow him.

I glanced back at the other reporters, hoping for expressions of jealousy and surprise. But the press horde was too busy trying to squeeze a juicy quote from Belsky to see me limbo under the police perimeter tape.

As we walked away, I heard them throwing questions at Belsky: "Did this have anything to do with the video?"

"Was this the result of the video?"

"Did the video drive him to take his wife hostage?"

I panicked. Every single reporter behind me in the fog knew more than I did.

What video?

As we walked, the crowd behind us disappeared in the gauzy mist. I asked Mike my own question. "What are they talking about? What video?"

He nodded. "I'll tell you when I meet you at Bricks for a drink."

"You know that I don't drink anymore."

"Then come watch me drink."

He knew that I'd quit, but I don't think he quite believed it. When we were dating, I was still quite the boozer.

We walked past the military-style SWAT vehicle and officers loading their equipment until we got to the driveway of a two-story colonial-style home with a broad front lawn and, near as I could tell through the fog, beautiful landscaping.

Dead ahead of us was a police cruiser, one of the few without the blues and whites flashing into the darkness. The dome light inside the car was on, and I could see there was someone in the back seat.

As we got closer, I saw Elliot Carlson, hands cuffed behind him. Instead of being perfectly groomed, his dark hair was tousled, and from the puffiness of his face, it appeared that he'd been crying.

"Can I go inside to take some pics?"

"Sorry, Genie. You'll have to be satisfied with taking some shots of the outside of the house."

In the fog, any shots of the house would be useless. I had a thought. "Any chance I can take a pic of Carlson?"

Mike glanced around to see if anyone was looking. "I'm going to check inside for a moment. I can't control what you reporters do when I'm not around. You can find your way back on your own?"

"Why you bein' so good to me, Mike?"

He stared for a second at the man in the back of the cruiser. "Carlson took some cheap shots at me last year on one of his broadcasts. Said my department was guilty of racial profiling. Payback's a bitch."

I smiled at him. "Bricks around ten?"

He grinned back. I could tell by the fatigue on his face that this hostage situation had been stressful. "I'll text you if I'll be later than that."

After he went up the steps to the front door and went in, I took the tiny digital camera out of the oversized bag I had hanging from my shoulder and crouched down to take a couple of shots through the window.

I got off two before Elliot saw me and turned to face the other direction.

Elliot Carlson handcuffed in the back seat of the police cruiser reminded me of the time I'd been arrested a couple of years ago for hitting a cop in a bar.

My career had survived. Barely.

I wondered if Carlson's would.

I smiled.

Pennysaver, my ass.

Chapter Three

It was shortly before nine when I called Laura Ostrowski to let her know I was on my way into the office. I wanted to knock out the piece about Elliot and Michelle Carlson in the *Sheffield Post* newsroom. I could have done it from my kitchen table and emailed it to her, but there's a certain comfort level I have when I'm in the newsroom. "Have you guys changed the code for the back door since I left?"

"No. Do you remember what it is?" She answered in her typical dry, sarcastic tone of voice.

Yeah, it's one-one-one-one.

"Hey, I've got a photo of Carlson in the back of a squad car."

"No shit?"

"Straight up. Exclusive."

"How's the bastard look?"

"Like crap."

"Get your butt in here, girl."

I knew that since the cutbacks, Laura worked insane hours. The *Post* had lost reporters and editors through attrition, and they weren't being replaced. More and more work was falling into fewer hands.

Newspapers are the dinosaurs of the twenty-first century—vestiges of a bygone era trying to keep up with twenty-four/seven internet news sites, losing readers to social media platforms. The old gray ladies were slowly dying.

I was terrified that good journalism was dying along with them.

The moment I walked into the dark newsroom, I felt like I was home. The mismatched desks and chairs, the stacks of newspapers and magazines on the coffee-stained, threadbare carpeting, and file folders stuffed with clippings and notes piled on the desktops were comforting. The computers with their moving screen savers bathed the room in flickering ghostly illumination.

Laura Ostrowski was sitting in her glassed-in cube, desk lamp on, the light from her laptop reflecting on her glasses. She glanced up at me as I walked through the newsroom. Involuntarily, she smiled.

Smiles didn't come easily to her. She'd been in the business all of her life, and her tired eyes and prison pallor were her reward. Laura had borne witness to some of the most exciting news stories in the last thirty years. But now she was watching it all slowly die.

When I'd started, working for newspapers was sheer joy for me. Now it was a business model gone bad, requiring cuts in production staff, cuts in reporters, reduced number of pages. I knew that Laura was counting the days before she retired, hoping the newspaper could stay afloat until she did.

One of the reasons I left the *Post* to go freelance was that Ben Sumner, the publisher, had come frighteningly close to selling the paper to a media conglomerate last Christmas. I'd met the corporate executives who would have become my bosses. They were soulless company zombies, unconcerned about how their purchase affected the community, focused purely on profits and not on employees.

When Ben discovered that an urban mall was being built right there in Sheffield, knowing it would be an advertising bonanza, he backed out of the deal, but not before an ambush of lawsuits slapped him in the wallet. He was in a litigation hell that he had little chance of winning.

I don't need that kind of chaos. I create my own.

I poked my head into Laura's cubicle. "Where can I knock out the piece on Elliot Carlson?"

"You can use Judie's computer. The password is *Outlander*."

I murmured to myself, "*Outlander*? Seriously?"

I noticed that Laura was streaming a news channel on her computer monitor.

She saw my line of sight and shrugged. "This hostage situation was tailor-made for television."

I recalled questions that Belsky had been asked. "They say anything about a video?"

Her eyebrows furrowed. "Only that all the broadcast stations apparently were sent a video of Elliot Carlson. Nobody is saying what's on it yet. But it doesn't sound like something that's going to get him a gig on the *Today* show. I've heard the word *salacious* multiple times."

It didn't take me long to hammer out the piece on the TV newsman gone nuts. All I had was a description of the crime scene, Mike's briefing, and a short bio on Carlson. It was all I could put together until I met Mike at Bricks.

Oh, and an exclusive photo of the perp in the cop car. There *was* that.

I hit the button to send the story to Laura's queue.

Once Laura gave it her blessing, she'd post it immediately online and then find room for it on the front page of the actual newspaper that would go to press at midnight. With a little luck, I'd get something juicy from Mike early enough that it would go both online and in the paper.

I glanced at the time on the computer screen, then turned my eyes to Laura, who I knew was reading over my copy. Finally, she gave me a thumbs-up, and I knew I could leave.

———

Bricks was an intimate pizza joint in South Sheffield with red brick walls, Tiffany-style hanging lamps, and red-and-white-checkered tablecloths. The air was filled with the pleasant scents of a woodburning oven, onions, tomato sauce, and garlic. It was primarily a take-out joint, so there were only ten tables in the dining area. If you were looking for a quiet place for an inexpensive date night, Bricks fit the profile.

The real attraction for me was the bar in the back. Away from the front windows, it was dark. In my drinking days, this used to be one of my favorite watering holes.

Mike was already there and had saved me a barstool. He noticed me in the mirror behind the bar and stood up to greet me with a kiss on the cheek. "Hell of a night, huh?"

I shrugged and sat down. The bartender came over and asked, "What will you have?"

By habit, I came damned close to ordering an Absolut and tonic. Instead, I told him, "Just a club soda and lemon, please."

Mike's eyebrows shot up. "You're serious this time."

There had been numerous times that I'd done my best to stay sober. The longest was for a year. It was right after my fiancé, Kevin, died. Before his death, he'd asked me to take care of his daughter if anything happened to him.

And then, tragically, it had.

At the time, Caroline Bell was thirteen, and I was suddenly in the mommy business. I felt I needed to stay sober for that.

But then the anniversary of Kevin's death rolled around, and

I threw it all into the crapper. I'd gone back to drinking with a vengeance.

So, what makes you think you can stay sober this time, Genie?

In spite of my own doubts, I answered, "Yeah, Mike. I'm pretty serious."

He picked up his bottle of Sam Adams and held it up in mock salute. "Good luck."

As the bartender placed my club soda on a coaster in front of me, I said, "So, what's the scoop on Elliot Carlson?"

He smiled. "This is off the record."

I hated it when he did that. But what I couldn't use from him as a source, I could use to independently track down the facts on my own. It still put me ahead of the other reporters out there. "Sure."

"According to Mr. Carlson, he was being blackmailed."

"By whom and for what?"

He took a swallow of his beer. "He claims it's an escort service called The Whisper Room. They have a video of him with a hooker in a hotel room. They claimed that if Carlson didn't pay them twenty-five thousand dollars, they'd release the video to his wife and the news media."

I shrugged. "A sex tape showing Carlson banging a hooker? In this day and age, that's not much to be blackmailed over anymore. We have politicians getting caught with more than that, and they're still in office."

"His wife showed me the video on her phone. It came with a message. It said the girl is only fifteen."

That took a dark turn, really fast.

"Let's stick a pin on the underage thing and come back to it in a minute. Carlson's wife showed you the video?"

"Apparently, Mr. Carlson called the blackmailers' bluff and refused to pay up. They sent the video to Mrs. Carlson and to Mr. Carlson's place of business."

"*WLTN News on Your Side* has a copy of the video?"

Mike took another swig of his beer, wiped his lips with a napkin, then answered, "And so do all the other broadcast news outlets in the tri-state area."

I put a hand up to my mouth. "No wonder there were so many news cameras out there tonight."

"I called the producer at WLTN, and she confirmed that a person or persons unknown sent them a copy of the video. She also told me that Mr. Carlson no longer is an employee of the company."

"Have you seen the video?"

"I have."

"Do you have a copy of the video?"

"Yes."

Sometimes he loved being obtuse. "May I have a copy of the video?"

There was the hint of a smile on his face. "Sure, but it won't come from me. It can't. It's evidence."

Dammit, every other news outlet has a copy of that video except me.

I glanced at my watch. It was time for the WLTN eleven o'clock news. I shouted at the bartender, "Hey, can you turn on the TV and flip to the news on Channel Seven?"

The young man picked up the remote and turned on the big-screen TV hanging on the wall above the corner of the bar. Immediately, I saw footage from where I'd been earlier in the evening. Blue and white flashing lights cut through the thick gauze of fog, the SWAT truck, and a thin, young brunette who looked to be barely out of high school was standing in front of the camera. "*Police confirmed that Elliot Carlson, anchor for WLTN's six o'clock news, has been arrested. Earlier this evening, in a standoff that lasted over an hour in which Mr. Carlson held his wife hostage, the Sheffield SWAT team was successful in talking Mr. Carlson into laying down his weapon and coming out of the house."*

Then the scene switched to a clip of Mike talking to reporters after the arrest.

Seeing himself on the big screen, Mike blushed crimson and glanced nervously around the nearly empty restaurant. The only diners there were a young couple out on a date and two women in business clothes who might have been working overtime and were grabbing a late dinner along with a couple of drinks.

Erin Frost, the young reporter speaking into the camera, reappeared with a serious expression. *"Police won't confirm that tonight's hostage-taking incident has anything to do with the video that WLTN received this afternoon. While we won't share the video at this time, it clearly shows Elliot Carlson in a compromising position with a female who might be underage. More to come on this story as it unfolds."*

So far, the station had shown uncharacteristic restraint. But I knew that within twenty-four hours, the video would be online and going viral.

After Erin Frost finished her piece on Carlson, Sonny Banks, the jovial weather guy came on camera to predict April showers in the morning. Seeing as his six o'clock news anchor had been arrested and the station humiliated, the weather guy was less jovial than usual. At the end of his forecast, he looked directly at the camera and stated somberly, *"While this station doesn't condone Elliot Carlson's behavior, we do wish his family well and send them our prayers."*

I asked the young bartender to switch the TV back off, and then I turned to Mike. "How did the evening get so out of hand at the Carlson household?"

"Once again, off the record. You can confirm this with Mrs. Carlson when you call her in the morning. She confronted her husband when he got home from work. She showed him the video on her phone and told him she was kicking his cheating ass out of the house."

Mike took another swallow of his beer. "Then she told him she was going take everything—the bank accounts, the cars, the house...she was going to leave him the way she found him. Poor and in the gutter.

"Mrs. Carlson said it got ugly after that. Screaming back and forth. The situation apparently escalated when she began throwing his clothes out of a second-story window onto the lawn. That's when her husband came into the bedroom with his rifle. She ran into the bathroom, locked the door, and called 911."

I drummed my fingernails against the wooden surface of the bar. "I've heard rumors about Carlson's temper."

Instead of saying anything more about Elliot Carlson, Mike switched gears. "So, are you still seeing that John Waters guy?"

He surprised the hell out of me. "John Stillwater?"

He snapped his fingers. "Stillwater. That's it. What is he, part Native American?"

I looked over at him. Mike had a lot of good qualities. He was handsome, brave, smart, and funny, but when the spirit moved him, he could be bitchy. I answered, not hiding the annoyance in my voice. "I don't know. I never asked."

"You still seeing him?"

I wondered why he was interested. "We see each other on occasion. You know, friends with benefits." I hoped that would sting a little. "Are you still seeing Vicki Smith, Girl Realtor?"

It was a not-so-subtle dig that she was much younger than Mike.

He shrugged. "The age difference keeps tripping us up."

I raised my eyebrows and gave him a "told you so" look.

He pursed his lips, then asked, "Any chance we might get back together again?"

Part of me was shocked, and part of me took his question as a compliment. I stood up, hung my bag over my shoulder, and gave him a coy smile. "Anything's possible. Call me sometime for dinner, and we'll see."

Walking out, I realized I could have given him a chance to make a date for dinner there and then while at the bar. But I hadn't.

I simply had no idea if I even wanted to see Mike again. At least in a nonprofessional setting.

While walking up the sidewalk to my car, I exhaled.

Genie, you don't know what the hell you want.

Chapter Four

By the time I got home, Caroline was already asleep. When I poked my head into her bedroom, there was enough light from the hallway that I could see her tucked under her blanket, her chest slowly moving up and down as she breathed.

Tucker, our Yorkshire terrier, slept alongside her and gave me little notice except for a brief side-eye.

Caroline is fifteen, going on sixteen in a couple of weeks. Although sometimes she acts like she's going on twenty. Why is it teenagers think they know more than the adults? I don't recall being that way when I was her age.

Of course, you were, Genie.

Caroline has golden hair and blue eyes like her father's. The older she gets, the prettier she is. I know that one of her classmates described her as the "hottest girl" in their class.

That worried me.

I quietly closed her door and went to my own bedroom. I shucked off my shoes, jewelry, and clothes and turned on the TCM channel. They were showing *Citizen Kane*.

For me, the hardest part of sobriety is at night. It's when I most want a stiff vodka tonic. It's when the monsters under the bed seem the most real.

I've discovered that a nice black-and-white movie with the sound turned low soothes the jangles in my nervous system and helps send me off to dreamland. When that doesn't work, meditation does—just emptying all the junk out of my mind.

I wasn't at the meditation portion of the evening yet. I just focused on Orson Welles.

Then I recalled what Mike had said about the text accompanying the video sent to Mrs. Carlson and all the broadcast news outlets in the area. It said that the girl in bed with Carlson was only fifteen.

The same age as Caroline.

———

The next morning, I crawled out of bed before Caroline woke up and went for a run down to the harbor and back under increasingly ominous skies. I trotted home, took a hot shower, meditated under the steaming spray, then fixed my face, brushed my hair, and went downstairs in my ratty bathrobe.

Caroline was already shoveling Cheerios and milk into her mouth with Tucker sitting off to one side, hoping she'd drop something. Swallowing, she managed to say, "What time did you get in last night?"

I filled the coffee carafe with water and poured it into the reservoir of my Mr. Coffee. "About eleven thirty or so. You were fast asleep."

"Soccer practice wiped me out."

"You got practice tonight?"

"Band practice."

Last year, Caroline had joined the band and was playing the trumpet like she was born for it. Her father and I had been childhood friends, and I couldn't recall him having any musical talent whatsoever. Maybe she got that from her deceased mom. I'd never met her, but if Kevin had fallen in love with her, and she'd been a good mother to Caroline, then she must have been a pretty good human being.

She'd died from cancer when Caroline was eleven. Then her dad died when she was thirteen. For a young lady who had gone through so much trauma, her head was on pretty straight. Most of the time.

Caroline reached down and gave Tucker a scratch behind the ear. "Can you pick us up after practice?"

Us meant Caroline and her best friend, Jessica Oberon.

"What time?"

"About four?"

"Sure." Jessica's two moms were usually terrific about ferrying the girls to school and back. If I needed to do it once in a while, it was a small price to pay. I asked, "When did riding the school bus become such a horrible thing?"

She rolled her eyes. "It is *so* not cool, Genie."

"And my picking you up is cool?"

"It's a lot cooler now that we don't have the Sebring."

I winced. The Sebring, as old and as beat up as it was, had been my faithful steed. And at the end, it had even saved my life.

After Caroline finished chewing another mouthful of cereal, she asked, "Did you sign the consent form?"

I gave her my *What the hell are you talking about?* face.

Seeing my confusion, she explained. "Driver's ed? I'll be sixteen in two weeks?"

"Oh, yeah. I'll sign it before you head off to school."

"I'm going to need some practice time beforehand. I don't want to get behind the wheel without having some experience driving. I'll look like some kind of dork."

I didn't like where this was heading. "Oh?"

She raised her eyebrows in anticipation. "I need to log a little practice time. You'll need to show me the basics."

Last February, my tried-and-true, eleven-year-old Chrysler Sebring had been totaled. The insurance company reluctantly sent me a small check, but at almost the same time, I'd received a very generous bonus from Nathaniel Rubin at Lodestar Analytics for an assignment I'd completed. I was able to put a few bucks into Caroline's college fund, buy some new shoes, and put a hefty down payment on the nicest car I've ever owned.

Caroline, being climate change–aware, wanted me to buy a Tesla. Definitely out of my price range. But a dear friend of mine, Shana Neese, who owned a small fleet of cars and had enough money to keep them garaged in downtown Manhattan, was selling her eight-year-old Lexus hybrid. It only had forty-thousand miles on it, got fifty miles to the gallon, had a pearl-white exterior, heated leather seats, and when you stepped on the gas, it ran like a jackrabbit on speed.

Oh…and it was a Lexus. Did I say that already?

Before I wrote Shana a check, I went online to see what a car like that was worth. She'd cut me a hell of a deal. Way below market value.

It is the best car I've ever owned in my entire life.

And Caroline is asking to drive it?

With some trepidation, I answered, "Sure. Maybe this weekend we'll go out to the industrial park so you can get a feel for it." While on the crime beat at the *Post*, I'd been out there investigating a meth lab in one of the warehouses. On Sundays, the place is essentially empty of traffic, a perfect place for a new driver.

A half hour after Caroline got a lift to school from one of Jessica's moms, my cell phone buzzed against the tabletop. "Yes?"

It was Laura Ostrowski, already in the office. "I got a call from someone who wants to talk to you. Michelle Carlson."

I was mildly surprised. I had planned to reach out to her after my system had the requisite amount of caffeine in it. "Is she pissed off about the piece I wrote last night? Or the photo of her husband in the back of the cop car?"

"Just the opposite. She's pissed off at the way the broadcast clowns are blowing it up. They've started showing clips from the video. The girl's face is blurred out and so are the nasty bits of Carlson's anatomy, but you can clearly see that it's Elliot Carlson. Mrs. Carlson said that the way you handled it was at least honest and straightforward. She wants you to interview her."

I whistled softly. "Well, how about that? Give me her phone number, and I'll set it up."

"Already done. Eleven o'clock. Can you make it?"

"Absolutely." I'd been there last night, along with a horde of newshounds, cops, and nosy neighbors.

I had some time to kill, so, recalling my conversation with Mike last night, I tried to track down an escort service called The Whisper Room. The only thing that popped up on my browser was a company that constructed and sold sound isolation booths.

Pretty sure that wasn't it.

I couldn't find any websites trafficking hookers under the name of The Whisper Room.

So, I punted. I called Shana Neese. I pictured her as I hit the Call button. In her thirties, tall, Black, athletic, with fierce brown eyes, full lips, sculpted cheekbones, she moved with the grace of a predatory cat.

Shana lives a dual life. She earns an extremely comfortable living as a professional dominatrix and owning an exclusive play space hidden in a four-story brownstone in downtown New York. She has nine women who work for her as paid dominants. Among the faux-dungeons were BDSM spaces including a schoolroom, dog kennel, doctor's office, and a special feminization room. All of them are outfitted with whips, chains, clamps, canes, and other BDSM paraphernalia.

Not my kind of thing, but apparently some people will pay big bucks to be spanked. Go figure.

The fourth floor of her building is her penthouse living quarters, complete with a beautifully appointed kitchen, two bedrooms, a fireplace, and Gerald, her live-in houseboy.

Hidden among the playrooms on the third floor is a special area where Shana works out and trains with her Israeli ex-pat ex-commando, Uri Tal. When she's not being a dominatrix, Shana heads up a discreet victim advocacy group called the Friends of Lydia. Working mostly in the shadows and on the fringes of legality, they rescue women who are being trafficked or abused. Sometimes, what she did got dangerous.

I've watched Shana train with Mr. Tal. She's supernaturally fast and vicious.

She is also my mentor, my advisor, and my Yoda. To keep me sober, she's been teaching me self-control over my mind and my body. If there is one person who knows control, it's Shana Neese.

"Geneva. What a nice surprise. How are you, dear?" She has a faint, dignified Southern accent and speaks as if savoring every word.

"Doing well. Look, I need to see if you've ever heard of an escort service called The Whisper Room."

"Why do you ask?"

"A man claims they were blackmailing him, and when he didn't pay up, they sent a video of him and a girl having sex to his wife and the news media."

"Are you talking about that news anchor in Connecticut who was arrested last night after a police standoff? Even the TV stations here in New York have picked up on it."

"Yes, and as an added bonus, the girl in the video might be underage."

There was a momentary silence. Then she said, "Yes, I know about The Whisper Room. I have a woman working for me who used to be an escort for them. She thinks that what we do here is much more lucrative."

"Do you know who runs The Whisper Room?"

"I don't, but if they're running underage girls, I'm damned well going to find out."

I had no doubt of that.

Shana added, "Bad for business."

"What's that? Running underage girls?"

"That's criminal. No, blackmailing your clients is bad for business. If that gets out, every client The Whisper Room has is going to be heading for the door."

So far, none of the news stories had mentioned The Whisper Room. They knew that someone was blackmailing Elliot, but they didn't know who. Once I got confirmation from Elliot Carlson's wife, I was going to write it up in a follow-up piece.

After that, the escort service would be all over the news.

"Oh, it's going to get out."

Chapter Five

In the subdued light of an overcast, slate-colored sky, I was able to get a better look at where Elliot and Michelle Carlson lived. When I'd been there the night before, the place was socked in with fog.

Before I left my kitchen, I'd done my homework and found that Elliot and Michelle Carlson didn't have children. In my opinion, that made their house much too big for just the two of them. At over thirty-five hundred square feet, it boasted three bedrooms, three bathrooms, two home offices, and a workout room. According to one real estate website, the home was worth slightly over a million dollars.

Does a local news anchor make that kind of money?

I pulled into the Carlson driveway and parked behind a black Range Rover. Another vehicle parked next to it was hidden under a silver car cover. I noticed they both sat in front of a two-car garage and wondered why they weren't parked inside.

The massive two-story colonial had a brick façade and plenty of windows. I tried to guess from which window Mrs. Carlson had thrown Elliot's things.

From the beautiful array of trees, plants, and bright flowers,

I surmised that the Carlsons had a landscaper. While studying the yard, I saw a small pile of men's clothing that presumably had been thrown onto the lawn near the far corner of the house and landed next to some bright yellow daffodils. Mystery solved.

Michelle Carlson opened the front door, dressed in black skinny jeans and a white oversized long-sleeved tee. "Are you the newspaper reporter?"

"I'm Geneva Chase. Michelle Carlson?"

"Come in." She sounded tired. I'm sure being held hostage had been emotionally, as well as physically, exhausting.

She closed the door behind me, and I followed her up four steps and into her spacious living room. It was appointed with an off-white fabric couch, two black leather recliners, hardwood floors covered in places by Oriental rugs, and a coffee table that held a glass vase filled with an explosion of colorful spring flowers. Vibrant, bright, modern-art paintings hung on the walls. Every item in the room seemed to perfectly complement the others. I wondered if Mrs. Carlson had done it herself or had a professional decorator.

Clearly out of place, a massive flat-screen television hung over the fireplace and dominated the room.

Michelle caught me staring at it. "Monstrous, isn't it?"

"Like bein' at the movie theater."

"Yeah, well, it's comin' down."

"Oh?"

"Elliot liked to sit in here and review video replays of his newscasts."

I noticed that she had said it in the past tense. "Liked?"

She nodded. "I'm not letting him anywhere near this house." Her brown eyes were bloodshot, probably from too little sleep and maybe too much wine. Michelle looked to be in her late forties and had the beginnings of age lines spider-webbing around her eyes and mouth. She wore her auburn hair stylishly short, the kind of cut that you can run your fingers through after getting out of bed and it looks like you just came from the salon. If she had any gray hair, her hairdresser had hidden it well.

"I understand," I replied.

There was a moment of awkwardness before she said, "Look, I was upstairs packing some things. I'm trying to stay busy. Would you mind if I did that while we talked?"

I smiled. "Not at all."

We climbed the stairs to the second floor, and I followed her down a short hallway to the master bedroom. On the comforter covering the king-sized bed were a suitcase and two cardboard boxes partially filled with clothing and toiletries.

I glanced around the room. Some of the framed photos on the walls were of Michelle and her husband posing in various locations around the world. Some were of Elliot, either in a tuxedo or suit and tie, receiving some award or emceeing some event.

Michelle gestured to an overstuffed chair in the corner of the room. "Make yourself comfortable."

I set my bag on the carpet and sat down while she stood in front of the bed, looking at the suitcase as if wondering what she should say or do next.

"You're packing Mr. Carlson's things," I said, stating the obvious.

"A judge has already issued a restraining order against Elliot. As far as I'm concerned, he'll never set foot in this house again." She looked me in the eye. "It's in my name, anyway."

"How did that come to be, Mrs. Carlson? Most couples have their home in both their names."

Her face registered an expression of disgust. "For all the face time he gets on TV, he doesn't make a lot of money."

I nodded in agreement. "Most journalists don't."

"Look, this marriage isn't my first time at the rodeo. Elliot is my second husband."

"I see." I've found that some of the best interviews happen when I listen more and ask fewer questions.

"When I was married the first time, I was twenty-one and still in college. The marriage only lasted five years. The one thing I learned from the divorce was to have as much in your own name as you can. It can leave you destitute if you don't."

I restated what she'd already told me. "So, Elliot Carlson is your second husband."

She didn't answer at first but went into what looked like one of two walk-in closets. When she came back out, she was holding a pair of slacks folded over a wooden hanger. "I met Elliot at a fund-raiser about fifteen years ago." She took the slacks off the hanger and dropped them into one of the boxes. "I'm an architect. I own Gold Coast Architectural Designs. Back then I was just getting the company off the ground, and exclusive Fairfield County fund-raisers were a good place to scare up clients. Clients with cash."

Fairfield County, Connecticut, is essentially a bedroom community for New York City. Wealthy towns like Greenwich, Westport, Darien, New Canaan, and Weston are where CEOs, actors, writers, sports superstars, and rock 'n' roll legends live, shop, and spend money. A lot of money. It appeared that Michelle Carlson had done well by them.

"That was where I connected with Elliot. When I met him, he didn't have a penny to his name. The only reason he was there that night was as the emcee. He did it to get a free meal." Michelle disappeared into the closet again and came back out with two shirts. "He struck me as being good-looking and charming, and he had ambition."

It was time to start taking control of the conversation. "So, how long after you met him did you get married?"

Michelle thought a moment. "It was about a year later. We took a long weekend and went to Block Island, stayed at a lovely little B&B that I paid for. That was where he got down on one knee and proposed."

"Sounds romantic."

"It was. I should have listened with my brain instead of my heart, though. I knew about his money situation, but he kept saying he was close to getting a network news job. He wanted to work in New York. That's when the big money would come in."

"Mrs. Carlson, why did you ask to speak to me?"

Slightly surprised by the change in conversational direction, she turned and studied me. "The other news outlets piled onto Elliot and me like rabid dogs. One thing about Elliot, he wanted to get ahead and didn't care if he made friends along the way or not. He's pissed off a lot of people in your line of work, Miss Chase."

"Please call me Genie. And, full disclosure, I was one of the journalists your husband pissed off."

She gave a head bob, apparently not surprised. "Call me Michelle. Anyway, you wrote a story that was straightforward and dispassionate. I want my side of the story made public, and I want someone who will do it right."

I offered up a small smile. "Fair enough. Can you tell me what happened last night?"

She took a deep breath and sat down on the corner of the bed. "It was while Elliot was in the studio doing the six o'clock news. I had the television on in the kitchen, watching the broadcast as I was making a quiche. My phone chimed. It does that to tell me I've gotten a text. When I took a look, this is what I saw."

Michelle pulled her cell phone out of her jeans pocket, swiped at something on the screen, then handed it to me. As I watched, a video played, complete with grunts, moans, and groans. It was clearly Elliot Carlson, naked and on his back, while a woman, also naked, straddled him.

It appeared that the video had been shot from slightly above them and maybe five feet away.

A hidden camera? Maybe from behind a two-way mirror?

As I watched, the girl and Elliot switched positions. She was on the bottom, and he was on top of her. The video then seemed to switch to a second camera that appeared to have been shot from an angle that best caught Elliot's face.

More than one camera in the room!

The girl was pretty, with long platinum hair, pouty lips, and wide azure eyes. Most of the time those eyes were closed. I'm not an expert, but she did look awfully young.

Yes, she looks like she might be Caroline's age.

I turned it off and handed the phone back to Michelle. Placing it on the bed, she said, "At the same time I got it, someone was sending it to all the news affiliates in Connecticut. Of course, I didn't know that then."

She nervously picked up the phone again, stared at the blank screen, then placed it back on the bed. "I glanced from that text to the television. At that singular moment, while Elliot was talking about lane closures on I-95, his career had died and so had our marriage."

I cleared my throat. "It must have been very upsetting."

She rolled her eyes. "Upsetting. I wanted to kill him. My first marriage ended when I caught my husband cheating on me. I thought Elliot was different."

"Why did you think that?"

Michelle chuckled. "Because he was so dependent on me. Or at least on my money. He has… What's the saying? He has champagne tastes but only makes beer money. He likes nice things, and I pay for them. That Porsche out in the driveway? I paid for that."

That must be what was under the silver cover. I nodded at the phone. "Looks like he had enough money for that, though." Meaning the hooker.

For a moment I thought she was going to spit on her cell phone. "Yeah, he had enough money to pay for an expensive whore."

That piqued my curiosity. "How do you know she's expensive? Or for that matter, that she's even a prostitute?"

Without answering my question, she said, "Before he left the studio last night, when the newscast was over, his producer showed him a copy of the tape that had showed up on her phone."

"I can only imagine the horror he must have felt when he saw that and realized what had just happened."

"Serves him right. When he came through the front door, he could hear the video playing in the kitchen. I had the volume turned up on my phone as high as it would go. Even though I was sitting at the kitchen table, I knew he'd stopped dead in his tracks in the living room trying to think of a way out of the mess he'd made."

"What did he say?"

She stood up and took one of Elliot's shirts off a hanger and started to fold it. Then she stopped. "He came into the kitchen and said that it wasn't what it looked like. Someone had photoshopped him into that video. That it was computer-generated. Then he admitted that someone had tried to blackmail him. But it wasn't him in the video."

She changed her mind about the shirt, wadded it up, and just dropped it into a box. Then she fixed me with her eyes. "And you know what, Genie? He told me this in that whiny voice of his that makes him sound like a victim."

I raised my eyebrows. "Did it work?"

Michelle gave me a scornful look. "Hardly. I asked him who

she was, the girl in the video. And was she really fifteen? There was a text that came with the video, Genie. It said that the girl's only fifteen."

Mike had already told me that, but I answered, "I don't know what to say."

She continued, "He had that deer-in-the-headlights look. He was quiet for a minute and then shook his head. He told me that the girl meant nothing to him. She was someone he ordered from an escort service."

I interjected. "Did he say it was something called The Whisper Room?"

"What? Yeah, Whisper Room. But he said that the people who ran the service didn't hire girls who were younger than nineteen. The girl just looked young."

I said, "I'm not sure that helped his case any, did it?"

She made that scornful look again. "No. I told him I wanted him out of my house and out of my life. He said he had every right to be there. That's when I came up here, opened the window, and started chucking his shit onto the lawn."

We both were silent for a moment. She took a breath. "When he came into the bedroom, I might have been a little hysterical because I remember screaming at the top of my lungs that I wanted him out of my house."

"Is that when he got his gun?"

"A rifle he bought last year *for protection*." She used her fingers to make air quotes. "Like he needed protection."

"Sounds pretty scary."

"I was freakin' terrified he was going to do something stupid. I ran into the bathroom and locked the door." She nodded to a doorway that I assumed was the bathroom. "After I was locked in, I looked down at my hand and saw that I was still clutching my cell phone. And you know what, Genie? That fucking video was still playing on it." She said it with a bitter laugh.

All I could do was shake my head.

She continued, "I called 911. Honestly, I was surprised how fast the cops came."

"What was Elliot doing?"

"Pleading with me. Begging me not to kick him out. That he'd learned his lesson. When he heard the sirens, he asked if I'd called the cops."

"What did you do then?"

"I told him I had. That's when he threatened to kill himself. I called 911 again. They told me to stay put. They said that SWAT was on the way."

I knew how this was going to play out. Michelle was right. The moment that video went to his studio, Elliot's career was over. But how would this affect Michelle Carlson's life? Would it affect her architectural firm?

"Michelle, how much of this do you really want me to put into my piece for the newspaper?"

"All of it." She sighed and then repeated, "All of it."

Chapter Six

I knocked out the Michelle-Carlson-Tells-All piece back in the *Post* newsroom using Judie's computer again. This time she was on the road covering a Wilton Gardening Club event, and hers was one of the few open desks in the office.

I was taking one last read-through before I sent it to Laura's queue when my cell phone rang. I saw it was Shana Neese and answered immediately. "Hey, Shana."

"I have the name of the woman who runs The Whisper Room."

I felt a tiny thrill and picked up a pen. "I'm ready."

"Her name's Stephanie Cumberland. I did some legwork for you. She's twenty-nine, never been arrested, and lives at 5B 148 Myers Drive, right there in Sheffield, Connecticut."

"Awesome. I think a visit is in order."

"One more bit of information that may or may not be pertinent."

"What's that?"

"She's the daughter of Joseph Cumberland, owner of Cumberland Custom Motorsports."

"Never heard of him or the company."

"Unless you have more money than you know what to do with and a raging midlife crisis, you wouldn't. They don't advertise. They don't have to. They sell every kind of expensive car you could possibly want. Maserati, Ferrari, Porsche, Jaguar, Rolls-Royce, Alfa Romeo. If they don't have what you want on the lot, they'll find it for you. If you want something special, they'll work with the manufacturer to have it custom-made."

Suddenly my sexy little Lexus felt low-rent. "Do you think Mr. Custom Motorsports knows what his daughter is up to?"

"I don't know. I just thought you might find that interesting. Who knows? Maybe it'll come in handy."

"How did you find all this out?"

"I told you. Brenda used to escort at The Whisper Room. Now she works for me and goes by the name of Mistress Scarlet."

That made me grin. "It suddenly occurs to me, Shana, that I never asked what you go by when you're working."

I could almost hear her smile over the phone. "Why, honey, everyone just calls me Goddess."

———

I sent the story over to Laura for her to edit. Then, fully expecting to go visit Stephanie Cumberland, I slung my bag over my shoulder and headed for the back door to the parking lot.

"Genie, wait a minute."

I turned around and saw Laura standing in the doorway of her cubicle with her cell phone pressed against her ear. Her face grim, she held up a single finger.

Against my better judgment, I slowly shuffled toward her.

Then she disconnected. "They found a body out in the sound, not far from Shea Island. They're bringing it in now. Can you cover this for me?"

"Still can't find Colby Jones?"

"I fired his ass when he came in with a raging hangover this morning." She gave me a defiant look. Laura had almost done the same with me about two years ago. "So, can you cover this for me?"

I glanced at my watch. It was almost two thirty, and I remembered that I needed to be at West High to pick up Caroline at four. I'd never hear the end of her whining if I was late. Doing some fast math in my head, I figured I had enough time. "Okay, but I may have to do the piece from my kitchen table."

"Not a problem. They're bringing the body by police boat to the dock in Columbus Park."

After a fifteen-minute drive through town to the harbor, I pulled into the parking lot and was greeted by half a dozen police cruisers, their lights all dramatically and uselessly flashing.

It was just beginning to rain as I got out of the car, so I zipped up my jacket and opened my UCONN Huskies umbrella. I saw EMTs roll a gurney carrying the body up from the dock to the back of a waiting ambulance. I knew they'd be taking it to Sheffield General Hospital, not for treatment, but to be stored in the morgue until the autopsy.

Mike Dillon emerged from a group of cops standing on the dock, apparently heading for his vehicle.

I got out of my car and trotted toward him. "Mike, hold up."

He glanced up, saw me, and stopped. He wasn't smiling. "Genie."

"Can you give me a statement? Was it a boating accident?"

He pulled a small notebook out of the pocket of his blue police windbreaker and flipped it open. "This is what we know for sure. Jane Doe, blond hair, blue eyes, wearing a black dress, the kind a woman might wear to a party. We think she's in her early twenties. Cause of death as of right now is unknown, but we suspect it's asphyxiation."

"Why?"

He looked away from his notebook and gazed out over the water. "Because when she was found, she had a plastic bag over her head, secured with a zip tie around her neck."

"Jesus, Mike. Any idea of the time of death?"

He shook his head. "No, but we think she's been in the water for at least twelve hours."

"Who found the body?"

"Couple of guys out fishing for blues saw something floating and went closer to get a look. Called us just as soon as they realized they'd found a body. They stayed with it until we got our guys out there."

"Any scars, tattoos, or body jewelry?"

"Once again, off the record for right now. We'll be making an official statement when we have more information." He pointed to his forearm. "A tattoo right here. It says, 'All of our knowledge begins with the senses.'"

I scrunched up my nose. "Sounds like a quote from something, but I don't know what."

He held up his iPhone. "I looked it up. It's from a philosopher named Immanuel Kant." He consulted his notebook again. "All of our knowledge begins with the senses, proceeds then to the understanding, and ends with reason. There is nothing higher than reason."

"Anything else you can tell me?" Seeing that it was raining harder, I tried to hold my umbrella so that it covered both of us.

"Not until we get more information. Did you go see Elliot Carlson's wife?"

"Yup. She confirmed everything you told me last night. The story should be up on the paper's website by now. It'll break in the print edition tomorrow morning. If Elliot's career wasn't over when that video hit, it's over now."

"Did you print the name of the escort service?"

I took a deep breath and nodded. "Yeah, if I were a client of The Whisper Room, I'd be looking for another escort service. When is Carlson being arraigned?"

"That was this morning. He's posted bail already."

"Was he charged with having sex with a minor?"

Mike chuckled at that. "We don't know for sure if the girl in the video is underage. We're trying to find a way to contact someone at this Whisper Room. Carlson says it's some kind of app you upload to your phone, but we've checked his Android and there's nothing there."

"An app? You mean like Uber for ordering hookers?"

He smiled. "Yeah, something like that. It appears that The Whisper Room has gone dark."

I toyed with the notion of telling Mike what Shana Neese had given me about Stephanie Cumberland. Hell, I even had the woman's address.

But I didn't tell. That wasn't my job.

I suggested, "Maybe once they heard that Carlson had gotten arrested, they took the app down."

Mike gazed out at the gray waters of the sound, pockmarked with falling raindrops. "If that didn't prompt them, then seeing their name pop up in your story certainly should have."

I had a hunch that Stephanie Cumberland, whoever she was, was going to be really pissed off at me.

———

The weather had turned into a full-blown rainstorm by the time I picked up Caroline and Jessica Oberon from band practice. Soaking wet, they climbed into the back seat, and I thought how lucky I was that the two of them played trumpet and not tuba. I dropped Jessica off at her house, then we went home.

Caroline, bless her heart, walked Tucker in the rain while I hammered out the piece on the dead woman the cops fished out of Long Island Sound and sent it via email to Laura back at the newsroom. Then I ordered sesame chicken, steamed dumplings, and fried rice from an excellent Asian restaurant on the Post Road with the understated name The Little Kitchen.

While waiting for Grubhub to deliver, I considered again The Whisper Room app on Carlson's phone. Ordering women, maybe men too, from your iPhone seemed so over the top.

But then again, why not? You can buy a car, get insurance, look for a house, shop for shoes, order up a ride, and purchase dinner and have it delivered. All from your phone.

Why not sex? How was this different from Tinder, OKCupid, or eharmony?

Except those are true dating sites. The Whisper Room was an app on which you *bought* companionship.

I looked up escort services on my laptop. Wikipedia defined an escort service as this:

> *"An escort agency is a company that provides escorts for clients, usually for sexual services. The agency typically arranges a meeting between one of its escorts and the client at the customer's house or hotel room (outcall), or at the escort's residence (incall). Some agencies also provide escorts for longer durations, who may stay with the client or travel along on a holiday or business trip. While the escort agency is paid a fee for this booking and dispatch service, the customer must negotiate any additional fees or arrangements directly with the escort for any other services that are not provided by the agency involved, such as providing sexual services (regardless of the legality of these services)."*

I turned on the TV in our kitchen to see if any of the broadcast stations had picked up my piece posted online about Elliot Carlson and a blackmailing escort service called The Whisper Room.

They had.

I'll admit, I got a little thrill watching the news anchors falling all over themselves while quoting from my story. I had written a fact-based but damning account of a husband philandering with a prostitute who was potentially underage. They added to the fire by running video clips, body parts appropriately blurred, but with Elliot's face clearly seen in the throes of ecstasy.

Funny thing, that. When you're having the most pleasure, your facial expression looks like you're in absolute agony. When Elliot hit the moment of climax, his face twisted in what looked like mortal pain.

But it was almost immediately replaced by a boyish grin, and there, on television, we could all hear him ask, "Was it good for you too, baby?"

I thought that could have been cut from the newscast.

When my phone vibrated against the top of my kitchen table, I was slightly startled. I didn't recognize the number and almost let it go to voicemail. "Hello?"

"Who the hell do you think you are?" a woman screamed, hysterically angry.

"I'm sorry?"

"Just who the hell do you think you are? I'm going to sue you and your penny-ante newspaper for every fucking nickel you have, do you understand me?"

Throughout my journalistic career, I've been accosted many times, both verbally and physically, but it was usually by someone I knew. "Who is this?"

"I don't blackmail my clients. Who the hell do you think you are, bitch?"

Okay, now I know who this is.

"Am I speaking to Stephanie Cumberland?"

That must have taken her by surprise because she was dead silent for a moment as she wondered how I knew her name. "How? Who?"

In a very calm but authoritative voice, I said, "Stephanie? Would you like an opportunity to tell your side of the story?"

There was another moment of silence, and I thought I could hear her conferring with someone. Then she replied. "Yes."

"Is now good?"

"Yes."

"I'll be right over. I already have the address."

Chapter Seven

I left Caroline some cash to tip the delivery guy, asked her to put my dinner in the refrigerator, and headed out. The rain had let up, but a stubborn drizzle continued to fall, and a cold front was moving in. Leaving the house, I zipped up my windbreaker and pulled my collar up around the back of my neck.

The townhouse I was looking for was technically in Sheffield but in an affluent enclave on the waterfront called Wilson Point. If you lived in Wilson Point, you would argue that you really weren't part of the town of Sheffield at all. Best described as wealthy, quaint, and artsy-fartsy, the village's biggest claim to fame was an outdoor production of a Shakespeare play every summer in their town park.

Coveside, Stephanie Cumberland's exclusive complex, was right on the shore of Bartlett Cove. Five buildings in all, holding three townhouses each, the complex boasted a tennis court, swimming pool, clubhouse, fully equipped gym, and its own marina.

Selling price of a two-story, three-bedroom townhouse at Coveside started at six hundred thousand dollars. Stephanie's was an end unit with an unfettered view of the water. That had to be worth at least an extra hundred grand.

This girl must be some kind of high-class madam.

I parked in the well-marked guest section of the parking area and climbed the steps up to Unit 5B. I rang the bell, and almost immediately the door was opened by an angry-looking woman with auburn hair tied back in a ponytail. She glared at me with piercing blue eyes. Judging from the well-toned musculature in her arms and shoulders, the woman was a regular in the weight room of the gym. In a voice that was all throaty growl, she asked, "Are you the reporter?"

"Are you Stephanie Cumberland?"

Before she could answer, a second woman stepped up. When she spoke, it was in a tense voice that was low and measured. "How is it you know so damned much about me?"

Stephanie Cumberland was about five-seven and slim, with black wavy hair that fell to her shoulders and dark-brown eyes that were almond-shaped, giving her a faintly exotic look. She wore a loose-fitting white top, black jeans, simple gold earrings, bracelet, necklace, and multiple rings on each hand. Her nails were lacquered black.

I glanced back at the other angry woman with auburn hair and was slightly amused that she had a gold chain with a cross dangling from it. Apparently, she thought religion and pimping went hand in hand.

"May I come in?"

Stephanie said, "Let her in."

I followed Stephanie into the house while the other woman closed the door behind me. I found myself in a spacious living area that flowed into the kitchen and then the dining room. The walls of the townhouse were sand-colored with white trim and the decor was a nautical motif. The living room sported a dark-blue couch with matching overstuffed chairs and end tables with brass lamps. Seascapes hung on the walls in the living area and what I could see of the kitchen. A large replica of a sailing schooner stood on the mantel over a red brick fireplace.

Sliding glass doors graced the living area and the kitchen and led out to a deck offering a stunning view of the cove and the marina. Even though the sun had sunk below the horizon and there was still a misty drizzle in the air, I could see boats tied to docks, bobbing in the water.

"You said I'd get a chance to tell my side of the story." She fixed me with her dark eyes, her face set with an expression somewhere between anger and suspicion.

"You're Stephanie Cumberland?"

"How is it you know my name and where I live?" she asked again in a testy voice.

I held up my hand. "I'm sorry, Miss Cumberland. I can't divulge my sources."

Stephanie spat, "Bullshit."

The other woman leaned in, her face uncomfortably close to mine. "We're off to a bad start."

I attempted a smile. "Look, my name's Geneva Chase. I already know Miss Cumberland's name, but I don't know who you are."

Stephanie put her hand on the woman's forearm, gently pulling her back. "This is my director of operations, Lorna Thorne."

Some names are more apt than others. This tall, brash woman was prickly. Thorne was the perfect name for her. I knew she'd already gotten under my skin.

Since she was still standing at the edge of my personal space, I suggested, "Is there somewhere we can all sit down?"

Stephanie gestured toward the couch. I spotted two glasses of red wine on the coffee table. Noticing my line of sight, she explained, "After reading your slanderous story online about my business, we both decided it was a good idea to have a glass of wine and try to calm down." She didn't ask if I wanted one.

As I lowered myself onto the couch, Lorna angrily lashed out, "Where the hell do you get off saying we were blackmailing that guy?"

While they seated themselves in the overstuffed chairs and picked up their glasses of wine, I pulled out my recorder. "I was only repeating what Elliot Carlson told the police and his wife."

Stephanie frowned. "He specifically said that we were blackmailing him?"

I replied, "And when he didn't pay up, he said you sent the video to his wife and the news media."

Lorna mumbled, "Bullshit."

Stephanie responded, "Do you have a copy of the video?"

Before I'd left Michelle Carlson's house, I'd asked her to email me the sex tape of her husband and the escort. I pulled it up on my phone, muted it, and pressed the Play button. As it rolled on my cell phone screen, I held it up for the two women to see.

Lorna reached out and took my phone, holding it closer to see it more clearly. They both watched through squinted eyes. Then Lorna handed the phone back. "She's not one of ours."

"One of your escorts?"

They glanced at each other for a moment. Stephanie answered, "You got it all wrong in your story. We're a dating app."

"The Whisper Room is a dating app? I couldn't find it anywhere online. And I'm damned good at finding things online."

Lorna sat a little straighter. Her words were filled with condescension. "You can't download it without our permission. It's very exclusive. It's for men and women of means."

I was getting tired of Lorna Thorne. "Look, Elliot Carlson gave a statement to the police that he ordered an escort from your service. Someone secretly shot a video of him having sex with one of your girls. And then someone tried to blackmail him. When he didn't pay up, the video was made public with the statement that the girl in the video is only fifteen."

Lorna growled, "Shit."

Stephanie's expression turned grim, and she sat back in her chair. She pointed to my recorder. "This part of our conversation has to be off the record."

Lorna's face registered shock. "Steph, what are you doing?"

Her voice was firm. "This part of this discussion has to be off the record."

I made a show of turning off my recorder and dropping it into my bag. "Okay."

Lorna turned to her friend. "Are you sure you want to do this?"

"We've got to find out who's framing us for blackmailing Elliot Carlson."

I jumped in. "So, you know Elliot Carlson?"

Stephanie answered, "Of course. He's a regular customer. But before we go any further, let me assure you we don't hire anyone unless they're nineteen or older."

Lorna cut in, "And we demand to see documented proof of age."

I was confused. "Let's get back to Elliot Carlson for a minute. You just said that your dating site is for men and women of means. That doesn't describe Carlson. He's a local news guy basically living above his means on his wife's dime."

Lorna shrugged. "I don't know where he gets his money, and I really don't care. As long as his credit card clears."

"So, to be clear. The Whisper Room really is an escort service."

Stephanie leaned in. "We prefer to think of ourselves as a dating app." She took a moment and finished her thought. "A full-service dating app." Then she added, "With all the bells and whistles."

Chapter Eight

The drizzle had stopped, and night had replaced twilight. The lights coming on from the other houses and condominiums perched on the shore of Bartlett Cove reflected off the dark surface of the water.

I prompted, "Where did the name The Whisper Room come from?"

Lorna glanced at Stephanie with admiration. "Stephanie is a marketing genius. She came up with the name. It sounds intimate. A room of whispers, of promises and deliverance. It just feels kind of naughty, doesn't it?"

I had to admit that it did. "Where did you get the idea of making it an app?"

Stephanie took another sip of her wine and answered, "You can do everything from your phone. Order food, book a hotel, get a rideshare, buy a car. Why not a dating service?"

"There's already Match.com, eharmony, and Tinder, and I'm sure there are at least a dozen more."

Lorna cracked her first real smile of the evening. "They're not full-service."

"What does that mean? Full-service?"

Stephanie held her hand up. "First, let me tell you how we started our business."

"Okay."

"Growing up, I was lucky. I come from a family that's pretty well off. My family lives in Greenwich, which ought to tell you something."

I knew that her father owned a company that sold the most exclusive automobiles available. I had a hunch her family was much more than well off.

She continued. "They paid most of my way when I was an undergrad at Yale. Even so, there were times when I was short on cash. And as I looked around me, I saw other students were going through the same money problems that I was, worse even."

Lorna sat back in her chair and gestured toward Stephanie. "Even though we come from completely different backgrounds, we were friends in college. We met in a class on entrepreneurship."

"Is that where you came up with the idea of The Whisper Room?"

Stephanie leaned forward. "Not right away. Lorna and I were paired up to come up with an idea for a business and then write a business plan for it."

Lorna smiled again. "We hatched a plan to launch an upscale distillery and restaurant. We'd target a market like Greenwich or Westport with an eye at franchising them in other affluent markets."

Stephanie's face adopted a pained expression. "We were both so taken with the concept that I went to my father to see if he would finance us. I pushed him hard for the money."

"He didn't bite?"

She shook her head. "My father is a control freak."

Lorna interrupted, "Your father's a prick."

Stephanie sighed. "He was bound and determined that I was

going to join him in the family business. He got so pissed off at me that he cut off my funds. I was essentially broke."

Lorna took a sip of her wine and said, "She found herself in the same predicament I was in." She glanced at her friend, then back at me. "That's when I told Steph that if she spent time with the right men, she could make some good money."

I wanted her to clarify. "What do you mean, 'spent time with the right men'?"

She placed her hands on her knees. "You know, go out with them, flirt with them, have dinner in a nice restaurant with them. Be nice."

"Did that include sex?"

Lorna pursed her lips and nodded slightly. "Sometimes. When I wanted to."

I turned my attention to Stephanie. "Did you do that too?"

She blushed and exhaled. "Yes. A few times. It was easy money." She waited a moment, then added, "And kind of an adrenaline high."

"Did you know these men?" *Certainly they didn't pick them up on the street.*

Lorna spoke up again. "My family wasn't helping me at all while I was in school. They couldn't. They just didn't have the money. So, on weekends, I tended bar at the Hamden Hill Country Club in New Haven. It's a pretty high-class place. Just the initiation fee alone is twenty-thousand dollars. The tips I got there were very generous."

"That's where you found the men to go out on your dates?" I tried mightily to keep the snark out of my voice when I said the word "dates."

Stephanie nodded. "Men of means and discretion."

I was suddenly curious. "What was your major at Yale?"

She answered, "Business, of course."

Lorna snapped her fingers. "Then one night over drinks, Steph had this brilliant idea."

"Originally, it was for a website," Stephanie explained. "But only clients we vetted would be able to see it. Unless we gave you permission, you'd never know it even existed."

"Lessening the chance of the law tripping over it," I said.

Stephanie ignored my statement. "Neither Lorna or I had the faintest notion of how to create or design one. Especially something so specific."

"When you say your clients are vetted, what does that mean?"

Lorna said, "We do background checks to make sure they can afford a date with one of our girls. And that they don't have an arrest record, you know, like for assaulting someone."

Stephanie tapped her finger against the fabric on the arm of her chair. "There was this guy I knew from high school in Greenwich. Total computer geek. I reached out to him and told him what we wanted to do. He was the one who pushed us away from creating a website and talked us into creating an app for your phone. And he could make the app absolutely exclusive to our clients. In order to download it, they'd have to have our digital permission."

"This computer geek, what's his name?"

The women glanced at each other again. Stephanie answered, "I don't think you need to know that. He works for us as a sub-contractor. He's not an employee."

"But you trust him."

"I've known him since high school. I'd trust him with my life. He's got his own tech firm now. He's very successful."

I took a breath, then said, "Where do you recruit the women?"

Stephanie grinned. "That's easy. We started with friends and classmates from Yale who we knew were struggling for cash. They saw how easy and safe it was, and they reached out to their friends, some of them attending other schools. All of our girls have at least taken some college courses."

"Classy." Once again, I was having a difficult time keeping the sarcasm out of my voice.

Lorna's voice took on an edge again. "Look, the women who work for The Whisper Room do so voluntarily."

"And men," Stephanie added.

"Right. Working for us is their choice. They're not working on the streets or having sex in some dark alley. Whether or not they sleep with someone at the end of an evening is always up to them."

"Where do you recruit the clients? Lorna's obviously not tending bar at the country club anymore."

Stephanie gave me a coy look. "That's a trade secret."

That made me want to know all the more. "Okay, tell me how The Whisper Room app works."

Lorna, the operations director, leaned forward. "It's seamless. If a client wants to go out on a date, he pulls up the app and scrolls down a directory of our girls."

That raised my eyebrows. "Oh?"

Lorna continued, "The client clicks on who he or she wants to go out with and then goes to our concierge page. That's where he picks out the type of date he's looking for. It might be dinner at a particular restaurant, tickets to a Broadway show, or a room at a specific hotel. Our app can even arrange a vacation to a tropical island, if that's what the client wants."

"Very high-tech. The client pays by credit card ahead of time?"

"And the charge comes up on the client's bill as the W.R. Foundation."

Stephanie stated, "That kind of service is what sets us apart."

That piqued my curiosity. "Apart from what?"

Lorna answered, "Any other services like ours."

"Do you have any full-service competitors that offer, you know, all the bells and whistles?"

Lorna scowled. "There's a start-up that's trying to do what we do. But their geek is far inferior to our geek because their site keeps crashing, and we hear from some of our clients who have used it that the girls aren't up to our high standards."

"I see. Do you keep records of all the transactions?"

Stephanie's eyes narrowed. "Of course, we do. But everything we have on file is encrypted."

"Okay, I'm up to speed on the business. I'm here to get your side of the story on Elliot Carlson. Can we go back on the record?"

The ladies looked at each other, and they both nodded.

I pulled the recorder back out of my bag. "You're certain that the girl in the video isn't one of your employees?"

Stephanie was emphatic. "I've never seen her before in my life."

Lorna added, "And I want to go on the record and state again that none of the women who work for us are under nineteen." She jabbed her finger into the arm of her chair for effect. "And, for the goddamned record, we don't blackmail our clients."

Stephanie chimed in. "The Whisper Room dating app is all about discretion and safety. Safety for our clients and our employees."

I thought for a moment. Then I asked, "Do you think this start-up competitor might have had something to do with this?"

Stephanie exhaled loudly, eyeballing Lorna. "What do you think?"

Lorna thought it over. "The only way Boca could have pulled that off is if he hacked into our app."

"Boca?" I asked.

"Matt Boca," Stephanie stated. "He worked for us as an escort two years ago. He's an ambitious little shit. I wouldn't put it past him. Boca's the one who's behind the start-up. He calls it the Midnight House. What a rip-off." She looked at Lorna and said, "Call Ian and tell him to check our systems for signs that we've been hacked. And can you get Gary on this?"

"I'm on it." Lorna jerked up out of her chair and stalked quickly out of the room, phone already in her hand.

I sighed. "I'm guessing Ian is your computer geek?"

She nodded silently.

"Is Gary a geek too?"

Stephanie gave me a sly smile. "God, no. Gary Racine is Lorna's boyfriend. He's a private detective. Has his own agency."

"Which one is that?"

"Racine Security."

I'd never heard of it, but replied, "Of course."

"If Boca is behind this, Gary will find out." Stephanie gave me an impatient expression. She was angry, but not at me. She was pissed off at her former employee gone rogue, Matt Boca. "How soon will your story be online? I want our clients to know we aren't blackmailers."

"I'll post this tonight. It'll be online in a couple of hours. It'll be in the newspaper by morning."

"Good. Is there anything else?"

I was about to play a hunch. "Are you missing any of your women?"

Her eyebrows knotted together as she wondered where I was headed. "Not that I'm aware of."

"How familiar are you with your employees?"

"Intimately. We vet them as closely as we vet our clients."

"This is probably nothing."

She leaned forward. "What?"

"The police found the body of a young woman in Long Island Sound this morning. She has a tattoo here." I pointed to my forearm. "It said something about all knowledge beginning with the senses."

She sat back as the blood drained from her face. Then she stared down at the floor. When she spoke again, it was barely a whisper. "Oh, my God. Mindy Getz. Mindy Getz has that tattoo."

Chapter Nine

As I sat in my car in the guest parking section of the town-home complex, I looked up Mindy Getz on Facebook, Twitter, and Instagram. She was a serial social media user. She'd put up online pictures of fancy restaurants and expensive meals she'd ordered. There were selfies of her outside Broadway theaters, on trips she'd taken to places like Key West and Atlanta, and of her skiing in Vermont and hiking in the Grand Canyon.

The selfies showed that she had long golden hair, blue-gray eyes, and was a pretty twenty-something. According to her profile, Mindy had gone to Columbia to study philosophy, and her current occupation was in the field of hospitality.

The one striking missing item in her vast array of photographs was that she'd never snapped a picture of any of her clients.

Or at least she never posted them online.

Interestingly, she had posted a few photos of herself and a young man with their arms around each other. He didn't appear to fit the profile of a Whisper Room client. He was in his early twenties, clearly needed a haircut, and was dressed in a Glass Animals-Dreamland Tour T-shirt and cargo shorts. In the photo, she was looking directly into the camera, and he was gazing lovingly at her. They appeared to be standing in front of a green Saturn.

Do they even make those anymore?

I glanced back at Unit 5B. When I'd left, Stephanie Cumberland was bereft. Tears flowing, nose running, sobbing uncontrollably in Lorna Thorne's arms. Lorna swore that if Matt Boca had anything to do with Mindy's death, she'd tear his heart out herself with her bare hands.

I was pretty sure she could do it.

I was able to get Mindy Getz's address in an online search, but before I set off, I called home to make sure Caroline was okay. She told me that she was fine, and took the opportunity to remind me that I'd promised she could practice driving this weekend.

Persistent teenager.

After disconnecting the call, I sat for a moment gazing out over the cove where houselights were reflecting like lazy eels on the surface of the water. I thought about Mindy Getz and Caroline and that they had similar features—blond hair and blue eyes.

And so did that girl in the sex video with Elliot Carlson.

I shook my head. I'd never let Caroline be put into a position where she would have to trade sex for money. But to hear Stephanie and Lorna tell it, no one had forced or coerced their employees into becoming escorts. They all did it of their own volition.

I sighed and thought of Mike Dillon. He didn't know the identity of his Jane Doe. I did.

I suffered a moment of conscience. Part of me knew the right thing to do was to call Mike Dillon and tell him who his Jane Doe was and how I got the information.

The other part of me wanted to get out in front of this story as far as I could. Having the police diving in would just slow me down.

Conscience be damned. I hit the Start button on the dash.

———

Mindy's condo was in a working-class section of Sheffield. Strawberry Woods Apartments were on Wolfpit Avenue, tucked behind a Stew Leonard's grocery story on Route 1. Streetlights offered enough illumination to see that there were five condos to a building and there were five buildings in the complex. Each condo was two stories, had a tiny front lawn, and shrubbery nestled against the foundation.

I knew that Mindy Getz lived in 4C. The windows to her condo were dark. The parking area marked with her condominium number was empty.

I pulled into it and sat for a moment, studying her unit. It was obvious that no one was home.

No, the owner is in the morgue.

An incredible sadness washed over me. Nobody knew she was dead. According to what I'd found online, both of her parents were alive and living in New Jersey. They were completely unaware that their daughter had been murdered.

Certain that I'd made the drive to Mindy's for nothing, I got out of my car anyway, walked up the sidewalk, and knocked on the door.

There was no answer.

I knocked one more time, more emphatically. No dog barked, no roommate or boyfriend came to the door.

The front door of the unit next to Mindy's opened and a tall, thin Black man leaned out. "Are you looking for Mindy?" His voice had a distinct British accent.

"Yes, I am. Do you know where she is?" I asked the question knowing full well that he had no clue where she was.

He stepped out of his condominium and crossed over the postage stamp–sized yard to where I stood. "She sometimes goes away for days at a time. Mindy has some kind of job in the hospitality business. Sometimes it takes her into the city, and sometimes she goes away on some lovely trips. But you probably know that already, don't you?"

He was eyeballing me, a curious expression on his face. The man was fishing. I reached out to shake his hand. "My name is Geneva Chase."

He smiled. "Charles Odom. Why are you looking for Mindy?" He was wearing a dark-green sweater, jeans, and house slippers. His dark hair was turning silver around his temples, and his large hand was warm and dry as it gripped mine.

I pulled a card out of my bag and handed it to him. "I'm a research analyst with Lodestar Analytics. Mindy is part of a survey I'm doing on the hospitality business."

I hated to lie to a man I had just met, but I couldn't tell him that I was a reporter looking into his neighbor's murder. I asked, "How well do you know Mindy Getz?" I was careful not to use the past tense.

He glanced at Mindy's front door. "You know, we're neighbors. We say hello to each other when we run into each other in the parking lot. When she goes on her trips, I collect her mail for her and feed her fish. She has a lovely aquarium."

"So, you have a key to her condo?"

He gave me a curious look. "Yes."

For the briefest of moments, I thought about asking Charles Odom to let me into Mindy's home to look around. Then I considered that her condo could very well be the place she was killed. If I went in there, I'd contaminate a possible crime scene.

The last thing I needed to do was leave my fingerprints or DNA in her condo.

"When did you last see her?"

He studied me with suspicion. "Yesterday afternoon. I was just coming back from the gym, and she was just coming home from grocery shopping. Why do you ask?"

"I was supposed to meet her last evening for the survey, and she didn't show up."

Lies upon lies.

He squinted at me. "I was given the impression she was going out on a date last night."

"I think she mentioned that she has a boyfriend. Do you know if she was going on a date with him?"

Charles chuckled. "Oh, she has a boy she sees off and on. Mostly off, I think. Mindy's a pretty girl. She likes to play the field. Mindy loves to tell me about some of the dates she goes on. And of course, I'm friends with her online. So, I get to see pictures of some of the fabulous restaurants she dines at. And the trips she takes."

I had the feeling that Charles Odom knew more about Mindy than he was letting on. "Does she ever talk about who she's going out with?"

He shook his head. "No, she keeps those cards pretty close to the vest, you know what I mean?"

"Discreet."

"Got to give her credit for that. Doesn't kiss and tell."

"Do you know any of Mindy's friends?"

Charles glanced at the next building over and nodded toward it. "Kristin in 2B. They're about the same age. Both nice girls."

I followed his line of sight. "Do you suppose she's home?"

"Her car's been gone for about a week now. I'm guessing she's on one of her vacations."

"Does she take a lot of them?"

Charles gave me a sly grin. "Both Mindy and Kristin travel a lot."

Mr. Odom knows more about their profession than he lets on.

Suddenly something caught Charles's eye. He squinted into the night, staring at a car parked in the shadows next to the dumpster. "That's odd."

"What's that, Mr. Odom?"

"That car. It was parked there a couple of nights ago. When I took out the trash, I must have made whoever was in it nervous, because the driver left in a huff."

I could just make out a vehicle sitting next to a dumpster that serviced the complex. I asked, "No idea who it belongs to?"

He slowly shook his head. "Didn't get a good look at it, sitting in the shadows like that. I'm going to call the head of our HOA, though. I don't like strangers hanging about." Then he focused on me again. "Sorry Mindy isn't here. Would you like me to tell her you were looking for her?"

I was still staring into the dark, trying to get more detail on the car that shouldn't have been there. "Sure."

He went back into his apartment, and I started in the direction of the mysterious vehicle. Before I'd gotten more than a couple of steps, the car headlights came to life, momentarily blinding me. Then it pulled out of its spot and drove quickly across the dark parking lot, only emerging into the light as it got to the road.

A Saturn?

Was that Mindy's on-again off-again boyfriend?

Could he be Mindy's killer?

Yes, I know the old trope about the criminal always returns to the scene of the crime. But I've been on the crime beat for a long time and know that's rarely the case.

No, he's looking for Mindy Getz. He doesn't know she's dead.

Chapter Ten

While I microwaved the plate of sesame chicken, fried rice, and a single dumpling Caroline had left me, I took a deep breath and punched in Mike's personal cell phone number. I wasn't looking forward to this call, but it was something I had to do if I wanted to look myself in the mirror again.

Driving home I had thought again about how Mindy's parents didn't have any idea where their daughter was. If something happened to Caroline, I couldn't stand not knowing.

Mike caught my call on the third ring. "Genie?"

"Hi, Mike. Look, I have some news, and you're going to want to ask me a lot of questions, but I'm not going to be able to give you a lot of answers."

Mike hesitated and the microwave dinged, telling me that my food was hot. As I opened the door and took out the steaming plate, he said, "Okay, tell me."

I placed my plate on the kitchen table. Tucker stared at me with hopeful brown eyes from his place next to my chair. "Your Jane Doe's name is Mindy Getz."

"And you know this how?"

"She was an escort, working for The Whisper Room."

I could visualize him opening his tiny notebook he carried everywhere and jotting down the girl's name. "The same escort service that blackmailed Elliot Carlson?"

I sat down at the table and sipped some water before answering. "It's the same escort service, but the owner of the service claims they weren't the ones who blackmailed Carlson."

"You know who the owner of The Whisper Room is?"

"Yes." I cut into the dumpling and popped it into my mouth.

"Are you going to tell me who it is?"

I finished chewing and swallowed. "Can't reveal a source."

I heard the anger in his voice. "You know that pisses me off."

"I feel the same way when someone tells me their statement is off the record." I took a bite of the chicken and chewed while he stewed.

Finally, Mike asked, "Did this pimp tell you if Mindy Getz was working last night?"

It was weird. Like Mike, when I'd started looking into The Whisper Room, I thought of the owner as a pimp.

But after meeting them, I didn't think of Stephanie Cumberland and Lorna Thorne in the same way. They were attractive, bright, erudite businesswomen. Their employees were college educated. Working as escorts was their conscious decision. The girls weren't being trafficked. They weren't being physically or mentally coerced. They went out on expensive "dates" with wealthy men.

But the two women were promoting prostitution.

"The owner said that Mindy Getz wasn't working for The Whisper Room last night. However, the owner also told me that from time to time, against their advice, their employees work freelance."

Mike thought for a moment, giving me an opportunity to shovel in a forkful of fried rice. I noticed Caroline leaning against the doorway leading from the living room into the kitchen. I winked at her.

"I need to get a list of clients from The Whisper Room and find out where they all were last night."

I thought I'd try to change the subject. "Was an autopsy done on the girl?"

"Do you really think I should tell you anything?" No question, he was angry.

I sighed. "Mike, I just told you who the Jane Doe is. C'mon. You'll be releasing the autopsy results in the morning anyway."

Caroline came into the kitchen and sat down at the table with me. She reached down and scratched Tucker behind the ears.

"The victim was asphyxiated."

I could tell Mike was really pissed off at me because he was making me work to get information. "Other than the ligature marks on her neck, are there any other bruises or signs that she struggled?"

"Bruises on her wrists, arms, and shoulders. Probably from when the killer zip-tied her hands together behind her back."

Her hands were tied behind her back? That's something you didn't tell me when they took her body out of the water.

"Think they'll get any DNA evidence?"

"They took scrapings from under her fingernails to see if they can get anything. Because she'd been in the water for at least twelve hours, I'm not sure what they'll find."

I took a final bite of the dumpling.

Mike said, "At least tell me *how* you found the pimp."

I watched Caroline's eyes widen and, with a sudden lurch of my stomach, I realized that she could hear both sides of the telephone conversation. "You have your snitches, and I have mine."

"It would really help to have a list of the escort service's clients. If Mindy Getz was a prostitute, then from what we can tell, she was probably working on the night of her death."

That piqued my interest. I wondered if the poor girl had been raped. "How's that?"

"Underwear. She wasn't wearing panties."

I saw Caroline blush.

"A lot of women don't wear panties. I might not be wearing any right now."

Caroline laughed out loud and clasped her hand across her mouth.

"The pimp told you that he wasn't the one blackmailing Elliot Carlson?"

I purposely hadn't told Mike the gender of the owner of the escort service. He'd just assumed that it was a man. "When the owner saw the video, they didn't recognize the girl who has having sex with Carlson."

"He could be lying."

"Yeah, that's possible. But I don't think so. Hey, does the name Matt Boca ring any bells?"

"Is that who owns The Whisper Room?"

"No, but he might be a competitor. It's possible that he somehow hacked into The Whisper Room's operational system. Then he planted his own girl with Carlson and filmed them."

I heard him scoff. "That's a hell of a stretch."

"Mike, I need one more bit of information."

"What?"

"Where is Elliot Carlson staying?"

He chuckled. "How the hell am I supposed to know that? He made bail this afternoon. I'm surprised you weren't there. There was a freaking media circus in front of the courthouse. We had to hustle him out the back of the building. His attorney was waiting to take him away."

"Okay, who's his attorney?"

"Dennis Russo."

Russo was a bulldog criminal lawyer. When he was in a court-room, he was relentless. He put on a good show, and I liked him. I was certain he liked me.

"Okay, thanks, Mike. Have a good evening."

Mike interrupted. "Wait a minute, there's dinner in it if you clue me in on who owns The Whisper Room. I really would like to get a list of their clients."

"I'll bet you would. No can do, but you can still buy me dinner."

In my head, I could see Mike smile. "I thought you said you were seeing that John Stillwater guy."

"I said that he and I were friends."

"With benefits."

I saw Caroline roll her eyes. I had purposely left the benefits out of my end of the conversation.

I gave her a guilty grin. "Have a good evening, Mike."

———

I finished eating while Caroline told me about her day. Thankfully, she didn't bring up the conversation she'd just overheard or talk about driving practice.

After she and Tucker went upstairs, I opened my laptop and banged out a story about my meeting with the owners of The Whisper Room and how they claimed they hadn't blackmailed Elliot Carlson. I left out Stephanie's and Lorna's names, of course.

I also left out the revelation that the girl the cops had pulled out of the water had been an escort for The Whisper Room. And I certainly didn't put Mindy Getz's name in the piece. Her next of kin hadn't been notified yet.

There are some lines even I won't cross.

Chapter Eleven

The next morning, after a run, twenty minutes of meditation, and a nice, hot shower, I sat in the kitchen with a cup of coffee and went online to see what I could find on Matt Boca.

I had suspected that the name Boca had been appropriated from the Florida town, Boca Raton. But, no, it was his real name. Matthew Daniel Boca was the son of Edward and Linda Boca, who were retired and living in North Carolina.

Matt was a millennial, thirty years old, and he did his share of social media postings. That was where I got the bulk of my information about him.

Be careful what you put online.

Matt's family was originally from Danbury, Connecticut, and he had graduated with a degree in psychology from the UCONN. From his selfies, I could see he had dark hair, brown eyes, carefully tended stubble shading his lower face, and a nice smile with perfect teeth. There was a photo of him in a bathing suit while vacationing in Belize that showed me that he had a lean, muscular physique complete with absurdly hard abs.

Stephanie had said that he'd worked for her as an escort for a while before going rogue and starting his own service. The only mention of what Matt did for a living in his profile was a line that said he was in the hospitality industry.

The same as Mindy Getz.

Then I tried to look up his fledgling escort service called the Midnight House. As with The Whisper Room, there was nothing I could find online. Either Matt was being particular, like Stephanie, about who could download his app or it had crashed.

Lorna had told me that his geek was inferior to their geek.

Then I looked up Dennis Russo's phone number and gave him a call.

A female answered, "Clemmons & Russo, how can we assist you?"

"I'd like to talk to Mr. Russo, please."

"Can I tell him who's calling?"

I grinned. "Genie Chase."

Seconds later I heard him pick up. "Genie. What a nice surprise."

"Hey, Dennis. How have you been?"

"No matter how dismal my day is, the sun is shining the moment I talk with you."

I visualized Dennis in my head. He's an imposing six-four and stocky. Attractive in a *Sopranos* kind of way. Balding, with sly eyes, he made me think of a television gangster in an expensive suit. "You make me blush."

"Do you still see Frank Mancini?"

That had been a mistake from my drinking days. I'd had an affair with a married man, an estate attorney by the name of Frank Mancini. Though some of it was a blur, I recall one drunken night in particular with Frank, Dennis, and one of Dennis's bimbos du jour. I'm pretty sure we didn't all end up in bed together, but like I say, the memory is a little fuzzy.

"These days, Frank and I are just friends."

"Does that mean you're available?"

I chuckled. "Depends on who's asking. Hey, I need you to do me a favor."

"If I do, you may have to let me buy you a drink."

Between Mike Dillon and Dennis Russo, I was feeling mighty popular. I should have told Dennis that I was on the wagon, but I didn't. It might ruin his flirtatious moment. "You're representing Elliot Carlson?"

His voice lost its warmth, and he became an attorney again. "Yes, I am."

"What're my chances of getting an interview?"

"Probably slim to none."

"Tell him I think I can help him find his blackmailer."

I heard Dennis laugh. "He already knows who his blackmailer is. The same people who ruined his life and sent that sex tape to the media."

"And his wife. Don't forget his wife."

"That fucking escort service, Genie. What's it called? Whisper House?"

"The Whisper Room. And I don't think it was them. I'd like to talk to Elliot."

I heard the attorney take a deep breath. "I'll ask him. If he agrees, I'd have to be there with him during the interview."

"That goes without saying."

Dennis promised to call me back when he got an answer.

While I sipped my coffee, I looked through my emails. One of them was from Nathaniel Rubin, the owner of Lodestar Analytics. It was single sentence asking me to call him.

I punched in his number. Seeing my name on his Caller ID, he answered by asking, "What are you working on?"

Most of the assignments I did for Nathaniel, while lucrative, were online background checks of political candidates, aides, lobbyists, or corporate types. Nothing particularly exciting. Once in a blue moon, he'd give me a job where I could actually use my investigative skills.

I wasn't officially doing any assignment for Lodestar at that moment.

I answered, "I'm doing some freelance work for the *Sheffield Post*. Why?"

"I got a phone call from a Charles Odom. Apparently, you stopped by to see a young woman by the name of Mindy Getz last night, whom Mr. Odom is very worried about."

I sighed. "He should be. She was murdered. Her next of kin hasn't been notified, and I didn't want to just blurt that out to her neighbor."

"You gave him your Lodestar business card. He called here to make sure you're really a research analyst for the firm."

"Sorry about that. Sometimes it's easier to be a researcher than an investigative reporter. What did you tell him?"

"I said you were an employee of mine, of course. Once I confirmed that, he asked me to pass something along. Was there some mysterious car parked out there last night?"

"Yeah. They took off when I started in their direction."

"Mr. Odom thinks he might have recognized the car when it drove away."

I felt a tiny kick of adrenaline. "He did?"

"He told me that his neighbor had an on-and-off relationship with a young man. He doesn't recall his name, but he does remember that he works for a car dealership in Greenwich. Mr. Odom stumbled when I asked which one. He said it could be Columbus or Columbo Motor Works. Something like that."

Then the adrenaline hit my bloodstream hard, and my heart started thumping. "Could it be Cumberland Custom Motorsports?"

"Sounds about right. Does it mean anything to you?"

"Sure does." I switched gears for a moment. "Hey, is John still on assignment?"

"Yeah, probably for another week or two."

John Stillwater is about six feet, trim, boyish good looks, pretty smile, dark hair always about two weeks overdue for a trim, and black-rimmed glasses that make him look super smart. Which he was.

He was also an ex-cop, so when Nathaniel has an assignment that could go south in a bad way, he sends John. When John is on a job, he's laser-focused.

Which was why I hadn't heard from him in two weeks. I knew it didn't have anything to do with me, but it still smarted a little.

Nathaniel spoke up. "If I hear from him, I'll tell him you asked about him."

"He's okay, isn't he?"

"Of course, he is." Nathaniel understood where I was coming from. "Look, you know John. He doesn't let anything distract him when he's on a job."

I sighed. "I know. Thanks, Nathaniel."

Disconnecting, I turned my attention to Mindy's sometimes-boyfriend. The lead on the young man who had hidden in the shadows last night was exciting. Was it a coincidence that the kid works for Stephanie Cumberland's father? I looked up the address of the dealership with the intention that it would be my next stop.

Then Dennis Russo called me back. "Mr. Carlson says he's willing to hear what you have to say."

"The conversation goes two ways, Dennis."

"He wants to meet with you this morning."

That meant the visit to the car dealership would have to wait. I did a mental calculation in my head. The police had most likely already figured out where Mindy Getz lived. They were probably working on getting a warrant to search her condominium, and while they were there, they'd interview the neighbors, including Charles Odom, who would tell them about the kid in the Saturn who worked for Columbus or Columbo Motorsports.

I knew Mike would eventually connect it to Cumberland Motorsports. He might even beat me out there, and I'd hate for that to happen.

But I wanted to talk to Elliot Carlson too. "Okay, where is he staying?"

I heard Dennis's snort of derision. "He's staying with his mom."

Ugh, that's gotta be a kick in Carlson's ego.

Chapter Twelve

Fairfield County has some of the wealthiest towns and enclaves in America—Greenwich, Westport, Darien, New Canaan, Wilton. But it also has one of the most impoverished cities in the state. During the early twentieth century, Bridgeport was Connecticut's hub for manufacturing and industry. Then, as companies closed or moved out, unemployment raged, and the city fell onto hard times.

Despite valiant rehabilitation efforts, Bridgeport is still the poor stepchild to the affluent rest of Fairfield County.

The address that Dennis Russo had given me was a trailer park on the eastern end of the city. You'd think that a place called Woodland Heights Mobile Home Park would have more than a few trees planted, but it didn't. It was just a few rows of double-wide trailers, placed more or less in permanence alongside each other. Some had elaborate wooden porches, some had flowers planted along their tiny sidewalks, and some had gas grills and picnic tables for outdoor dining.

And then there was Wanda Carlson's trailer. Her trailer was mostly gray with hints of mossy green from its advanced age. There was no attempt at prettying up what tiny plot of land came with the monthly rent. A dusty maroon Hyundai sat in the cramped parking spot alongside the trailer.

I figured it was most likely Wanda's car.

A far cry from the Porsche that Elliot's wife had bought him.

When I got there and parked my car at the side of the narrow avenue, Dennis was already there in his black BMW. As I got out, he quickly exited his car and hustled over to me, whispering, "Make sure you lock it."

I glanced around, pulled my bag closer to my side, and hit the button on my key fob, hearing the satisfying click when the car locked itself. "This doesn't look so bad."

He leaned over. "There was a shooting here just three nights ago. The cops said it was a drug deal gone bad." Then he straightened up and gave me a broad smile. "It's good to see you."

I gave him a grin. "You, too, Dennis. You look like life is treating you well." It looked like he'd packed on about twenty pounds since the last time we'd run into each other. But I couldn't very well say that.

He sighed and then mumbled, "C'mon, let's do this."

We walked up the short, dusty walkway. Then he climbed up on metal steps and knocked. A moment later, I saw Elliot Carlson open the door. He glanced from side to side and then waved us in.

The interior of double-wide mobile homes always surprised me. It looked much bigger inside than it did from the outside. The living area and kitchen were essentially the same room separated by a countertop. The walls were cheap wooden paneling decorated with framed needlepoint designs. The fabric of the brown-and-tan plaid couch looked frayed on the arms, and a gash in a leather recliner exposed white stuffing beneath repeated efforts to stitch it back together with Scotch tape.

A tiny voice from the kitchen sang out, "Hello, Mr. Russo." Elliot's mother, Wanda, was stirring a pot of chili. "I'll have lunch ready in a few minutes if you're hungry." She was a petite woman with blue-gray hair and wore a green tracksuit, the kind that had been popular back in the eighties.

While Elliot looked better than the last time I saw him in the back of the police cruiser, he still looked pretty awful. His hair was tousled, he had dark circles around his eyes, and he hadn't shaved since yesterday.

I went first. "Thanks for taking time to see me, Elliot."

He ran his fingers through his hair. "Dennis says you have information to share."

Wanda shouted, "Don't be rude, Elliot. Everyone, come in here and sit down at the table. Can I get anyone coffee?"

Dennis declined, and Elliot already had a cup in his hand. I shouted, "I'll have some, Mrs. Carlson."

As we sat down at the kitchen table, Wanda poured me a cup and handed it to me. "Thank you." I took a sip and focused on Elliot. "How are you doing?"

He blinked at me with incredulity. "My career is over, my marriage is over, I spent a night in jail, and the media is having a field day dragging my name through the fucking mud. How the hell do you think I'm doing?"

I nodded. "That's kind of how I thought. Look, I tracked down the owner of The Whisper Room."

"And?"

I glanced up at Elliot's mom and wondered how much she knew.

Elliot caught me. "Mom knows everything."

She turned around and gave me a smile. "I know everything."

Dennis had a notebook out and was clicking a ballpoint pen. "I'd like that name, please."

Elliot growled menacingly, "So would I."

I shot the attorney a look but purposely ignored Elliot. "Sorry,

Dennis. I can't reveal a source." Then I turned my attention back to Elliot. "I showed the owner the video, and they told me that the girl isn't one of theirs."

Elliot's expression was one of disgust. "What else would they say?"

"They think it might have been a competitor who had hacked into their app."

Dennis's eyebrows shot up. "Can you give me *that* name?"

This was to be the second time I would throw someone under the bus without really knowing who it was. "Guy by the name of Matt Boca. A former Whisper Room employee who's trying to get his own escort service off the ground."

Elliot shook his head. "By blackmailing me?"

"By scaring off The Whisper Room's client base."

Dennis scowled. "Is there any evidence of that?"

"The Whisper Room people are having their IT guy take a look to see if they've been hacked."

Wanda piped up. "The chili is ready. Does anyone want some?"

From the expectant expression on her face, I just knew that if we said no, she'd be disappointed. We gave her a collective, "Sure."

As she began to ladle it into bowls, I asked, "Could you just walk me through the night the video was obtained?"

He glanced at his attorney, who gave him a simple nod.

Wanda placed a bowl of steaming chili in front of me and handed me a soup spoon and a napkin. Then she did the same with the two men. "Hope you enjoy it."

Then she walked out of the kitchen and down the hallway.

Elliot watched her. "It's time for her stories. That's what she calls her soaps."

I said, "She's sweet."

"I worry about her. I think maybe she might have early onset dementia."

"I'm sorry."

Elliot stared down at his chili bowl. "One more thing to worry about. I have an older brother, but he's an alcoholic and lives in California. If she's got Alzheimer's, he's not going to be any damned help at all."

I wanted to get him back on track. "The night the video was shot?"

He glanced around the interior of the trailer. "I'll be living here for the rest of my life, collecting unemployment, taking care of Mom."

Dennis put his hand on Elliot's arm. "Tell Miss Chase about the day the video was shot."

Elliot wiggled his shoulders, as if shaking the gloom off. "Right, it was actually an afternoon. It was maybe two weeks ago. I had some time to kill before prepping for my six o'clock newscast. I pulled up The Whisper Room app on my phone."

I interrupted. "From what I understand, the clientele for that service is very exclusive. It's not available to just anyone. The service has to give you permission to download it. Can I ask how you came to have it on your phone?"

He shrugged. "I don't know. Maybe someone at Whisper Room saw me on the news. One day I got a text explaining what the escort service was and asking if I wanted to download the app."

I gently tapped the top of the table with my fingers. "So, you did."

Both Dennis and I had notebooks sitting next to our bowls of chili. I didn't want to spook Elliot by pulling my recorder out of my bag.

"Sure, it was free. Why not?"

Free? It was the most expensive mistake you've ever made, dumbass.

I tasted Wanda's chili. It was spicy. Taking a tentative swallow, I asked, "Tell me what happened last night at your house."

Elliot glanced at his attorney, who scowled. Dennis said, "This part is off the record."

I knew I was treading on shaky ground, so I nodded and closed my notebook.

"I finished my six o'clock broadcast and was in the process of packing up my things to go home when Nancy, my producer, waved me over. She held up her cell phone and showed me what someone had sent her."

"A copy of the video?" I asked.

"I thought I was going to throw up. All I could do was say that it wasn't me."

"But obviously it was."

"Before I sprinted out of the studio, I told her some bullshit about it being computer-generated."

"When did the blackmailer originally reach out to you?"

He looked down at the bowl of chili, then stared out the window over the kitchen sink. "I'll never forget it. The bastard sent me a copy of the video about nine days ago. They said if I didn't pay up, they'd send the video to my wife and all the news outlets."

"How much did the blackmailer want to be paid?"

"Twenty-five thousand dollars."

"And you didn't have it."

He slowly shook his head. "Even if I had it, there was no guarantee that they wouldn't be back for more money."

"So, you gambled that if you ignored him, the problem would go away?"

Elliot gave me a sad look. "What choice did I have?"

I took another taste of Wanda's chili. "Tell me what happened when you got home on the night the video was released."

Dennis interrupted. "I just want to reiterate that this is off the record. What we say here may be part of Elliot's testimony at trial."

"Of course. Elliot?"

"When I got home, I could hear the video playing in the kitchen. I knew right there and then that my marriage was over. The bastards had sent it to my wife."

"She confronted you?"

"When I went into the kitchen, she was holding her phone in one hand, held it up so that I could see the screen when I walked in. Then I noticed one of the kitchen knives in her other hand."

Michelle Carlson had either left that part out or else Elliot was embellishing.

"But it was her face that scared me the most. The only way I can describe her expression is grim. Her eyes were cold, like she wanted me dead."

He stopped for a moment, then continued. "In a calm voice she asked me why she shouldn't cut my balls off. I tried telling her that the video was a fake. That it was photoshopped somehow. Computer-generated. That I was being blackmailed."

He glanced at his attorney, who nodded at him.

Elliot said, "It just escalated after that. She was screaming. I was screaming. She wanted me out of the house. Then she ran upstairs and started throwing my things out the bedroom window. My whole world was collapsing. It felt like there was an iron band around my chest, squeezing. I couldn't breathe. There was no light at the end of the tunnel."

"Is that when you got your rifle?"

"I don't even recall getting it. But there I was standing in our bedroom with the rifle in my hands."

I asked, "Was it loaded?"

"Yes. When I walked into the room, the look on Michelle's face was absolute horror. She was afraid of me, terrified. Of me.

That's when she ran into the bathroom and locked herself in. I told her that if she didn't come out and talk to me that I'd kill myself."

"Did you threaten your wife?"

He shook his head. "No, but I guess just my showing up with the gun was threatening enough."

I didn't need to hear anything more about that night. "Let's go back to the day the video was shot. You said you had time to kill before your newscast."

He poked his spoon into his chili and moved some of it around but didn't take a taste. I guessed he didn't have much of an appetite. "Yeah, I pulled up the app's directory and ordered a girl."

Unbidden, I felt my face flush with anger. "Just like you'd order up a hamburger driving up to McDonald's."

Elliot seemed oblivious to the sarcasm. "Yeah, something like that. Anyway, they have an algorithm that learns your preferences. Mine were petite, blond, preferably young."

"How young?"

His eyes were wide, and he shook his head. "Not fifteen. The app says up front that all the girls are over nineteen and college educated."

"Elliot, how many times did you use the app?"

He glanced over at his attorney, who shook his head.

Dennis offered, "That's not pertinent to this conversation."

I sighed. "What else did you order? I understand they'll make reservations at a restaurant or a hotel for you."

"That's right. I didn't need reservations at a restaurant, I'd already had lunch. I was just looking for a roll in the hay, so I had them book me a room."

"What hotel?"

"The Hilton on Route 7."

"Is that where you went?"

"No, the app told me that the hotel had no vacancies. They booked me into the Sheffield Inn on East Avenue, instead." He took a spoonful of chili, blew on it, and then dropped his spoon back into the bowl.

"Then what happened?"

"This is when I should have figured out that something wasn't right. I was supposed to meet the escort in Starbucks. But the girl I met there wasn't the same girl I'd ordered from the directory. But since she still fit my profile, I didn't ask any questions."

"Your profile?"

He raised his eyebrows. "She fit my preferences."

I repeated what he'd told me. "Petite, blond, and young."

"We talked for a few minutes, we hit it off, and then walked to the hotel."

"Then?"

He shrugged again. "We had sex. When it was over, I tipped her, thanked her, and she left."

"You've done this before."

I saw him blush. "Yes."

"Was anything about this encounter different than the others you've had through The Whisper Room?"

Thinking back, he slowly shook his head. "Other than it was a different girl than I'd chosen from the directory, no."

"And you didn't get the room you originally asked for."

"Yes."

Dennis spoke up. "No clue whatsoever that you were being filmed?"

"No."

I had to ask. "One last question. What was the girl's name?"

He blinked. "No idea. I never asked."

Chapter Thirteen

I hopped onto I-95 and immediately merged into bumper-to-bumper, stop-and-go traffic. Knowing that my trip to Greenwich was going to take longer than I'd hoped, I used the time to make some hands-free phone calls.

Stephanie answered on the second ring. From the high pitch of her voice, I could tell her nerves were pulled tight. "Geneva Chase? Do you have any information about Mindy? Have they made an arrest?"

"Not yet. Has your computer guy checked you out for signs of hacking?"

Then her voice went low and angry. "Ian thinks that our system might have been compromised."

Cool way of saying you were hacked.

She continued, "He's installing additional firewalls and security."

While watching an Audi move slowly by me, I asked, "Can he find out who did it?"

"Maybe. But I can already tell you it was that son of a bitch Matt Boca."

I saw flashing lights up ahead on the left telling me that a traffic accident had one of the lanes blocked. "Any idea where I can find Mr. Boca?"

"If I did, I would have already had him put down."

I thought that was an interesting turn of phrase and wondered how serious Stephanie was. She'd probably send Lorna Thorne to do the deed. "Do you think your computer guy can locate him?"

It sounded like Stephanie had put her hand over the phone and was conferring with someone. Probably the imposing Miss Thorne. Finally, she came back onto the line. "We don't know. There are ways to keep your electronic address hidden. Ian knows all about that. It's how we can stay exclusive and available only to our clients and employees."

And another way to keep off the cops' radar.

I was getting closer and closer to the flashing lights. I could see an ambulance among the police cars. "Tell me a little about Ian. He sounds like he knows what he's doing."

He also sounded to me like someone who could easily be the blackmailer. After all, he had access to their system.

"I've known Ian Minor almost my whole life. We went to high school together. He was kind of a nerd back then." She attempted a chuckle. "Nerds are in demand now, aren't they?"

"Yeah, where would we be without nerds?"

"When he developed our app, he was just getting his company started."

"What kind of company is that?"

"Quantum Digital."

"Quantum Digital. Where have I heard that name before?"

"They're the company that created the *Final Apocalypse* game series."

I knew of it. Violent and misogynistic as hell. Parents and church groups from all over the country had called for it to be banned. It only made the games more popular.

"So, it's a gaming company."

"Oh, way more than that. They create apps, websites, computer networks, write code. I don't know how many people Ian has working for him now, but his headquarters is a three-story building in Westport. He travels all over the world, working for some major league corporations."

It does sound like blackmail would be a little beneath him.

But so did doing computer grunt work for an escort service. "And he still does IT for The Whisper Room?"

She chuckled. "He says we'll always have a special place in his heart. Frankly, I think he's still got a crush on me."

"Is this Ian married?"

"Only to his company."

I thought I'd go out on a limb. "So, in your mind, there's no possibility that this guy is the blackmailer?"

"He makes a ton of money, Geneva. Blackmailing a local news anchor would be a waste of his time and talent. No, the blackmailer is Boca."

"Is Matt Boca capable of murder?" I was thinking of Mindy Getz.

Her voice turned grim. "I think that son of a bitch is capable of anything."

"Stephanie, what are my chances of getting a list of Mindy Getz's regular clients?"

"Why?"

"The cops say she was wearing a black dress, like the kind you'd wear out on a date. And she was missing her panties."

"Oh, my God. Was she raped?"

"The autopsy didn't find evidence that she was, but she was in the water for at least twelve hours, so they don't know for sure."

Her voice got cold and professional. "Lorna and I will review her regular customers."

Without further explanation, she disconnected. I thought again about giving Stephanie's name and contact information to Mike Dillon. He'd get a warrant and force The Whisper Room to give up its client information.

But I didn't, and I concentrated on driving. Traffic had resumed its normal pace, slow in some places and breakneck in others. No wonder that this part of I-95 is one of the deadliest stretches of road in America. I told my phone to call Shana Neese.

After five rings, it went to voicemail.

"Hey, Shana, I need another favor. Have you ever heard of a man by the name of Matthew Boca? Maybe running an escort service called Midnight House? Any help you can offer would be appreciated. Talk later. Bye."

As I drove, I wondered if Shana was with a client and smiled as I visualized her paddling the hell out of some hedge fund manager.

———

Cumberland Custom Motorsports has a massive three-story showroom with floor-to-ceiling windows so that even if you drove past it, you'd easily see gleaming, expensive toys for the rich and super-rich. A unique architectural feature was a bank of four elevators. Two were large enough to carry a vehicle, and two were meant to move only people.

No cars were parked outside like at a regular car dealership. These vehicles were much too valuable to be left outside.

I pulled into their lot, but instead of parking, I drove around to the back of the building, where I figured the employees kept their cars. I was greeted by an eclectic group of Fords, Chevys, Toyotas, and Hyundais. There were two exceptions to the mundane mix. One was a Ferrari, and the other was a dark-green Saturn.

I parked my car in the employee lot next to the Saturn and caught sight of the back entrance to the building. Getting out of my car, I went to the door and pulled on it.

Locked.

Then, as luck would have it, a man in khaki slacks, white shirt, and black sport coat came out, almost running right into me.

"Oh, I'm sorry," he said, smiling.

I held the door open as he came out. He was holding an unlit cigarette in his hand.

The man asked, "Can I help you?"

"Yeah, I have an appointment to meet with Joseph Cumberland."

He gestured down a hallway that I could easily see from the door. "Second office on the right."

Then I glanced back at the Saturn. Pointing, I asked, "I didn't think they made those anymore."

The name tag on his jacket said the man's name was Mark. He chuckled. "They don't. That belongs to Timmy, one of our detailers."

"Thanks." I left Mark to his cigarette, and went inside.

Joseph Cumberland's workspace was much like every other sales office I've seen in an automotive dealership. A lot of glass and stainless steel. Looking through his doorway, I saw a man in his late fifties, full head of salt-and-pepper hair, face cleanly shaven. He wore a white shirt, sleeves rolled up to his elbows. A stack of files was piled high next to an open laptop on his desk.

With no visible secretary or gatekeeper, I pulled the glass door open and went in.

He looked up at me with dark-brown eyes and a broad car salesman grin. Standing up behind his desk, he said, "Can I help you?"

"I'm sorry to be a bother, but I just wanted to meet you and maybe ask you a few questions. I'm Geneva Chase with the

Sheffield Post. Could I take a few minutes of your time? I have some questions for a story I'm working on."

"What kind of story?"

I smiled back. "You have a unique inventory. I'm doing a story on what your typical customer might look like."

He gestured that I take a seat. "I'm not sure I want to let my competitors know who my customers are."

When we'd both sat down, I asked, "Do you have competitors?"

He raised an eyebrow. "Anyone who sells cars is a competitor. Buyers have choices. They don't have to come here and buy from me, Miss Chase."

I noticed a photograph on the wall of Joseph Cumberland and an Asian woman I surmised must be his wife, Stephanie's mother. "They have to buy from you if they want the best, Mr. Cumberland." It didn't hurt to butter the roll a little.

He continued to grin and nod. "Well, that's true. Look, my demographic is typically male and usually over forty."

"And men who can afford these vehicles."

He held up a hand. "I won't lie. My customers are kind of an exclusive fraternity. They're men of means."

I was suddenly struck by how Joseph's customer profile was exactly the same as his daughter's.

He continued, "We do have some younger clientele as well. Young men who have come into an inheritance or entrepreneurs who have done very well very quickly."

Like the CEO of Quantum Digital—Stephanie's computer geek?

I prepared to ask my next question. "Mr. Cumberland…"

"Please, call me Joe." I noticed that he had a twinkle in his eye. He didn't look like the control freak his daughter Stephanie had described.

"Call me Genie." I pointed to the photo on the wall. "Is that your wife?"

He turned and followed my line of sight. "Yes, that's Chantana. I met her when I was vacationing in Thailand nearly thirty years ago."

"Any children?"

"My daughter, Stephanie."

"Does she work here? Is she part of the family business?"

His eyes turned sad. "No. She really didn't have an interest in cars. Steph worked here for a few summers when she was in college. Went to Yale," he said proudly. "I really hoped she'd come into the family business with me."

"What's she doing now?"

"She and a couple of her friends developed some hospitality software. Her company is called W.R. Systems. I know they're doing well because she bought a beautiful townhouse out on Wilson Point right on Bartlett Cove, and I know those are not cheap. And one of her subcontractors, Ian Minor, who also owns another software development company, bought a Maserati a few months ago when he got back from a job in Chicago."

I whistled in appreciation. "I'll bet that's not cheap either."

"When we're done, I'll have Jan show you one. She's my top salesperson out on the floor."

"A little more than a journalist can afford, I'm sure. What did your daughter do when she worked here over her summers?"

"Grunt stuff mostly. She didn't like interacting with the customers face-to-face. She'd rather sit in front of a computer. It was primarily data entry."

That's when it hit me. The Whisper Room was able to recruit clients when Lorna was in college and working at an exclusive country club. When they couldn't do that anymore, Stephanie needed to find another roster of "men of means."

What better list could she have than the men who could afford her father's cars?

That means that to keep her list current and recruit more clients, Stephanie had to have access to her father's customer list.

And then it occurred to me how Elliot had been targeted to receive the exclusive Whisper Room app. His wife had purchased a Porsche. I was willing to bet they'd bought it from Cumberland.

———

I asked a few more questions, then dropped my recorder into my bag. Before I could stand up, Joe picked up the phone on his desk, pressed a button, and I heard him say, "Jan, can you stop by my office? I'd like you to show someone around the floor. A reporter."

By the time I had my bag over my shoulder, I turned and was greeted by a tall brunette coming through the door of the office. She wore a white blouse, a pencil skirt, and a black jacket with the Cumberland logo on the lapel. She was made even taller by the black leather Louboutin pumps on her feet.

Jan flashed me a smile and gave me the once-over. "I'm Jan."

I was wearing jeans, a blue sweater, and running shoes. Probably not the attire of her usual client.

Joe said, "This is Genie. She works for the *Sheffield Post,* and she's doing a story about us. Do you mind showing her around?"

"Not at all." She glanced at me. "Follow me, Genie."

We walked down a short, carpeted hallway that opened up into the spacious ground floor of the showroom. We stopped, and I gazed out over the gleaming inventory of Ferraris, Porsches, Bentleys, Aston Martins, and Lamborghinis. If it was exotic, fast, and expensive, it was there.

And this was just the ground floor. There were two more above us.

"Is there anything I can show you?"

"Just out of curiosity, how much is that little number right there?" I nodded toward a red Maserati.

"Good eye. That's a Quattroporte Trofeo with a twin-turbo V8, five hundred eighty horsepower, eight-speed automatic transmission. Just to sweeten the package, the cabin is appointed with leathers, silks, and woods. It goes for one hundred and forty thousand dollars."

I raised my eyebrows.

Jan noted my expression. "While we don't do deals, we can offer a lease at three thousand a month for thirty-nine months, ten thousand due at signing."

I smiled. "Not in my price range. I'm on a newspaper salary. What kind of customer can afford something like that?" I glanced around the ground-floor showroom. All the salespeople were attractive women. One was showing a Bentley to a man who appeared to be in his fifties, dressed in khaki slacks and a mint green polo.

Jan adopted a slightly bemused expression and leaned in, keeping her voice low. "Mostly older men who have money and want to pretend that their testosterone levels are still high."

I took another look, and sure enough, most of the customers kicking the expensive tires were over forty and dressed in high-end clothing. I turned back to Jan. "Do you have an employee here who drives a Saturn?"

She put a hand over her mouth and stifled a laugh. "Timmy."

"What's funny?"

Jan regained her composure. "I'm sorry. I love Timmy to pieces, but he's kind of a hot mess."

"How so?"

She leaned in again. "At our last Christmas party, he brought a date." Jan got even closer to my ear, and her eyes got wide. She whispered, "A hooker."

I must have given her my slightly confused expression.

Jan clarified. "Rumor has it, he spends all of his money on her, and that's why he drives that car." When she said the words "that car," she rolled her eyes.

I decided that I really didn't like Jan.

"Where can I find him?"

It was Jan's turn to look confused, but I didn't explain why I'd asked the question. She pointed to one of the glass elevators in the corner of the vast showroom. "Take that to the basement. It's where the mechanics maintain the inventory. Timmy works in the detailing room."

"Thanks." As I walked away, I was glad that I wasn't buying a car from her. I wouldn't want her to get the commission.

Like I could afford something here.

Reaching the basement, the elevator door opened onto a spacious garage where a half dozen expensive vehicles were being worked on by men wearing denim work shirts with the Cumberland logo above the pocket.

I shouted out to one of them. "Where's the detailing room?"

He seemed a little surprised to see me there. "You're not supposed to be here. Insurance rules."

I gave him a thumbs-up. "Jan said it was okay."

The mechanic seemed angry at that but pointed toward the other end of the garage. "The detailing room is over there."

I walked across the concrete floor, amazed at how clean the garage was, and noticed the wide ramp leading up to the ground level where these cars came and went. The doorway to the detailing room was clearly marked.

When I walked in, I saw a young man in a blue T-shirt with the Cumberland logo across the chest steam-cleaning the engine of a gleaming black Bentley.

I announced myself. "Hi, I'm Geneva Chase with the *Sheffield Post*. Do you own a green Saturn?"

When he stood up straight and turned off the steamer, I saw that he was a tall, slim man, about thirty with a black hipster beard, a prominent Adam's apple, and warm brown eyes. The same young man on Mindy Getz's Facebook page. In that photo, while she was geeking into the camera, his eyes had been on her.

His voice was wary. "Yes."

I decided to go straight at him. "Were you parked next to a dumpster last night, watching Mindy Getz's condo? Are you stalking her?"

I watched as his eyes glistened with tears. He took a deep breath, put a hand to his forehead, and then asked, "She's dead, isn't she?"

Chapter Fourteen

I wondered, did this young man only suspect Mindy Getz was dead or was he making a statement of fact?

Glancing around the hot detailing room with a humidity level akin to a sauna, I noticed there was no place to sit down, other than a single upholstered stool next to a tool counter. "Is there somewhere we can talk?"

The young man stared at me, blinking, rubbing his eyes already glazed with shimmering tears, waiting for me to confirm or deny that Mindy was alive or dead.

I took a breath and repeated myself. "Is there a bench or some chairs somewhere?"

He nodded slightly, glanced up at a clock on the wall, and said, "The break room should be empty."

I took my bag off my shoulder and fished around until I found a tissue that was barely used. "Here, why don't you just wipe that off?" I pointed to the wet trails on his cheeks.

He nodded, took the tissue, and dutifully dried his face. Then he blew his nose.

Dazed, he held it out, thinking I wanted it back, and mumbled, "Thank you."

"Keep it." My heart broke for the young man.

We left the detailing room and trudged slowly through the garage. With their heads under open hoods or facing the underside of vehicles on lifts, not one of the mechanics took notice of us.

Tim led us into a small kitchen complete with a microwave, refrigerator, a small table with four plastic chairs, and an overused coffeepot stained beyond cleaning. As much as the garage space was super tidy, the kitchenette was nasty. Not wanting to put my bag on the floor, I hung it on the back of one of the chairs and sat down. Then I stared up at him, waiting for him to do the same.

Eyes still glistening with welling tears, he lowered himself slowly onto a chair, stretching out the moment, not wanting to hear bad news.

I gave him my most sympathetic smile. "I've already told you that I'm Geneva Chase. What's your full name?"

He cleared his throat. "Timothy Reed."

"Do you like to be called Tim, Timmy, Timothy?"

"Tim," he whispered.

"Do you mind if I ask what your relationship is with Mindy Getz?"

He blinked and was silent for a moment. "Boyfriend. Sort of."

I wondered what Mindy Getz had labeled him.

Tim asked, "Is she alive?"

"Why do you ask that, Tim?"

Tim was silent again, thinking. Then he said, "She does dangerous things."

"What kind of dangerous things?"

He rubbed his eyes and his forehead. "Do you know what she does for a living?"

I nodded. "She's an escort."

"I hate it. I hate that she goes out with men for money."

I glanced up at the doorway leading out into the garage, hop-ing nobody would come in for a snack or a cup of the sludge floating at the bottom of the coffeepot.

"How did you two meet?"

"We met in college. She was studying philosophy, and I was a biology major. I had some crazy idea I'd go to med school and become a doctor." Timothy gave me a shy smile. "That didn't happen."

"And there's not much of a job market for someone with a philosophy degree."

"She was turning tricks while she was still in college, so I knew what she was doing."

"Did you ever live together?"

"We tried it. But every time she got a notification from The Whisper Room, I couldn't stand it. I couldn't stand thinking of her in bed with another man. I left her." He looked down at the table. "But I always came back. Always."

"Why?"

"Is she alive?"

I wasn't sure if I was ready to tell him that yet. "Where were you two nights ago?"

"I was home."

"Where is that?"

"I have a studio apartment on Water Street in Norwalk."

"Any roommates?"

"I live alone."

So, no alibi.

"She called me that night. Mindy said she was going out on a date with someone who wasn't a Whisper Room client."

"Did she know this guy?"

"She didn't say. We each have a tracking app on our phones." He took out his cell phone and showed me the screen. "Being an escort made her nervous sometimes. She dated really rich guys and ate dinner at the best restaurants and, once in a while, one of her customers would take her on vacation. She said she mostly felt safe, but she liked that someone knew where she was."

He sighed. "Something must have made her nervous, because Mindy asked me to keep an eye on her location that evening."

"Where did she go?"

"She said she was meeting this guy at the Z-Bar in South Sheffield." He pulled his phone out of his pocket and punched at the screen, pulling up the app, showing me a map of Sheffield with a red dot where the Z-Bar was located.

"Then where did she go?"

He shook his head. "I don't know. That's where her signal ended." He gazed at me sadly again. "When I saw that, I got into my car and drove to the Z-Bar as fast as I could. Nobody recalled seeing her, including the bartender, Tony. He and Mindy are friends, so he'd know if she'd been in there."

I wondered if I'd have any better luck if I went to the Z-Bar myself and poked around.

When he asked his question again, it was barely a whisper. "Is she alive?"

I took a deep breath. "They found her body in Long Island Sound."

The young man's head dropped into his hands as tears streamed down his cheeks. "I knew it," he gasped.

I watched, my heart aching for the young man. He had fallen in love with an escort, a woman who would never bring the young man anything but pain. But it didn't matter. He'd been in love with her. The fact that she was an escort didn't deaden his anguish over her death.

As his sobs subsided, I asked, "You said you lived together; do you still have a key?"

"No."

"You came back the next night and parked outside her condo?"

"I was hoping she'd come back." He glanced up at me, recognizing me. "You were there last night, talking to Charles."

"Do you know the names of any of Mindy's regular clients?"

He thought for a moment. "She was very discreet. It's one of The Whisper Room's strictest rules."

"No names?"

"I know one of them is the CEO for Branfil Pharmaceuticals."

"How do you know that?"

"When I was still living with her, she came home after a date with a bag filled with plastic bottles of anxiety medicine made by Branfil. She told me that guy she saw that night ran the company."

I wrote that down. "Anything else you can remember?"

He thought about it again. "There's one guy who owns a dozen restaurants in New York and Connecticut. I don't know his name, but one of the restaurants was one Mindy bragged about, Firefly in Stamford. She brought me home a doggy bag from there one night." Then Timothy glanced up at me. "Oh, and that guy who did the news. The guy who held his wife hostage."

"Elliot Carlson?"

He nodded. "Yeah, she said that in real life he isn't anything like he was on television. He's a jerk."

Seems to be the consensus.

"I'm sorry, that's all I can remember."

I handed him one of my old cards from the newspaper. "If you think of anything else, please let me know. Just a heads-up, by now the police are searching Mindy's place, and I'm sure they'll be talking to the same neighbor I talked to last night. He'll tell them that you're her on-again off-again boyfriend. They'll want to talk to you."

He mumbled, "I understand."

As I stood up, he did too and asked, "Do you know if she suffered?"

I put my hand on his forearm. "I don't think so, Tim."

Sometimes a lie isn't a bad thing.

———

I stopped by a little coffee shop about three blocks from Cumberland's vast warehouse of overpriced cars and ordered a latte and a chicken salad sandwich on toasted rye. I found a table, opened my laptop, and while I ate, looked up the CEO of Branfil Pharmaceuticals. William Janik, fifty-seven, had worked his way up from being a pharmaceutical salesman to the head of the corporation. The photo on the company's website showed a handsome man, clean-shaven, with salt-and-pepper hair, twinkling eyes, and a broad smile with white, even teeth.

The bio said he was married, had one grown son, and even though Branfil Pharmaceuticals was based in Danbury, Connecticut, Janik lived in Greenwich.

Of course.

It didn't say anything about him being a regular client of Mindy Getz, dead escort.

Having finished my sandwich, I sipped at the latte, and researched the owner of Firefly, the trendy restaurant in downtown Stamford. In 1959, Theo Andino's parents moved from Mykonos, Greece, to the United States, where Theo and his three younger brothers and two sisters were born.

Theo, now sixty years old, opened his first restaurant in Brooklyn when he was nineteen. Since then, he'd owned eleven other restaurants, including, of course, the trendy Firefly. There were a number of news stories about his success as a restaurateur and many of them included photos. He was balding, around five-nine, weighing in at about two hundred seventy pounds, and not particularly handsome. His eyes were too small, his lips too thin, his face too round.

There was one story about a sexual harassment lawsuit brought by a former employee that had been settled out of court. I wondered what Mindy had thought about him, especially during sex.

I imagined what it must be like. The vision of him on top of me, naked and sweating, made me gag a little.

There were three leads I wanted to follow up on. William Janik, Theo Andino, and Elliot Carlson.

I snapped the lid onto my cup of latte and took my phone out of my bag. My immediate intention was to call Branfil Pharmaceuticals and get an appointment with the CEO.

Before I could punch in the number, my phone vibrated, and I saw that it was Shana Neese. "Shana?"

"Hey, Genie. I got your message."

"Have you ever heard of Matthew Boca?"

"Oh, yes. The Friends of Lydia have an interest in Mr. Boca."

"Sex trafficking?"

"Possible. He runs Panache. It's an upscale gentleman's club."

"A strip joint?"

She chuckled. "Rumor is it's financed by some Mexican investors."

"Cartel cash?"

"Well, it's a good place to launder money, isn't it? The dancers at Panache are a combination of local girls and girls from Guatemala, El Salvador, and the Philippines. The word is he also uses them for an escort service he's running."

"Got an address?"

"Yeah, I'll text it to you. It's in Danbury."

That was a convenient coincidence. I was headed up that way to tour a pharmaceutical company and talk to a guy who was a client of The Whisper Room.

Chapter Fifteen

After a quick check on my phone, I saw that Panache opened for lunch at noon. I was willing to bet that my coffee shop chicken salad was way more palatable than what would be served in a strip club.

Lunch, really?

I'd save my visit to Boca's gentleman's club until after my meeting with William Janik.

I called Janik's pharmaceutical office and, knowing how he'd worked his way up the corporate ladder, told his receptionist that I was a freelance reporter and that I wanted to do a profile on her boss. On how William Janik had shown that the American Dream was still alive. How the average Joe can scratch and claw his way up to the top and become the CEO of a legal pill mill.

While researching Janik, I'd seen about a dozen similar stories in other publications. I was betting that Janik loved talking about himself and having his ego stroked.

The receptionist left me on hold and I listened to Kenny G while she checked to see if Janik had time to meet me that afternoon. A few minutes of cool jazz later, she was back on the phone to say that Mr. Janik would make time to see me. Would one thirty work?

Of course.

Branfil has research and development labs in three states, two manufacturing plants in India, and a massive headquarters on the outskirts of Danbury. Set on a hill outside of town, the seven-story brick building was an imposing square block surrounded by trees. I was certain that the managers called this their "campus." I'd also heard rumors that the "campus" was secured with armed guards, none of whom I saw as I motored up the long drive.

After parking the Lexus in the guest lot, I hoofed it to the front doors where I was met by a smiling woman behind a large counter. That's when I did spot an armed guard standing in front of a bank of elevators. Unlike the receptionist, he wasn't smiling.

I told the woman I had an appointment with William Janik; she phoned his office and looked dutifully impressed when she found that I had told her the truth. I was certain that she was used to dealing with expensively dressed salespeople trying to sneak in and get time with the CEO. Wearing my usual windbreaker, jeans, and sneakers, no one would mistake me for a well-dressed pill executive.

She gave me a visitor's badge. "Mr. Janik's office is on the top floor."

The guard gave me a nod as I walked by, and I took the elevator to the seventh floor. When the door slid open, I found myself in a spacious waiting area with couches, chairs, and coffee tables. About a dozen men and women were there awaiting appointments with other Branfil executives.

"Are you Geneva Chase?" I turned and found myself face-to-face with an attractive woman, about five-eight, trim, and dressed in a smart black skirt, white top, and heels.

"Yes."

"I'm Rochelle, Mr. Janik's assistant. Would you come this way?"

I followed her down a long hallway to a spacious glassed-in office. We walked by what was most likely Rochelle's tidy desk, and she ushered me into the impressive inner sanctum of the pharmaceutical CEO.

William Janik was a large man, tall at about six-four, and overweight by about fifty pounds. He had on a white dress shirt, red power tie, black slacks, and what looked to be Gucci leather oxfords. His face broke into a practiced grin as he hoisted himself out of his chair from behind his glass-and-stainless-steel desk. For such a large man, he came around to greet me with surprising speed and grace. "Miss Chase, I'm William Janik. Please call me Bill."

I smiled back as he took my hand into his own. "Call me Genie."

He motioned to a leather guest chair. "Please sit down. Who did you say you worked for again?"

"I'm freelance. I thought getting to know a man of your stature who's lifted himself up by his bootstraps would make a great piece for a publication like the *Atlantic* or possibly the *New York Times Sunday Magazine.*"

He rubbed his large hands together as he moved back around his desk. "Yes, yes, many people have found my story to be inspiring."

While he lowered himself back into his chair, I took my tiny recorder out of my bag and placed it on my lap. "I hope you don't mind if I record this?"

He grinned again. "We want to get it all right, don't we? Can we get you something to drink? Coffee?"

Already hopped up on my latte from the coffee shop, I shook my head. "No, thank you. Okay, let's start with something easy. How's business?"

"I'm proud to say that last year was our best year ever, and the first quarter of this year is already outperforming expectations."

From the looks of his expensive shoes, his bonus must have outperformed expectations as well. "Your shareholders must be very happy."

"It's not just the bottom line, Genie. It's the work we do. Healing the sick, easing people's pain and anxiety, constantly searching for better medicines. That's what it's all about."

One of the stories I'd read about Branfil was about how they'd been part of the opioid crisis, pushing pills, ignoring the effects of addiction, and the rising death toll. There was a class action suit pending. But I wasn't there for that.

"Your family must be very proud."

He picked up a framed photo from his desk and turned it around so I could see a picture of him in a tuxedo alongside a woman in a blue gown who must have been his wife, a younger man, also in a tuxedo, and a woman in a bridal dress and veil. "This is from my son's wedding last year. Yes, Genie, I think my family is happy with the life I've given them. It's all about family, isn't it?"

Slightly tired of his hypocritical bullshit, I leaned forward. "Look, is your office private?" I glanced back to the closed door. "Rochelle can't hear what we're talking about?"

Confusion clouded his face. "I'm sorry? What?"

"No matter. Do you know a woman by the name of Mindy Getz?"

Bill blinked his eyes twice. "Who?"

"Mindy Getz. She's an escort for a service called The Whisper Room. You're one of her regular clients."

Slightly pale, he undid the top button of his shirt and loosened his tie. "Who are you?"

I leaned back in my chair. "Before you call security, I need to ask you some questions."

He pointed at me. "You're one of them, aren't you? I've already met your demands. You can't keep coming back to squeeze me for more money."

Now I was the one who was confused. "I'm sorry. What?"

His voice was louder, angrier. "You can't keep coming to me for money."

"Who do you think I am?"

"One of those blackmailing bastards at The Whisper Room."

"You're being blackmailed?"

His face was mottled red as he sneered. "I saw what you goddamned people did to that TV news guy. Humiliated him. Ruined his career. Ended his marriage. I paid you, goddamn it. Now leave me the hell alone."

I held up a hand. "I'm not with The Whisper Room. I really am a freelance reporter. I'm trying to find the people behind the blackmail."

As he sat in silence, waiting for me to continue, I could feel the hostility radiating in my direction.

I kept my voice level as I said, "Mr. Janik, the owners of The Whisper Room believe their operations system was hacked. They suspect a competitor is trying to scare their clientele away."

"Well, they're doing a damned good job. I'll never use them again."

He didn't say he'd never hire an escort again. He'd only said that he wouldn't use The Whisper Room.

"Let me guess, you ordered an escort from their app and a different girl showed up instead. And instead of getting the hotel you wanted, the app said there was no vacancy, and it set you up with a room at the Sheffield Inn."

His face had taken on the look of someone who had just witnessed a magic trick. "Who are you? Really?"

"I really am a crime journalist. I'm trying to find out who

blackmailed you and, even more, find out who killed Mindy Getz."

The man's angry scarlet face abruptly changed expression. His mouth opened slightly, and his eyes went soft. His voice was barely a whisper. "Mindy's dead?"

"Murdered. And you were one of her regular customers."

He didn't answer.

"Did you ever meet with Mindy without going through The Whisper Room?"

He slowly nodded. "A couple of times. She told me that I could save some money by contacting her directly. And she didn't have to split her cut with the service."

"Did she ever tell you about any other men she had arrangements with?"

"No."

"Where were you two nights ago?"

He had to think. "I was home with my wife. We had friends over for dinner."

Does that scratch him off my list of suspects?

"Did the blackmailer send you a video?"

He glanced down at his phone, sitting on his desktop next to his computer keyboard. "Yes."

"Can I see?"

His eyes went wide, and his mouth opened as a look of terror crept across his face. "Dear God, no."

"Is the girl petite and blond?"

"Yes. When they sent me the video, they claimed the girl's only fifteen. But when I met her, she told me she was nineteen. And The Whisper Room guarantees that all of their escorts are over nineteen."

"Did she tell you her name?"

He thought again. "Piper. She said her name was Piper and

she was studying to be a nurse. She was taking classes at Norwalk Community College."

"You said you already paid the blackmailer off? How much?"

He scowled. "A hundred thousand dollars. Wired from my account to an account in the Caymans. Money shoved down a rabbit hole."

That was considerably more than they'd demanded from Elliot Carlson. But then again, there was a wide difference in what a local news anchor earns and what the CEO of a pharma makes.

"And they haven't contacted you again?"

"I thought you were one of them."

"Am I right about the hotel?"

Reluctantly, he nodded his head and agreed. "Yes, it was the Sheffield Inn."

"Do you recall the room number?"

He shook his head.

I almost asked him if he'd ever had a beer at a strip club called Panache, but I'd already gotten more than I thought I would from Mr. Janik.

Better if I leave with what I have.

Chapter Sixteen

"No unescorted ladies in the club." His words were as much a snarl as a statement. At six-five, around three hundred pounds, the bouncer's square frame was as imposing as the boxy, brick, windowless building he was guarding. He wore a black blazer, gray shirt, black bow tie, work boots, and jeans; his head was shaved, and his eyes were open wide and seemed a little too wild and crazy for me.

Maybe that was the look he was going for.

I had to shout to be heard over the heavy bass of the music coming from inside the club. "That sounds discriminatory to me."

"The owner doesn't want any trouble with single ladies sitting at the bar."

"Actually, I'm not here to stare at your girls or start any trouble. I'm here to talk to Mr. Boca. Is he in?"

His eyebrows lifted. "You got an appointment?"

"Tell him I'm here to talk about the Midnight House."

His eyes compressed to tiny slits as he studied me. Finally, he said, "Just a minute."

I stood in the lobby of Panache and waited. The lighting in the small foyer was dim, the carpeting was a neon blue, and framed, glossy photos hung on the red velvet-covered walls. Apparently, they were images of women who had performed at Panache. All of them were naked, at least from the G-string up.

The bouncer disappeared through a doorway covered by a red curtain. On the wall next to it hung a sign that said that you must be twenty-one to enter and there was a two-drink minimum.

While I waited, I listened to the song "American Woman." The bass was loud enough to make my teeth vibrate.

A few moments later, the bouncer returned and motioned that I should follow him in. The interior of Panache was decorated in much the same way the lobby was, except it was devoid of glossy photos. And it was darker. Most of the lighting was directly over the stage; multicolored spotlights focused on the woman, wearing only the tiniest of thongs, twisting and writhing around the pole, her sweat-covered skin glistening in the illumination.

The dancer was in her late twenties, athletic, her brunette hair cut in a bob with bangs, and she would have been pretty except for the general boredom in her eyes.

At that time of day, she only had an audience of two men. One was in his thirties, dressed in a business suit, tie loosened, and a bottle of beer in front of him. The other was a guy maybe in his sixties with a ponytail, wearing a Pink Floyd T-shirt and jeans, also with a bottle of beer positioned on the counter.

They were both gazing up at the dancer, hypnotized, fantasizing.

The two men glanced at me, but seeing I was fully clothed, immediately turned back to the woman running her hands up and down her body on the stage. As I followed the bouncer through the club, I couldn't help but notice that the upscale gentleman's club smelled like stale beer and sweat, mixed with urine and despair.

The bouncer opened a door on the far end of the bar, letting me into Matt Boca's office. Slightly smaller than the lobby, the room's walls were stucco, the carpeting was an emerald green, and the desk that Boca was seated at was gun-metal gray. Behind him, three large monitors hung on the wall. On the desk in front of him was an open laptop. He closed it and stood up, studying me from head to toe and back.

He was wearing a Tommy Bahama light-blue long-sleeve T-shirt and khakis. He had dark-brown eyes under thick black eyebrows. About thirty, he was handsome with even features framed by dark stubble on the lower half of his face. He smiled, showing a set of perfect, insanely white teeth. "Leo tells me you're here about the Midnight House. Are you applying for a job as an escort?"

He struck me as being a jackass right off the bat. "That's almost flattering. Aren't I a little mature to be an escort?"

Meaning too old.

"Oh, I think you're pretty enough, and I'd be willing to bet you have some experience around the bedroom."

I felt my face redden.

Then he added, "And some of my clients have a mommy thing going on."

"I think I just stopped being flattered."

The big man, Leo, behind me asked, "You need me anymore, boss? There's nobody watching the lobby."

Boca waved him out.

When the door closed, I noticed that none of the musical din from the club could be heard. I guessed that his office was soundproof.

He asked, "You are?"

"Geneva Chase." I handed him a Lodestar Analytics business card.

"Lodestar Analytics?"

"We do research."

His dark eyes met mine. "And what, Miss Chase, are we researching today?"

"Please, call me Genie. Can I sit down?" Without permission, I dropped my bag to the floor and sat in a leather chair.

He squinted at me and sat back down behind his desk. "By all means. Call me Matt."

"I'm looking into escort services. I understand you're the owner and operator of one called the Midnight House."

He propped his elbow on the top of the desk and perched his chin in the palm of his hand. Not too convincingly, he said, "It's more of a dating service. An app you can download on your phone or on your computer." He gestured toward his laptop. "Mainly for people of means."

"So, it's a lot like The Whisper Room."

He studied me again, wondering what I was really doing there. "It's still a work in progress, but once I'm finished, it'll be better than The Whisper Room."

I nodded toward the three computer screens behind him. One displayed closed-circuit shots of the exterior and interior of the club. One appeared to be scrolling stock prices from around the world. The middle one was computer code gibberish. "Looks like NASA in here. Are you the one who's doing the programming?"

He glanced behind him. "Self-taught while I was at Yale."

"What was your major?"

"Partying."

"I tried to find your app online."

"Oh, you need to know the URL."

I pulled out my phone.

Matt gave me his trademark smile. "Punch in www .midnighthouse.com. What's your phone number, and I'll give you permission to download it." He opened his laptop up again.

I gave him my number, he punched it into his laptop, and up popped a website welcoming me to the Midnight House. On a background that looked like black silk, it claimed to be the full-service, exclusive dating app guaranteed to match the user with the most beautiful women and men in the tri-state area. "What more do you have to do before it's completely finished?"

"It's already functional, running, and profitable. But it's still a little buggy. It crashes at inopportune times." He leaned forward in his chair, his chin over his desktop. "Want my opinion?"

"Sure."

"I think Stephanie has her geek dumping viruses and shit into my site. There's a thing going on between them."

"A thing?"

He rolled his eyes. "You know. A thing."

"Between Stephanie Cumberland and her computer guy?"

"Yeah."

"Is it true you used to work for The Whisper Room?"

He grinned. "For a while. It's where I got the idea for the Midnight House. I really didn't like being an escort. I got tired of humping middle-aged women, and men who claimed they weren't gay. I decided to start my own escort service."

"Dating app," I corrected him, smiling.

He nodded his head. "Dating app."

"It feels a little like you might have stolen their concept."

He shrugged. "So, sue me."

I glanced around his office. The only thing hanging on his wall was his diploma from Yale. There was a bookshelf but no books. Instead, it held vintage toys, mostly from the seventies. *Star Wars* and G.I. Joe action figures, tiny Hot Wheels and Matchbox muscle cars, all of them still in their original packaging.

I asked, "Do you own this place?"

"Panache? I have partners."

"Did these partners give you the start-up cash for the Midnight House app?"

"Are you a cop?"

"I'm a research analyst."

"I call bullshit but that's okay. My partners enjoy my business acumen."

When the door to Matt's office suddenly swung open, cacophonous music flooded into the room, followed by a man in tan slacks, loafers, and a white button-down shirt, open at the throat. He was about five-eight and muscular, balding, with a ruddy complexion. He was also wearing a tacky gold chain around his thick neck. "Leo stopped by my office and said someone was in here asking questions about Midnight House."

Matt looked slightly perturbed and gestured toward me. "Ernest Ruiz, meet Genie Chase."

He glanced down at where I was sitting, then looked back at Matt. "What's she here for?"

Matt pointed to the business card. "She works for something called Lodestar Analytics. She's curious about our dating app."

Ernest studied me with unblinking eyes. "I've heard of Lodestar Analytics. They dig up dirt on politicians and leak it to the press."

I hated being associated with that misconception. "That's not us. I'm here because a news anchor was blackmailed, and he thinks the people at The Whisper Room did it."

Matt chuckled. "I saw that on TV. It's freaking hilarious. Stephanie and Lorna must be crappin' in their stilettos."

Ernest never cracked a smile. "What's that got to do with us?"

He was in my personal space, and I felt that he was standing over me. "Us?"

He answered. "We have an interest in Matt's businesses."

Remembering that Shana heard Matt was bankrolled by cartel

money and that strip clubs were perfect fronts for money laundering, I asked, "We? Who's we?"

Ernest declined to answer, moved to one side, and dropped into the chair next to mine. He never took his eyes off me. "So, I repeat, what's somebody being blackmailed got to do with us?"

"The owners of The Whisper Room believe they've been hacked. They think it was Matt here who was behind it and that he blackmailed the news guy. And maybe others as well."

For the first time since I met him, Ernest cracked a tiny grin. "And why would we do that?"

"If clients of an escort service find out they might be targets for blackmail, they're going to dump that service like a bad habit. A start-up like Midnight House could benefit by the losses of its competitor."

The two men glanced at each other. Then Matt shrugged and looked back at me. "Wish I'd thought of it. It's not us, though."

Ernest reached over and put his hand on my forearm, genuinely creeping me out. "Look, you're a pretty girl and all, but I don't think it's a good idea for you or Lodestar to sniff around our business anymore."

I felt the heat of anger rising inside me as I felt his clammy hand on my skin. "Why? Are you going to sic Leo on me?"

He sneered. "Lady, Leo is a dream date compared to the nightmare we could make for you."

Chapter Seventeen

I took Route 7 south from Danbury, and just as I was hitting the Wilton town line, I got a call from Nathaniel Rubin. I answered, "Hey, Nathaniel." It was never Nat. Never Nate. Always Nathaniel.

"I got a call from Shana. We're going to do a pro bono job for the Friends of Lydia."

The nice thing about doing a pro bono job for Lodestar Analytics? Nathaniel worked pro bono. I still got paid. And I liked doing work for the Friends of Lydia. The Lydia organization was named for Shana's sister, who was beaten to death by a pimp when she was still just a teenager. It was Shana's motivation for rescuing women who were being trafficked or abused.

And when she did it, it wasn't always according to the rule book or even the law. For Shana, the end really did justify the means.

"What's the job?"

"You said you were looking into an escort service owned by Matt Boca. Shana wants us all in on that."

I smiled. "Timing is everything. I just came from Boca's strip club in Danbury. Had a sit-down with him and a guy by the name of Ernest Ruiz. They claim they had nothing to do with blackmailing Elliot Carlson."

"Blackmail's not our concern. We want to know if they're trafficking."

It was a noble cause, of course, but it added to my overfilled plate. I was already looking for a blackmailer and a killer. "This Ruiz guy has already warned me to quit looking into their matters. Lodestar, too."

"What, are you handing our business cards out like Halloween candy?"

"I don't have any from the *Sheffield Post* anymore." That part was a lie. "And it's easier to get my foot in the door if I'm a research analyst rather than a nosy reporter." That part was the truth.

"They threatened you?"

"In a matter of speaking. Well, no, literally, yes."

"Well, Lodestar won't be nosing around their businesses. It'll be the Friends of Lydia. John's flying back tonight. He finished his Portland assignment last night."

My heart took an extra couple of beats. Since February, John and I had a couple of pleasant dinners followed by a couple of enjoyable if not athletic adventures in his hotel room. Hearing that he was coming back to Connecticut made my temperature rise a little.

"Are you putting John on this?"

I wondered how much Nathaniel knew about John and me.

"Yes. Shana too. She wants to be hands-on with this one."

"Do we know what our end game will be?"

"To find out as much as possible about Matt Boca and his operation. If he's trafficking, we're going to shut him down."

"Did Shana tell you who's rumored to be his financial backers?"

"Cartel money. You worried?"

You bet your ass, I'm worried.

"Let's call it a healthy concern."

I could almost hear Nathaniel smile over the phone. "Good, I want to keep you healthy. Keep me posted."

I glanced at the clock on my dash. It was about three thirty. I knew that one of Jessica Oberon's moms would pick up Jessica and Caroline from soccer practice...or was it band practice again? All I knew for sure was it meant I didn't need to hurry home.

I also knew that the lunch rush at the restaurant called Firefly was long over and the kitchen staff would be prepping for that night's dinner crowd. It was time for me to stop by to meet another one of Mindy Getz's regular customers.

———

Downtown Stamford is known for its eclectic mix of restaurants. Depending on one's mood or taste buds, they could choose anything from Italian to Spanish, Japanese to Brazilian, French to Tex-Mex.

Firefly was about as upscale as Fairfield County got. Which means that even when I get a bonus from Lodestar, I can't afford to eat there. It also means that it's extremely popular, and reservations are often booked up months in advance.

When I walked through the front door, the place was empty. The warm earth tones, marble floor, black tablecloths, crystal goblets, the faint scent of garlic and tomatoes were all as welcoming as an old friend. There was no hostess to greet me, so I strode parallel to the bar along the left side of the dining area, threading my way around some of the empty tables until I got to the kitchen doorway.

I carefully pushed open the door and peeked inside. A half dozen men and women in white jackets, hairnets, and cloth caps were chopping, cutting, marinating, and prepping for the evening's dinner crowd.

I went in and let the door close behind me. The closest kitchen employee was cutting carrots at an eye-blurring speed. I didn't want to spook him for fear he'd cut off a finger, so I moved around to where he'd see me in his peripheral vision. When he stopped what he was doing, I asked, "Is Theo Andino here?"

He blinked at me. "Chef?"

From the way he said the word, I suspected that English was a second language for the man. "Yes, Chef."

He pointed toward the rear of the busy kitchen where a short man the shape of a fireplug was watching a tall woman in a hairnet add spices to a large, steaming pot. Theo Andino was wearing the same white jacket as everyone else, but he was also wearing a black leather duckbill cap. From where I stood, I could see his closely cropped salt-and-pepper beard and deep creases at the corners of his gray eyes and sides of his mouth.

I left the carrot chopper to his work and walked along the series of stainless-steel tables and other preppers who openly stared at me as I passed them. When I got close enough, I gently said, "Chef?"

He turned, gave me an angry look, and shouted, "Who the hell are you and why are you in my kitchen?"

The entire kitchen stopped and gawked at me, mouths open, eyes wide.

I gave him a sincere grin, or at least as sincere as I could muster because I'd taken an immediate dislike to Chef Theodor Andino. "My name's Geneva Chase, and I'm a reporter for the *Sheffield Post*. I'm working on a story about Mindy Getz."

I wanted a reaction, and I got it. His dark eyes went wide, and he blanched at the sound of her name. "Look, let's step out into the dining room." He glanced over at the tall woman stirring the pot and mumbled, "Just keep doin' what you're doin.'"

Then, without another word, he moved quickly through his kitchen with me behind him. He pushed through the door to the dining area and walked briskly to the bar, where he sat down on one of the stools, gesturing that I should do the same. Then he growled, "Who the hell are you again?"

I repeated, "Geneva Chase. I work for the *Sheffield Post*, and I'm doing a story on Mindy Getz."

He put his elbow on the maple surface of the bar and rested the side of his head in his hand, trying to look as casual as possible. "What's that got to do with me?"

I smiled again. "I understand you're a regular customer of Miss Getz."

He jerked as if he'd gotten a mild static shock. "I don't know what you're talking about."

"She's dead, you know." I didn't have to blurt it out. Her name hadn't yet been publicly associated with the Jane Doe fished out of Long Island Sound. I could have eased into the news with Theo, but I was pissed off at the way he shouted at me in the kitchen.

His ruddy complexion went pale, and he sat up straight, his confidence shaken. "How?"

"Murdered. Where were you two nights ago?"

"Here. I'm always here. We're open every night except for Mondays."

"What time do you go home?" I already knew that the restaurant closed at ten.

I saw that he was still trying to wrap his mind around the fact that a prostitute he frequented, and might have had feelings for, was murdered. "I don't know, eleven maybe. Sometimes I don't get out of here until after midnight."

Still, more than enough time to meet with Mindy and then kill her. "Tell me about Mindy."

He glanced nervously around the dining room. "What makes you think I know this woman?"

"Did you know that Mindy had a boyfriend?"

He was silent.

"She used to brag to him about your food."

His shoulders sagged when he realized he'd been outed. Theo sighed. "She was a nice girl. Whenever I used The Whisper Room dating app, I always chose her. She was sweet and very smart. Philosophy major. I'd meet her and take her a nice meal from the kitchen."

"Where did you meet?"

He hesitated. "Different places."

"Different hotels?"

"Yes."

"Ever been to the Sheffield Inn?"

He looked at me suspiciously. "Yes. Not my favorite meeting place."

"Oh, why not?"

He scowled. "The rooms seem a little dated."

"When's the last time you saw her?"

He took a deep breath. "I don't know. Maybe a week ago? My schedule is a blur."

"Was there anything different about her? Was she nervous or anxious about anything?"

He slowly shook his head. "No, not that I can recall. I took her a petite filet and fingerling potatoes and a bottle of wine. She ate while we chatted."

"And?"

He scowled and glanced around again, clearly uncomfortable. "And what?"

"Did the two of you have sex?" I really didn't have to ask that. Of course, they had sex. She was a paid escort, and they were in a hotel room.

In a low voice, he answered. "Yes."

"Do you know if she had any enemies?"

"No, but she told me about that boyfriend. She said that the two of them had a contentious relationship. She said he sometimes followed her and would park his car outside her condo. I told her I have friends who could talk to him. Maybe get him to leave her alone."

"Was she worried that he might get violent?"

Timmy the detailer was still on my list of possible suspects.

He shrugged. "She never said. She just told me that it bothered him that she did her kind of work."

"One more question. Has anyone ever tried to blackmail you?"

His brows knitted as he considered my question. "You mean like that TV news guy?"

"Yeah."

"Did The Whisper Room really try to extort money from that guy?"

"No."

At least that's what they keep telling me.

"They better not try that with me. I've got friends who'd track them down and make sure they'd never be seen again."

That was the second time he'd talked about his mysterious "friends."

"Okay."

"I've already got enough problems. One of my part-time waitstaff filed a sexual harassment suit against me."

Another one?

Looking at him, I didn't doubt that for a minute. He struck

me as being a dog who thought he was a player. "Does she have a case?"

"Of course not. Look, will any of this be in the papers?"

"No. But something for you to think about. If I can track you down as one of Mindy's regular customers, the cops can too."

Chapter Eighteen

I brought home a caprese salad with blackened mahi for me and a double bacon cheeseburger and onion rings for Caroline. No, it wasn't from Firefly.

Placing the paper bags on the kitchen counter, I went back into the living room, stripped off my windbreaker, and hung it up in the hall closet.

Tucker must have heard me come in because the terrier came rushing down the stairs in a blur of brown and tan fur. I swept the little guy up into my arms and hugged him close while his tail wagged at a furious pace and he licked at my face.

Caroline stood at the top of the steps and called out, "Hey, Genie. How was your day?"

I looked up at her. She's on the cusp of being sixteen and there were some evenings she'd barely grunt at me, some evenings she'd try to start an argument, and some evenings when she'd be chatty as hell. At that age, it was a crap shoot; you just never knew what you're going to get.

"Productive, how was yours?"

Wearing one of her father's old T-shirts, pajama bottoms, and slippers, she plodded down the stairs. "It was okay. Hey, I aced my calculus test."

"Ugh, I hated calculus."

"And I got a B-plus on a chemistry quiz."

"Awesome."

"What's for dinner?"

And just like that, the subject of our day had been derailed. "Double bacon cheeseburger from Farley's."

She grinned. "Love me some Farley's. Onion rings?"

I chuckled. "Wouldn't be Farley's without onion rings."

Without another word, she went into the kitchen. She called back at me. "What do you want to drink?"

Vodka and tonic.

I shook that off and carried Tucker into the kitchen and put him on the floor. "Just a glass of water."

Caroline had already opened the bags and removed the Styrofoam containers of food. "We should really be insisting that when we get takeout, they use eco-friendly materials. This stuff literally lasts forever in landfills."

"The next time I'm in Farley's, I'll let them know." My tone was only slightly sarcastic. The kid was right, after all.

Caroline sat down at the table with Tucker at her feet, watching her chew and hoping that she'd drop something. Wiping her lips with a paper towel, Caroline said, "Kayla Daniels is having a party Friday night. Can I go?"

I brought my salad to the table and sat down, opening my own container. "Will her parents be there?"

She bit into an onion ring and closed her eyes in a moment of oily bliss. "I guess," she answered, still chewing.

"You guess? Is Jessica going?"

"Yup." Caroline took a bite of her cheeseburger, a dribble of ketchup on her chin.

I stabbed at a tomato nesting in my salad. "You can go, but I need to make sure that Kayla's parents are going to be there."

She rolled her eyes and whined. "They'll be there. Why don't you trust me?"

Before the argument had a chance to begin, my phone buzzed against the tabletop. When I went to answer it, Caroline already had hers in her hand and was texting someone.

"Hello?"

"Geneva Chase?"

"Yes?"

"Hey, bitch, it's Elliot Carlson." He'd been drinking. His words were slurring.

"Hi?" It was really all I could think of saying. I had no earthly idea why he'd be calling me.

"You know my life is over."

Yes.

He sounded like he'd been drinking *a lot*. "Is there someone you can talk to, Mr. Carlson? Maybe Dennis Russo? I can call him for you."

"There's nothing anyone can do, Geneva Chase. My life is over and there's nothing anyone can do."

"Are you at your mom's place?"

"No. I'm home. My home. My house."

I felt a sudden chill. "Where's your wife?"

"I don't know. I sat outside and watched the house until she left. Now I'm inside," he chuckled at his own drunken joke. Then he added, "How would you like the biggest story of your miserable career?"

I felt a sudden chill. "What are you talking about, Elliot?"

"Get your scrawny ass over here in the next fifteen minutes, and you'll find out. The front door is unlocked. Just let yourself in."

He hung up.

My hands were cold with terror. My heart was thumping hard with adrenaline.

What did I know for sure? That he'd driven from Bridgeport to Sheffield and had sat, hidden, outside his home until his wife left. Then he broke into his house. No...he most likely still had a key to the front door.

And I knew he was drunk.

Did he have a gun or had the cops confiscated it?

I called Mike Dillon.

"Genie? What's up, I'm kind of busy."

"It's Elliot Carlson. He just called me. He's inside his house here in Sheffield."

He took a breath. "Shit. Is his wife in there with him?"

"He says she's not. He says he sat in his car watching his house until she left. Then he somehow got back into his house. And something else, Mike. He's sounds like he's hammered."

"That's just great. I'll have someone go over there. It's going to be a few minutes. I have two massive accidents. One on I-95 and one on the Merritt. Traffic is backing up for miles. That's sucking up most of my manpower for the moment."

I glanced at my watch. "He said that if I got there in fifteen minutes, he'd give me the story of my career."

Mike growled, "Don't go anywhere near there, Genie. Stay where you are. We'll take care of it."

"Did you confiscate his rifle?"

"Yes, but that doesn't mean he doesn't have another gun hidden in the house somewhere."

He disconnected, and I saw Caroline, burger in her hand, face frozen. "I heard all of that."

"I've got to go."

"Genie, no."

"I've got to go." I stood up. My legs were weak. I went into the living room, grabbed my jacket, hung my bag over my shoulder, and started for the door.

Caroline came into the living room. "Genie," she pleaded, "no."

I offered a wan smile. "I won't be long." I reached for the door but stopped and turned around to look at her. "I love you."

I could see tears welling in her eyes. "I love you, too, Genie."

———

It took me twelve minutes to get to the Carlson house. Parking in the driveway next to the Porsche still hidden by the silver car cover, I considered my options.

Sit in the car until the cops got there.

Or I could go to the front door.

The last thing Elliot Carlson said to me was that the front door was unlocked, and I should let myself in.

He may have a gun, and he's definitely been drinking.

I could think of nothing good that could possibly come out of this. Other than Elliot was right. Catching him in his wife's house would make a good story. Good ink. And good ink was my job.

I got out of my car and closed the door as quietly as I could. There seemed to be only one light on in the house, in the upstairs master bedroom.

I looked up at the window and my heart stopped.

Elliot Carlson was staring down at me, grinning.

In a particularly unnerving moment, he waved me to come inside.

Genie, if you go in there, you're the stupidest person on earth.

A siren wailed in the distance, getting closer. Mike was true to his word. He was sending someone by to check on the situation. From the sound, the police cruiser would be there in minutes.

There wasn't much time.

If you're going to do this, do it.

I willed my feet to move forward, staring up at the window.

I was stunned to see Elliot was no longer staring down at me. He was gone.

Waiting for me?

I took a deep breath, trying to gauge from the sound of the siren how long it would be before the cops got there.

When I opened the front door, the hallway was pitch black. I reached out, scrabbling at the wall, trying to find a light switch. Feeling it, I flicked it up and the hall light came to life.

I felt a little better, more in control. I had mastered the darkness. At least there in that part of the house.

I peered up the short set of carpeted steps leading to the dark living room. I quietly climbed them, shuffled carefully across the living room floor, and went to the stairway leading to the second floor.

Frozen at the bottom of the steps, I shouted, "Elliot?"

Silence. I half expected to see him appear on the landing, gun pointed down at my head.

"Elliot?"

I jumped when the deafening sound of a gunshot echoed down the stairwell.

My heart jackhammered hard against my chest. My hand rested on the banister leading up to the living room. I was paralyzed. I couldn't move.

The siren was getting closer.

I stared up the stairs, into the darkness on the second floor.

I turned on the light switch and willed my legs to slowly climb the steps, cringing at every creak and squeal of wood.

The police siren was closing fast.

I called out. "Elliot?"

Dead silence.

"Elliot?"

I crept down the hallway to the door to the master bedroom. "Elliot? Are you in there? The police are almost here."

The siren had stopped, red and blue lights erratically flashed on and off through the windows.

I pushed open the bedroom door.

He was sitting on the floor, head cocked at an unnatural angle, gripping a handgun that rested on the carpet.

Blood and tissue were just beginning to trickle down the wall where the bullet had ripped through the top of Elliot Carlson's head.

Chapter Nineteen

"I think I corrupted the crime scene." I could hear the nerves in my voice.

Mike's temperament wavered between anger at me for having entered the house at all and sympathy for having seen the gruesome tableau. "How did you do that?"

"I puked in the master bedroom."

He sighed. "Why did you even go in there?"

"Chasing down a story, Mike."

"I thought you were out of the newspaper business."

I offered him a weak smile. "You never really get out."

He crossed his arms. "Have you finished giving Officer Davison your statement?"

"Yes."

"Can you drive yourself home?"

I turned and took one more look at the house where Elliot Carlson had ended his life. "Yes. Has anyone contacted his wife?"

"While you were in the back of Davison's patrol car, she came home." He sighed again. "I was the one who broke it to her."

I glanced down the road to where the police had, once again, set up barricades. Mobile news crews had their cameras out and they were trained on where Mike and I were standing. "How did she take the news?"

"Better than I anticipated. I think she was more pissed off about the mess he made in their bedroom than the fact that he's dead."

"I think that with everything she's going through, distancing herself from the pain might be a coping mechanism."

He stared at me. My observation seemed to amuse him. "Well, thank you, Dr. Chase. I think it's time for you to go home. Are you sure you're steady enough to drive?"

I waved at him. "Piece of cake." I stole one more glance at the house. "Sorry about the mess in the bedroom." I, of course, meant my vomiting on the rug.

He gazed up at the bedroom window where detectives were busy documenting the scene. "Yeah, a gun blast to the head can really be ugly." He glanced back at the television cameras up the road. "I'll radio Cummings to move the barricade when you drive up to it. I don't think you want to stop and do any interviews with those vultures, do you?"

"No, thank you." It occurred to me as I got into my car, that I was one of those vultures.

Congratulations, Genie. You got your freakin' story.

———

I could have driven home, but I didn't. I drove to South Sheffield instead and parked on the street in front of Bricks. The bar at the back was empty except for one lone guy sitting at the end, watching the news. He was somewhere in his sixties and was wearing a tropical shirt and jeans. His eyes were glassy like he'd been there for a while.

The young man behind the bar was someone I hadn't seen before. "What can I get you?"

I hesitated. Then I noticed how my hands were shaking. "Vodka tonic."

Jesus, Genie. Really?

I've written a lot of stories in my life that have altered people's lives. Some in a good way. More than not, some in a bad way.

There are people who will say that they had it coming. They broke the law. They ignored society's moral codes. They betrayed the public trust. They thought they could get away with something.

I was the one who held up the light to expose those injustices. That had been my job.

But I'd never written something that had driven a person to suicide.

I know. I wasn't the only journalist on Elliot Carlson's story. I'm not sure what it was that made him single me out. Maybe it was because his wife had talked to me.

Maybe that made it more personal to him.

I glanced up at the television screen. The news anchor who had replaced Carlson was an earnest-looking forty-something with graying hair and expressive eyes. I couldn't hear what he was saying, but I saw that the program had gone to video showcasing the scene outside of the Carlson house. At first it was of police cars, their lights flashing, then a clip of an occupied body bag strapped to a gurney being wheeled out to an EMT vehicle, followed by short sound bites with the neighbors.

Then another clip showed me driving past the camera crews while Officer Cummings moved the barricade. My name crawled across the screen in a chyron. GENEVA CHASE, CRIME JOURNAL-IST, FOUND THE BODY.

This was the second time in three days that the Carlson household had been a crime scene. The first was when Michelle

Carlson locked herself in the bathroom while her husband threatened to kill himself with his rifle.

The second was when he actually did it.

The bartender brought me the tumbler of vodka, tonic, and ice. "Anything else I can get you?"

I shook my head, eyes still fixed on the television screen.

The guy at the other end of the bar, seeing that I was watching the news, held up the remote. "Want me to turn it up?"

I didn't need to hear it. "No, thank you."

I didn't need to see it either. I'd already seen too much. I don't think I'll ever get the sight of Elliot's body slumped down on the bedroom floor out of my head.

A professional photograph of Elliot Carlson appeared on the screen. The man at the end of the bar pointed to the TV. "That poor news guy. Talk about someone crashing and burning."

I didn't answer.

He was right. Elliot had it all. Beautiful wife who made a ton of money. A high-profile job. Perfect house in a nice neighborhood. A Porsche in the driveway.

And he threw it all away. For an afternoon with an escort.

Then the man at the bar said in a low growl, "But you know, anyone who has sex with a fifteen-year-old deserves what he gets. I guess that Carlson guy didn't like his turn in the spotlight."

The man at the end of the bar started me thinking. One, it was the blackmailer who had said the girl was fifteen. That was yet to be proven.

And two, had the media driven Elliot to suicide?

Was I complicit in his death?

I reached out and touched the glass in front of me. It had already fogged over with condensation. I drew a line on the tumbler with my finger.

Is that why he called me to bear witness to him blowing his head off?

The broadcast outlets had made his downfall a circus. I'd tried dealing with him as fairly as possible.

So, why do I feel like such a shit?

I picked up the glass, feeling its cold comfort in my hand. I knew all about guilt, and I also knew that Absolut would help take it away.

Temporarily.

My cell phone rang, and I put the tumbler back down on the bar. Pulling the phone out of my bag, I saw that it was Laura Ostrowski's private number. "Laura?"

"Genie. I'm home watching the news. Are you okay?"

I hesitated. "Yeah, a little shook up. It was pretty ugly."

"I'll bet. Look, there's no way we can get out ahead on this. The TV jockeys are all over it already. But we'll need something for the morning edition. Can you put something together? Or I can ask Bill to do it."

She was a pro and knew that this had taken an emotional toll on me. But it was my job to hammer something out. "No, I'll do it. I'm on my way home. I can do it from my kitchen. I'll have something to you in about an hour."

As I reached into my bag to get my wallet, Laura asked, "Are you sure you're okay?"

Dropping some money on the top of the bar, I pushed the vodka away. "Yeah, I'm okay."

Chapter Twenty

By the time I got home, Caroline had seen the newscasts about Elliot Carlson's suicide and me finding the body. Her friends had texted her multiple times. And by then, copies of video had made it onto the internet. Not only was my name mentioned, but the name of the escort service as well, The Whisper Room.

It had all started with The Whisper Room.

When I opened our front door, she was there, her arms out, ready to give me a hug. And I was more than ready to get one. "Are you okay?" she asked.

Everyone keeps asking me that.

"About as okay as I can be."

"It must have been awful."

"It wasn't pretty."

"What do you think made him do it?"

"You mean what drove him to suicide? I don't know, sweetie."

I think I did. He'd reached the tattered end of his rope. He'd lost everything. He'd gone from respected newsman to a punchline.

Before I could get my jacket off, my phone was buzzing again. I picked up, "This is Geneva."

"Genie, this is Dennis Russo. I just saw what happened on the news."

Please don't ask me if I'm okay. "What the hell set him off, Dennis?"

Caroline picked Tucker up from the floor and held him tightly. She gave me her "I'm worried about you" look.

I tried to offer her a reassuring smile and walked into the kitchen. I kept my voice low. "Something must have put him over the edge."

"He called me. It must have been shortly before he called you."

"What did he say?"

"That he'd gotten a text from someone claiming they had proof he murdered Mindy Getz."

After everything else that had happened, I had to sit down. "Is there?"

"What?"

"Evidence that Elliot Carlson killed Mindy Getz?"

I heard the big man sigh. "I think that whoever blackmailed Elliot was coming back to hammer him one more time."

"Jesus Christ, Dennis. They didn't squeeze any money from him the first time, what the hell did they think they were going to do with him this time?"

"I have a hunch it was revenge."

I put my hand up to my head. "Revenge for what? It was his life that someone ruined."

"Look, I don't know for sure, but this Whisper Room escort service must have taken some damage when the story got out that they're blackmailing their clients."

"So, Elliot thought this was someone from The Whisper Room?"

"And that wasn't all. The text said that they were sending the evidence to you."

"Me?" I saw Caroline standing in the doorway again, listening, that concerned look still on her face. I should have taken the call upstairs in the bedroom.

"I think that's why he specifically called you. You know… when he decided he was going to…"

Take the top of his head off.

I finished Dennis's sentence while I glanced up at Caroline. "Kill himself."

"Yeah."

"Jesus." There was a certain logic in that. I was the only journalist that Stephanie Cumberland knew personally. Dennis was correct that the escort service was in damage control once Elliot publicly accused them of blackmailing him.

But it was also true that I was most likely the only journalist that Matt Boca knew as well. What better way to point the finger back at The Whisper Room again?

I rubbed my eyes with my free hand. "So, Dennis, did Elliot kill Mindy Getz?"

"He told me he knew her, but no, he didn't kill her."

"But he'd had sex with her."

"Using The Whisper Room app. But he wasn't with her on the night she died."

I looked up at Caroline again, wishing she wasn't standing there. "Could he account for his time? Did he have an alibi?"

I could hear that Dennis wasn't comfortable with this. Attorney-client privilege and all of that. But his client was dead, and Dennis knew that I was feeling lousy about it all. "He said that on the night she was murdered, he did his newscast and then went straight home. The night after that, he was arrested."

"So, he could account for his time on the evening Mindy Getz was killed?"

"I didn't push him on it."

"Where do we go from here, Dennis?"

He was silent for a moment and then he said, "I just want to know the truth, Genie. So do you. Look, Elliot could be a jerk, but he wasn't a bad guy. Not really. Just weak."

———

Before I made my next move, I went upstairs, stripped off my clothes, and took a long, hot shower. While under the steaming spray, I practiced controlling my breathing, emptied my mind, and willed my body to relax.

It wasn't working.

The gruesome sight of Elliot Carlson slumped on the floor, his blood and brains dribbling down the wall, was a horror movie that kept rudely intruding on my thoughts.

The feelings of guilt snuck back in as well. I was the one he called to come "get the story of my miserable life." I was the one he wanted to find his body.

Not the broadcast news people.

Me.

I thought about the vodka tonic I'd ordered but didn't drink. I wished I'd never quit drinking.

You don't mean that, Genie. You can't.

I dried off, put on some sweatpants and a T-shirt, and sat down on the bed, holding my phone, wondering what the best way to move forward might be. Deciding to do it head-on, I called Stephanie Cumberland.

"Hello?"

"Stephanie, it's Geneva Chase."

"I saw the news. It's awful."

I wondered which part of it was the most awful for her. The fact that one of her clients had killed himself or hearing the name of her escort service spoken in a derogatory tone again. "Was Elliot Carlson a regular client of Mindy Getz?"

"Why do you ask?"

"I already know that William Janik and Theodor Andino were her regulars."

She was silent for a moment. "How do you know that?"

"I also know that William Janik was blackmailed the same way that Elliot Carlson was. Except he paid up. I'm betting he hasn't been on your app lately."

"Was Chef Andino blackmailed as well?"

"He said he wasn't."

Even though she covered her phone and her voice was slightly muffled, I could hear her saying to someone in the room, "There's been another client who was blackmailed. Bill Janik. It's Geneva Chase, she says he paid up. Can you check and see when he last used the app? And check and see when the last time Theo Andino was on the app."

Stephanie came back onto the line. "Lorna is checking the last time he used the app. How do you know all of this?"

"It's my job. I also know that the alibis of all three on the night that Mindy was killed are pretty shaky. But again, I need to confirm if Elliot Carlson was a regular client of Mindy Getz?"

"Why? Do you think he killed her?"

"He received a text tonight from the same people who blackmailed him. They told him that they have evidence proving he murdered Mindy and that they were going to send it to me."

"Did they?"

It suddenly occurred to me that whoever it was must have been bluffing. "No."

Then I heard Lorna in the background say, "Janik hasn't used the app in two weeks. That's not like him."

Stephanie snarled, "This is insane. We're going to have to

take the entire app down. Close shop. Start fresh under another name."

Lorna was still in the background. "Let's not get ahead of ourselves. We still have clients using the app. We're still making money. Let's see how this unfolds."

I asked, "Stephanie, do you know for sure who's bankrolling Matt Boca?"

She was silent for a moment while she struggled to get herself under control. "I've heard it's cartel money."

Lorna spoke up again. "Ask her about Kristin."

I reacted. "Kristin?"

"One of our girls. One of our clients ordered her up from the directory. She didn't respond. When that happens, we get an alert online."

My stomach began to twist. "Did you try calling her?"

"Of course. Lorna went out to her condo. She's not there."

I pulled out my reporter's notebook. "What's her name?"

"Kristin Breese. She's a Fairfield U. undergrad. Majoring in economics."

"Can you describe her?"

"Five-six, about one hundred and ten pounds, blue eyes, blond hair. I'll text you a picture."

Kristin Breese sounded an awful lot like Mindy Getz. "When's the last time you know she was with a client?"

Lorna said, "Four nights ago."

"Who was the client?"

"Theo Andino."

I thought for a moment, then asked. "Was Elliot Carlson a client of this girl?"

"Yes. She was his type."

Chapter Twenty-One

The next morning, I didn't turn on the television. I knew the morning news broadcasts were going to be running the same film clips as last night for the folks who went to bed early and missed them. The last thing I wanted to do was relive walking into that bedroom and seeing Elliot's body.

I skipped going for a run, and as I went downstairs to the kitchen, I thought about what Stephanie Cumberland had told me. She had another girl missing, and the last client to see her alive was Chef Theo Andino.

He'd also been a regular client of Mindy Getz. That's an interesting coincidence.

Caroline had already gone to school, and I was on my second cup of coffee when I got a text from John Stillwater: I hear we're working together again.

I started texting back, autocorrect butchering what I was trying to type in, and then muttered, "Screw this." I punched in his number.

"Genie?"

"I don't like to text. I have monkey thumbs."

He chuckled. "Monkey thumbs?"

"It takes me forever to type anything into my phone. Yes, we're working together again." I know I sounded miffed, and I'd tried to keep it out of my voice, but while he'd been out of town on assignment, he hadn't called me once.

Shana had warned me that John Stillwater was laser-focused when he was working. That's what had made him a good cop when he was with the NYPD.

He seemed oblivious about my angry edge, though. "Awesome. Want to catch me up?"

I filled him in on Elliot Carlson's being blackmailed and the incriminating video of him with a hooker going to his wife and the press. "Worse, the text that accompanied the video claimed the girl was only fifteen."

John muttered, "No wonder Shana is all up in this."

I told him about The Whisper Room, Stephanie Cumberland, and Lorna Thorne and how they denied attempting to blackmail their clients. How they believed a small-time hood, Matt Boca, and his big-time cartel financial backers, were guilty of blackmail in an attempt to put The Whisper Room out of business.

I told him about Mindy Getz, found murdered, most likely working on her own as an escort when it happened. I described two of her regulars, Elliot Carlson and William Janik, CEO of Branfil Pharmaceuticals, who had also been blackmailed. A third return client, Theo Andino, was a celebrity restaurateur who claimed that he had not been blackmailed.

"I'm concerned about another one of The Whisper Room's escorts. Stephanie Cumberland can't reach her. I'm going to head out to her place this morning."

"Have you talked to the police?"

"Not yet."

"What do you want me to do?"

I thought it was interesting that he had placed himself in a subordinate role on this case. I was certain that was temporary. "Do the Friends of Lydia or Lodestar Analytics have access to facial recognition software?"

"We even have someone who's an expert in using it."

I didn't ask who the expert was or if he or she was a cop. I'm not sure I wanted to know. "I'm going to send you the video of Elliot Carlson and the girl. Carlson didn't know her name, but Janik said that her name is Piper and that she told him she was nineteen and a nursing student at Norwalk Community College. That's all most likely bullshit, but you never know. You think your guy might be able to find out who she is?"

"It depends how clear the video is."

"Oh, it's high def. The blackmailer wanted to make sure they got a clear look at Carlson's face as well as his backside."

"And if any of what this girl told the client is true, it'll make my job easier."

"Fingers crossed."

"I think I'll also do a little digging and see who's bankrolling Matt Boca."

"Everybody thinks it's cartel money. Watch your back."

"Want to grab dinner tonight? It looks like I'm coming to Connecticut."

The temperature in the room felt like it rose dramatically. When we did dinner, we often finished the evening in a hotel room.

I couldn't very well bring him back here now, could I?

"I think I'll book a room at the Sheffield Inn. Isn't that where you said both Carlson and Janik had been filmed?"

Check it for cameras.

"Yeah. There's a nice place just up the street for dinner. Mostly pub food, but it's cozy."

I almost added, *"Then let's go back to your hotel room and film our own video."*

But I didn't.

After we disconnected, I spent a few minutes looking up Kristin Breese on the usual social media sites. Like most millennials, she was a heavy user. From her photos, she could have been Mindy Getz's sister. Long golden hair, sparkling blue eyes, pretty smile, and the bikini shots she'd taken when she was in the Bahamas showed she had a killer body. She had abs to die for.

Also, like Mindy, she took a lot of photos of food—meals from some of the best restaurants in Connecticut and Manhattan. I like food as much as anyone else, but I have never taken a photo of any meal I've eaten to share with my friends.

Ditto a bikini shot. None of anyone's business what my abs look like.

———

The day was overcast, and a cool breeze blew from the direction of Long Island Sound. I parked in one of the guest spots at the complex, got out of the car, and zipped up my windbreaker. Even though April had arrived, spring sometimes comes late to Connecticut.

I knocked on Kristin's front door.

No answer and no surprise.

Glancing behind me, I noticed that her parking spot was empty. I knocked one more time.

Still no answer.

Deciding to go to my favorite gadfly neighbor, Charles Odom, I went across the lot and knocked on his door.

Charles answered, dressed in a black sweatshirt and jeans. I noticed he was wearing the same slippers he had on the other night. He smiled when he saw me. "I recognize you. The research lady."

"Geneva Chase." I gave him a coy grin. "You called my boss."

His smile disappeared, and he gave me a concerned look. "Oh, I hope I didn't get you into any trouble."

"Not at all. It just showed him that I was on the job."

The smile returned. "Excellent." Then his smile faltered again. "Horrible what happened to Mindy."

I nodded. "It was."

"The night you were here, you knew, didn't you? That she was dead?"

I lied. "I didn't know for sure."

He let my words hang in the air for a moment, then he said, "Is there something I can do for you?"

I turned and pointed to Kristin's front door. "What can you tell me about the woman who lives there?"

His face took on a pained expression. "Kristin? I don't know her well. See her once in a while, just to say hello when we're passing each other. Is she okay?"

"I think that the last time I was here, you said Kristin and Mindy were friends?"

His face turned serious again. "Oh, my God, Kristin's not dead too, is she?"

"We can't locate her. When's the last time you saw her?"

I watched as he searched his mind. "I really can't say. I haven't seen her car parked out front for about a week, I guess."

I repeated my question. "Do you know if Mindy and Kristin were close friends?"

"I think they were. Young girls, the same age, same kind of business."

"Same kind of business?"

"Hospitality."

Thinking about the young man who did detailing at Cumberland Motorsports, I asked, "I don't suppose you know if Kristin has a boyfriend?"

He slowly shook his head. "Not that I've noticed. No room-mate. No pets. In some ways, she was almost the opposite of Mindy. Mindy was outgoing and gregarious. Kristin's kind of an introvert."

Opposites, yet very much the same. Two escorts, sex-workers, living in the same condo complex. One was dead, and one was missing. Other than where their homes were located, there was one other common factor.

Charles Odom.

Oh, and Theo Andino.

"Well, thank you, Mr. Odom. You've been helpful." Then I feigned a failing memory. "Tell me again what you do for a living?"

The smile came back one more time. "I'm a software engineer."

"Sounds like an interesting profession."

"It can be. I like it because I can mostly work from home. Once in a while, I have to hop the train into the city for a meeting with the corporate types. Now and then they send me out of town to set up a network."

"Who do you work for?"

"Quantum Digital."

Another coincidence that made me uneasy. The company owned by Ian Minor, the same guy who did IT work for The Whisper Room because he had a "thing" for Stephanie Cumberland.

Mr. Odom had the know-how to hack into The Whisper Room database, and he knew Mindy Getz as well as the missing Kristin Breese. Charles Odom had just become an official person of interest.

Chapter Twenty-Two

Charles went back into his condo, and I started across the parking lot when a black Bentley Bentayga SUV, worth about two hundred-thousand dollars, pulled up into the parking lot and stopped. The window rolled down, and a stocky man with a sunburn under his dark stubble leered at me. "Geneva Chase?"

That piqued my curiosity. How would anyone know where I was? "Can I help you?"

Mr. Sunburn, sitting in the passenger seat, was somewhere in his thirties, with a military-style haircut. His voice was low and deep. "My employer wants to give you a message."

I glanced around to see if anyone else was in the parking lot. When I realized I was alone, I silently hoped that Charles Odom might be spying out of his front window. "Oh?"

I shuddered when he pulled out a handgun and placed it on the dash.

I felt fear gripping at my chest. With a false bravado, I asked, "Is that supposed to scare me?"

He grinned. "Don't come to Panache anymore."

I dredged up some courage. "No worries. Strip clubs aren't really my cup of tea."

"And quit nosing around Mr. Boca's businesses."

I tried to get a look at the driver, but he had sunglasses on and was staring straight ahead, as if I were of no consequence. I asked, "Is Mr. Boca your employer?"

His scary grin disappeared. "This is your only warning. The next time you won't see me."

With that, the tinted window went up, the SUV moved forward, circled the lot, and drove past me and out onto the road.

I wondered what Mr. Sunburn had meant.

You won't see me.

Is that like you never see the bullet coming that kills you?

Then I wondered, yet again, how these guys knew where I was. I got into my car and called Stephanie.

"Hi, Genie. Did you find Kristin?"

"No, one of the neighbors says he hasn't seen her in days. But he says that Kristin and Mindy Getz were friends."

"Well, Ian and Gary are here. He's going to see if he can track her through her phone."

I quickly recalled that Ian was the computer whiz, and Gary was Lorna's boy toy, who also happened to be a private detective.

"Mind if I come over? I'd like to meet them."

———

Lorna let me into the townhouse and pointed across the big open space that was the living room and dining room that opened into the kitchen. "Everyone's in there."

Before I took another step, I drank in the gorgeous view of the cove, alive with sailboats and seagulls. The sliding glass doors were open. A breeze was coming in from Long Island Sound, but the water in Bartlett Cove was relatively calm, the sun glistening like twinkling diamonds on the surface.

Lorna led the way. "Coffee?"

"Love some. Black."

Seated at the table were Stephanie and two men. All three had open laptops in front of them. Stephanie glanced up. "Hey, Geneva. This is Ian Minor and Gary Racine."

They both stood up.

Ian, apparently in his late twenties, wore a green T-shirt under an unzipped gray hoodie, jeans, and sneakers. He was the epitome of the clichéd computer nerd. Ian's eyes were penetratingly brown under thick black eyebrows. He had a disarmingly dazzling smile. "I've heard a lot about you, Miss Chase."

"Please call me Genie."

Older, in his forties, Gary was dressed more professionally, yet casually—blue button-down shirt, khaki slacks, leather loafers. Unlike the others at the table, his cup of coffee was in a green recycled paper cup with a blue-and-red coffee shop logo saying it was from Cool Beans. Gary's receding brown hair was neatly combed to one side and his face sported the prerequisite stubble that women find sexy. His blue eyes fairly sparkled when he smiled at me. "So nice to meet you, Genie."

I could see what Lorna was attracted to. He emanated charm, even though he was probably at least ten years older than her.

I peered at him. "Lorna tells me you're a private detective."

He grinned, showing me a mouthful of perfect teeth. "I do a lot of security consulting."

Eyeing his Breitling watch, I considered that security work must pay him well.

Stephanie said, "Sit down, Geneva."

As I did, I noticed that the kitchen tabletop was a lovely gold-and-silver-colored mosaic in a Buddhist theme. I pointed at it. "What a beautiful design."

Stephanie rubbed her fingers lightly over the tabletop. "It's from Thailand, where my mother's from."

That explained her exotic eyes. I said, "I hope to see Thailand someday." Then I turned my attention to Ian. "You guys are trying to track Kristin's phone?"

"Done. We did the same thing with Mindy's phone."

I told them, "The last place she was seen was the Z-Bar in South Sheffield."

Ian gave me a quizzical look. "How do you know that?"

"Her boyfriend...ex-boyfriend...and Mindy both had tracking apps on their cell phones. How are you able to track her?"

Ian smiled. "Once you've downloaded The Whisper Room app onto your phone, we're able to track the user wherever they might be."

I turned my attention to Stephanie. "So, you can track not only your girls, but your clients?"

She nodded. "Correct."

"Were any of the clients at the Z-Bar that night?"

Gary answered. "Not according to their cell phones. But it's possible one of them could have met her and left his cell phone home."

Lorna shot Gary an evil look and placed my cup of coffee on the table in front of me. "We're confident that whoever killed Mindy, it wasn't one of our clients."

I sighed. "Like Gary said, unless he left his phone home that night."

She and Stephanie exchanged glances.

Ian continued. "About five minutes after Mindy got to the Z-Bar, she left, and then her signal ends."

"What about Kristin Breese?"

"Five nights ago, she left her condominium at about nine, drove to Norwalk, and went into an Irish pub called O'Neill's. A few minutes after she arrived, she left, and then her signal stops." He looked over at me. "That's not a good sign."

I muttered, "Not good at all. Any of The Whisper Room's clients there that night?"

Gary answered again. "Nope."

Just then, the thought of the two thugs in the SUV threatening me in the parking lot of Kristin and Mindy's condo complex popped into my head. "I think someone is tracking my phone." When I said it out loud, even I could hear the paranoia in my voice.

Ian raised one of his bushy eyebrows. "You would have had to download something that had malware on it, like a website or a photo that someone might have sent you."

I sat up straight. "I went to Danbury to talk to Matt Boca in his sleaze club. While I was there, I downloaded the Midnight House website onto my phone."

Ian held out his hand.

I rustled around in my bag until I clutched my cell phone, then dropped it into his hand. While he fiddled with it, I turned my attention to Stephanie. "Two thugs tracked me down and threatened me to stop sniffing around Boca's businesses. I think they were sent by whoever is bankrolling the strip club and his escort business."

Stephanie put her coffee cup on the table. "We hear it's the Mexicans."

Lorna was leaning against the kitchen counter. "Gary heard it's the Guatemalans."

I mumbled, "Whoever it is, they're seriously scary."

Gary glanced up at Lorna, who was leaning against the kitchen counter. He said, "I told you this is all coming from Boca. He's behind the blackmail, and I'll bet he was the one who had Mindy killed."

I toyed with the idea of telling them that the Friends of Lydia was doing a deep-dive investigation on Boca but held my tongue for the moment.

Gary closed his laptop with a gentle snap. "I'm going to head back to my place and reach out to some friends who might know who's backing Matt Boca."

As Gary stood up, Ian did the same. "And I'm going to go out on the balcony to enjoy a little sunshine and quiet while I try to exorcise the demons from Genie's phone."

I watched Ian slip out the sliding glass door onto the deck. Then Lorna and Gary left the kitchen, and I heard them whispering to each other in the living room. Once the front door closed behind her boyfriend, Lorna joined us in the kitchen and sat in the empty chair across from me.

I glanced at Stephanie, "Did you say you went to high school with Ian?"

Stephanie gazed out at the deck, where he was standing with my phone in his hands. "I've known him since ninth grade. We kind of gravitated to each other. His mother is from Syria, and mine is from Thailand. When you're growing up in Greenwich, that kind of makes you an outsider. We've always been tight."

"It's nice that he owns this big company but still finds time to help you." I still found that curious.

She shrugged. "He might be a rich computer genius, but he's still one of my best friends."

When Stephanie's phone vibrated against the tabletop, we all jumped. She glanced at the screen. "It's Daddy. I'd better take it. I'll just be a minute."

She walked out of the kitchen and into the living room, leaving Lorna and me alone at the table. I took a sip of my coffee.

"There's more to the story." Her voice was low, conspiratorial. "About Ian and Steph."

Curious, I leaned in to hear better. "There is?"

She took a breath, as if considering whether she should tell me or not. Then she whispered, "Ian's mother and Stephanie's mother were both sex workers when their fathers met them."

I blinked. "Really?"

"Steph's dad went to Bangkok and basically bought her mom from a pimp. Ian's dad met his mom at a massage parlor in Florida. Ian and Steph both know what their mothers used to do. They share a little bit of trauma drama, if that's what you want to call it."

So they both started an online brothel? How twisted is that?

"Have you met their parents?"

Lorna glanced at Stephanie, who was pacing in the living room, phone to her ear.

"I've met Steph's parents. Her dad's a controlling asshole, but her mom's a sweetie." She turned her eyes toward the glass doorway, staring at the man seated at the patio table overlooking the cove, my phone in his hand. "Ian's father died when he was ten. I've never met his mother, but I've heard she's demanding as shit. Nothing Ian did when he was growing up seemed to please her. She kept pushing him to succeed. She didn't want him to have to grovel or demean himself for money. You know, like she had to before she met his father."

So, Lorna saw Ian's mom prostituting herself as demeaning? But not the girls who worked for The Whisper Room? Hell, even Lorna turned tricks while in college.

"Doesn't sound like either one of them had happy childhoods. It's nice they've stayed so close all these years."

"Yeah, well, Ian had a crush on Stephanie in high school, and I think he still does. I don't think he's interested in any woman other than her."

"What about Stephanie?"

"In a strange way, I think she's looking for a guy like her father.

The problem with that is she's very strong-willed, and if both the man and woman are strong then you have two alpha personalities in a relationship, and that just never works out. I keep telling her to go out with Ian. He's making money hand over fist, and he's a nice guy. She's an alpha, he's a beta. It would be heaven."

I grinned. "How about you?"

Lorna smiled. "Gary and I have been a couple now for about eight months."

"How did you two meet?"

"We both like the cinema. We met in New York at a Lawrence Kasdan retrospective. We were sitting next to each other. After the showing of *Body Heat*, he turned to me and told me that I looked just like Kathleen Turner."

"That's quite a compliment." When I glanced at Lorna again, I saw that she did bear a resemblance to a young Kathleen Turner.

She continued, "Gary's really smart and a hard worker. And his business is going really well."

I gave her a coy grin. "So, is he a keeper?"

Lorna rolled her eyes, clearly embarrassed. "We've talked about going in together and buying a sailboat. You know, maybe cruise around the Caribbean on an extended vacation."

"Sounds serious."

She frowned. "I'm not sure if the money's going to be there. With all this trouble, I don't know what's going to happen with our company."

"The Whisper Room?"

"The bad publicity is killing the business. We're losing clients left and right."

When Stephanie came back into the kitchen, we fell into an awkward silence. She looked at the two of us and then complained, "Dad's being a pain in the ass again. He's pushing me to have Easter dinner with him and Mom."

Just then, Ian came back into the kitchen from the deck. He handed me my phone. "All clean."

"So, we know that at least two of your clients were blackmailed. Is there any way we can find if there were any more?" I asked.

Ian shook his head. "Let's hope it was just those two. There's no way someone is getting inside this system again. I installed extra firewalls. It's virtually unhackable."

I'd heard somewhere that nothing is unhackable, but I kept my mouth shut.

I glanced at Lorna and Stephanie. "Look, I have someone who's trying to identify the girl in the blackmail video. I showed William Janik the clip of her and Carlson, and he said it was the same girl in his blackmail tape. Same hotel, too, the Sheffield Inn."

Lorna's voice was low and menacing. "When you find out who that girl is, let us know. We'll handle it."

That isn't going to happen.

"One more thing. There's an organization called the Friends of Lydia that combats sex trafficking. They're looking into Matt Boca's businesses. Eventually, they'll find out who Boca is working with."

Lorna stood up and folded her arms across her chest. "How about if Gary works with your Friends of Lydia people? He's pretty good at this sort of thing."

So far, he hasn't helped The Whisper Room at all.

I glanced at my watch but didn't answer her. It was nearly lunchtime. "I'm going to drive down to O'Neill's. Can you text me a photo of Kristin? Maybe somebody there will remember seeing her. And who she left with."

Chapter Twenty-Three

O'Neill's is warm and comfortable with wood paneling, a stone fireplace, and an oak bar. When I got there, the place was filled with diners. The only spot left, the hostess told me, was at the bar.

In my checkered past, that would have been the perfect place for me to drink my lunch. But now that I'm on the wagon, it felt awkward.

But I sat on a barstool and ordered the shepherd's pie and an iced tea. When the waiter brought it to me, I showed him a photo of Kristin. He didn't recall seeing her. Neither did the bartender, the other two waitstaff, or the hostess.

Other than the lunch, my trip to Norwalk had been a complete waste of time.

I was nearly finished eating when my phone buzzed against the wooden surface of the bar. I saw that it was Laura Ostrowski from the *Post*.

"Genie?"

"Hey, Laura."

"They found another floater in the sound."

"Shit. Have they brought the body in yet?"

"Not yet. According to the scanner, they're bringing the body to Columbus Park."

Just like the last body they found floating in Long Island Sound.

I held up my credit card to get the bartender's attention. "I'm on my way."

———

The last time I was at the city's waterfront park it was raining. This afternoon the sun was shining, and the air was clear. People who had been playing tennis out on the courts, hiking some of the trails, and sunning on the beach were now curious onlookers, being asked to stay back by two uniformed officers.

I parked my car and threaded my way around the police cruisers in the lot. By the time I joined the onlookers, the police had already brought up the body and placed it into the waiting ambulance.

Mike Dillon was on the dock, talking with the officers who had retrieved the body and Dr. Foley, the medical examiner. Foley, with his ample girth and handlebar mustache, resembled a walrus in a hazmat suit. I watched in silence as he leaned into the assistant chief of police to discuss his preliminary findings.

Glancing around me, I noticed that I was the only member of the press there on the shoreline. I sighed. It had already been ascertained that the last body pulled out of Long Island Sound was that of Mindy Getz, an escort, a prostitute. It saddened me that dead hookers don't generate a lot of news interest.

Most likely, the prevailing wisdom was that this floater was a sex worker as well.

I caught Mike Dillon's eye, and he nodded. Once he finished up with Foley, he trudged down the dock, onto the sidewalk, then to where I stood in the parking lot behind the police tape.

I asked, "Man? Woman?"

"Woman," he answered. "No ID. Early twenties, maybe. Blond, blue eyes, petite."

I sighed and pulled my phone out of my bag, punched up the photo of Kristin Breese, and showed it to Mike. "Is this the girl?"

His mouth opened in surprise. "How did you get that?"

"Her name is Kristin Breese. She lived in the same condo complex as Mindy Getz. They were friends."

"Was she an escort too?"

I nodded.

"Working for The Whisper Room?"

"Yes."

He stood in front of me, legs apart, arms folded against his chest. "Genie, I want to know who's running The Whisper Room. And don't give me any bullshit about not revealing your sources."

"I'll have her call you, Mike. Fair enough?"

"Her?"

"A woman, two actually, run The Whisper Room."

We watched as the ambulance carrying the body pulled slowly out of the parking lot. "When?"

"I'll call her once you and I are done talking. Was Kristin murdered?"

He nodded. "Looks like the same way Mindy Getz was killed. Foley says she was asphyxiated and dumped into the water postmortem."

"Plastic bag over her head?"

"Yeah."

"Were her hands zip-tied behind her back?"

Mike replied, "Yes."

"How was she dressed?"

"Wine-colored minidress. No shoes, no panties. Can't be sure if she'd been raped. Foley says she was in the water longer than

Mindy Getz was. The longer a body is in the water, the harder it is to get good evidence."

"Do you think the same person who killed Mindy Getz also murdered Kristin Breese?"

He shrugged. "I don't like to jump to conclusions, but it sure looks that way, doesn't it?" He relaxed his stance. "I've got to go start the paperwork on this. Have your lady pimps call me as soon as possible."

"Are you going to bust them for promoting prostitution?"

"That's not my main concern right now." Mike gazed out over the water. "I want to find whoever killed these girls."

I studied him. His face was grim. I've known Mike for a few years and there's nothing that drives him harder than to catch a murderer. "I understand, Mike. I feel the same way."

As we walked away from each other, I turned and stared back at where Mike had gone to the edge of the water. He was just standing there, staring at the horizon, thinking.

Mike was a good cop. He took the job seriously. I knew he wanted to solve this, and I also knew he had precious little to work with at the moment. He needed to talk with the owners of The Whisper Room.

I punched in Stephanie's number.

"Geneva?"

"I have bad news."

There was only silence for a moment. Then, "What?"

"Kristin Breese is dead."

Her voice was barely a squeak. "How?"

"Murdered. Same as Mindy."

"Oh, my God." She must have put her hand over the speaker on her phone because I could hear muffled voices.

Finally, Lorna Thorne took the phone. "What should we do?"

"I'm going to give you a phone number. It's for the assistant chief of police here in Sheffield. His name is Michael Dillon. He's not interested in your business, but you need to call him. Right now."

There was more silence as Lorna thought about what I'd just said.

"Lorna, listen to me. All Mike wants to do is find who's killing your girls."

Lorna sounded pensive. "He's going to want to know who our clients are."

"Probably. He thinks one of them is a killer. And he's probably right." I gave her the number of Mike's cell phone.

She argued, "No, it's Matt Boca."

"Ya gotta call Mike Dillon."

Lorna was silent for a moment, then answered, "Let us talk it over."

She disconnected.

I stood next to my car. The cops were packing up, the ambulance carrying Kristin Breese's corpse had already left, and the onlookers had dispersed.

Mike was still standing on the shore, staring out at the water.

I watched until he took his cell phone out of his pocket and answered a call. He turned, looked at me, then gave me a wave.

The Whisper Room was officially out of business.

Chapter Twenty-Four

On my way back to the *Sheffield Post* newsroom, I was struck with a strange melancholy, a vague, nagging sense of depression.

Two young women were dead. That alone was enough to send me into a dark funk.

But for some strange reason, I also felt bad about the demise of Stephanie Cumberland's business. Stephanie and Lorna, two young female entrepreneurs in a male-dominated business that generally abuses the women who work for them.

They weren't forcing their women to do anything they didn't want to do. If the escorts decided to opt out of having sex with a client, that was their decision. The escorts were there by choice. They weren't being coerced by threats, drugs, or violence. If they decided they wanted to go back to school or take a job somewhere else, they were free to do so.

It was a business for consenting adults, plain and simple.

I shouldn't feel sad about the end of an escort service.

But I did.

As I pulled into the newspaper parking lot, I sighed. The Whisper Room's legacy would now be one of blackmail and murder.

———

"Where do you want me?"

Laura pointed across the newsroom to an empty desk and computer. "Paul's covering a chamber of commerce workshop." Her demeanor was somber. "Does this one look like murder?"

"Yeah. Looks like she was killed the same way."

"Is this one an escort for The Whisper Room too?"

"Yeah."

"Jesus."

I studied the newsroom. At that time in the afternoon, nearly every desk was occupied as the reporters knocked out stories for tomorrow's newspaper. Then I leaned into Laura and whispered, "Looks like The Whisper Room is out of business."

Laura put her hand on my shoulder and pulled me into her glassed-in cubicle. Standing just inside the doorway, she said in a low voice, "I just got a little bad news myself."

I looked at her. Her normally pallid face was paler than usual, and her expression was grim. I asked, "What's wrong?"

"Ben threw in the towel. He's stopped fighting Galley Media. They'll take over ownership of the paper starting next week."

I felt my stomach roll, and I was suddenly filled with dread. Galley Media was known for their Draconian cost-cutting measures. Even though I knew all along that the sale had gone too far for Ben to try to call it off, I'd kept up hope, despite not being a full-time employee anymore. I'd met those icy-cold, bloodless corporate executives. Even before the deal was completely done, as they were introducing themselves, they were sharpening their knives.

They were part of the reason I had decided to go freelance.

Laura sighed. "Maybe it's time I hung it up too. I've been doing this way too long. Want your old job back?" She waved at her own desk.

Up until the holidays, I'd had Laura's job as editor. Galley Media had wanted me back on the crime beat, and they wanted Laura to be the single editor for both shifts.

I gave her a sad look. "I think I'll stick to working freelance."

Without another word, I drifted over to Paul Brown's desk. For a guy who was an outstanding business and government beat reporter, I would have thought he'd keep his workplace a bit tidier. There were notebooks and file folders piled up on almost every square inch of desk space that wasn't being used by his monitor and keyboard. Surrounding his swivel chair were more piles of folders, old newspapers, and magazines.

I took my bag off my shoulder and placed it on the threadbare rug. Then I sat down and began to write the piece about the murder of Kristin Breese. Her next of kin hadn't been notified, so I couldn't use her name, and Mike had asked me to embargo the information about the plastic bag over her head and the zip-tied hands.

Once I'd finished writing what I knew, I did some more digging into Kristin Breese's life. Like Mindy, she was an over-user of social media, posting photos of herself in fancy restaurants, flying off to Caribbean islands, and sunning next to a beautiful pool. There were even a few photos of Kristin and Mindy posing together in bikinis.

Then I dug deeper and found out that she had graduated from the University of Connecticut with a degree in biology. Like with a psychology degree, if you didn't plan on going to grad school, there weren't going to be a lot of well-paying jobs coming your way.

She'd grown up in a little town outside of Danbury called Bethel. Both of her parents were still alive, and she had a younger sister and an older brother.

They're going to be devastated when they find out.

I was overwhelmed with a sense of crushing depression again. It wasn't unusual for me to get the blues. Back when I was drinking, I could self-medicate with a few vodka tonics and eventually just black out.

Now I had to try to push through it on my own.

There was one last item about Kristin I found interesting. While still in college, she'd been arrested for solicitation.

It must have been before she joined The Whisper Room.

After spending two nights in jail, she posted bond. A month later, her case came up for trial. She got a suspended sentence and a small fine.

That must have been the reason she joined Stephanie's company. She didn't have to worry about vetting her clients or accidently soliciting an undercover cop.

As I hit the button to send the story to Laura's queue, the theme song for *Mission Impossible* played from inside my bag. It was the ringtone I used for John Stillwater. It somehow seemed appropriate. We were friends with delicious benefits, but I knew that I'd always be second fiddle to whatever assignment he was working on.

I answered, "Hey, John, calling about dinner tonight?"

"Yeah. But first, I want to show you something. Can you meet me at the Sheffield Inn?"

I smiled. "Really? It's midafternoon. Isn't it a little early for a quickie?"

I heard him chuckle. "It's the best time for a quickie. But not today. I want to show you something."

"This still sounds sexual to me."

"Girl, get your mind out of the gutter. Meet me in the lobby in a half hour?"

———

The Sheffield Inn is a single-story hotel with a red brick exterior, a lovely, laid-back reception area, a full-service restaurant and bar, and a patio overlooking a garden and pool.

The inn is a holdover from a slower time. The lobby boasts a gleaming marble floor, a polished oak check-in counter, and an opaque glass wall separating the reception area from the bar and restaurant. There were flowers and chocolate chip cookies on the front counter, and when I walked in I was greeted by a young lady with a warm smile. "Good afternoon. How can I help you?"

Just then, John came into the lobby from the hallway leading to the rooms. Glancing at the receptionist, I replied, "I'm meeting this handsome man."

At six feet, John is a few inches taller than me. He's got the athletic body of a forty-year-old New York ex-cop who works out on a regular basis and a handsome, clean-shaven face. The lines around his blue eyes and his mouth gave him character, and his brown hair, as always, looked like it was two weeks past due for a trim.

He was wearing jeans and a gray button-down shirt rolled up at the cuffs. Black-rimmed glasses gave him a handsome college professor appearance.

The woman behind the counter gave us both a knowing smile. "Please let me know if there's anything we can do for you."

I knew what she was thinking. The same thing had popped into my mind when John had called—a little afternoon hanky-panky.

John leaned in and whispered, "Follow me."

I walked slightly behind him down the carpeted hallway until we reached Room 21. He waved the key card in front of the lock, opened the door, and gestured me into the hotel room.

I've been a guest in many hotels. The rooms all look pretty much the same. This one had a king-size bed, a bureau, a large-screen television and generic seascape paintings on the walls, and a large window framed by green curtains. On either side of the bed were built-in shelves, each with a brass lamp and a digital alarm clock. On the wall closest to the door hung a full-length mirror. On the window side of the bureau, a shelf meant to be used as a desk was attached to the wall. On the shelf was a charging station for cell phones and laptops.

I gazed around the room. "Is this where they were filmed?"

He smiled. "The young lady at the front counter is a hundred dollars richer for telling me the room number The Whisper Room rents when it uses the Sheffield Inn."

I folded my arms against my chest. "She's sure it's The Whisper Room?"

"It's charged against the company card."

It was looking more and more like someone from The Whisper Room had blackmailed Elliot Carlson and William Janik. Still, I had my doubts. "If someone can hack into their operational system, hacking a credit card is child's play."

"True."

"Where's the camera?"

"Cameras. Plural." John pointed to the charging station on the desk. "There." Then he gestured toward the two clocks on either side of the bed. "There and there." He turned and looked at his reflection in the full-length mirror. "And there."

"Are they on now?"

"I don't think so. Only when they know a mark is in here. They're clever. Motion-activated, the cams can record and send via Wi-Fi to an off-site computer. Should the mark turn off the lights, they have night vision."

"Where does someone get these?"

"Oh, hell, a dozen places on the internet. You can buy spy cams from Amazon."

"Well, we're not coming back *here* after dinner."

John laughed.

I gazed around the room again. "Do you think someone from the hotel is in on this?"

"I doubt it. Anyone can rent a room and bug it. Keep that in mind the next time you're traveling."

"So, now what?"

"I have a room at the Hilton Garden Inn. I'm going to shower and change. Then, what do you say we grab an early dinner?"

I looked at him quizzically. "Why an early dinner?"

His face grimaced. "I'm going to be working tonight."

"What? I haven't seen you in weeks."

"I'm on assignment."

"Looking into Matt Boca's business."

"Businesses. Plural."

Suddenly I realized what he was going to be up to. "You're hanging out at Boca's strip club."

He seemed slightly embarrassed. "Technically, it's a gentleman's club."

"It's a titty bar."

"It's my job."

Suddenly I was very pissed off. "Let's skip dinner. We'll do it another time."

There was a reason I'd assigned John the *Mission Impossible* ringtone on my phone. We were never going to be anything more than friends...coworkers...with occasional benefits.

Occasional to the point of it being a rarity.

Chapter Twenty-Five

Rather than a flirty dinner with John Stillwater, I picked up beef souvlaki from Santorini's, and Caroline and I ate it in our kitchen. She was in one of her quiet moods and trying to draw her into a cogent conversation was pissing me off even more than knowing that John was sitting in a strip club watching some babe in a G-string slide up and down a metal pole.

I had hoped that some scintillating exchange of ideas over dinner might distract me from that unsettling image in my head. Unfortunately, Caroline ate in relative silence.

"How was your day?"

"Okay."

"Anything interesting happen in school?"

"Not really."

"Got any homework?"

"A little."

Frustrated, I decided to shake up her up a little. "Did you see where they found another body in Long Island Sound?"

That got her attention. She looked up from her Greek food and her phone, her big blue eyes blinking at me. "I saw your story online. Another murder?"

"Yeah. Depressing."

"Asphyxiation?"

"Yes."

Caroline finished chewing a cube of beef, swallowed, and then asked, "Do you think Sheffield has a serial killer?"

I felt myself sit up a little straighter. Until then, I had suspected that the girls were being killed by one of Matt Boca's thugs. A brutal way to eliminate the competition.

But serial killers often targeted prostitutes. In spite of what they tell the press, cops are more likely to expend energy and resources on someone they care about. Hookers don't necessarily get the same treatment.

I answered her honestly. "I don't know."

After dinner, we adjourned to our bedrooms, where I opened my laptop and began checking homicides by asphyxiation in other cities and states. Unfortunately, like with these two murders, if the victims were killed by placing a plastic bag over their heads and the killer taking their underwear for trophies, those details weren't being reported to the press.

I widened my search. I typed in "homicide" and "prostitutes."

That list was lengthy. It would take some time to cull through them and try to find some sort of pattern.

Instead, I called Mike Dillon's cell phone.

"Hey, Genie."

"I see you released Kristin Breese's name."

"Yeah, the next of kin were notified. The chief wanted to make it public in time for the six o'clock news."

"When's he going to retire, and they give you the job as chief of the Sheffield Police Department?"

He chuckled. "Not soon enough. Did you see on the news where Michelle Carlson is blaming the media for her husband's suicide?"

I felt that pang of guilt stab me in the chest again. "Did she mention me?"

"She said it was no accident that Elliot invited you to the house to witness his death."

"Christ."

"She's not being fair, Genie. Everyone was tearing into that story."

I tried to shake it off. "Hey, I can't stop thinking about those two young women. Do you think we're looking at a serial killer?"

He was always careful when he talked to me professionally. "Look, this is off the record. I'm home and I've already had a couple of beers. The last thing I need is something in tomorrow's paper because I got a case of Budweiser lips."

He made me smile. "Cross my heart. This is between me and you."

"The manner in which the murders were carried out, the way the girls' hands were tied behind their backs, the way the plastic covering was placed over their heads and tied around their necks, the fact that the killer may have taken their underwear for trophies—I have a suspicion that we're looking for someone who isn't new to this."

My depression morphed into a feeling of fear and unease.

Mike continued, "Plus, the way he discards the bodies into the water. He knows that the longer they're in the water, the harder it is to get solid evidence."

"Do you still think it's a Whisper Room client?"

He didn't answer my question. "One more thing about the water, Genie. Whoever it is, I think he wants us to find the bodies."

"Why is that?"

"If a killer wants the bodies to stay hidden, he'll weigh them down, but first he'll puncture their bodies with a knife. Multiple times. Over and over."

That made my stomach twist. "Why?"

"As a dead body decomposes, the result is the creation of putrid gasses. With no place to escape, the gasses make the body more buoyant. Stabbing the victim before placing them in the water is like letting the air out of a balloon. No, the killer wants us to find the bodies."

"Why?"

"I don't know. Maybe he's proud of his work? But right at the moment, I'm just spitballing."

I took a cleansing breath and went back to my earlier question. "Do you still think it's a Whisper Room client?"

"I've got access to Stephanie Cumberland's database, and we're looking at all of them. Discreetly, of course. A lot of these guys are heavy hitters. Actors, athletes, corporate CEOs, politicians. She catered to some very powerful people."

"So she told me. And one of them is possibly a killer. Does this mean that Matt Boca is off your radar screen?"

"For now. As far as I'm concerned, he's a small-time hood. Murder is a little above his pay grade."

"But not necessarily his financial backers."

"True, nothing is off the table. But right now, we're focusing on the johns."

I held the phone to my ear with one hand and rubbed my eyes with the other. "Hey, how's Vicki?"

"She's busy as hell. The market is red hot."

"I meant between the two of you."

He hesitated. Then he replied, "She's talking like we should take this to the next level."

I frowned. "What's that mean?"

"Jesus, Genie, I shouldn't be telling you this."

A smile crept back onto my lips. "If you can't talk to me, who can you talk to? I probably know more about you than anybody, and that includes your ex-wife."

He sighed. "She wants us to purchase a house together."

"Like for both of you to move into?"

"That's the idea. She's also talking about buying investment property."

I inwardly grinned. "Sounds like a long-term commitment. Are you ready for that?"

The irony was that Mike and I broke up when he wanted me to make a long-term commitment and move in together. That's not what I was looking for. It hadn't been two years since I'd lost Caroline's dad, Kevin, and I sure as hell wasn't ready to shack up with anybody, even with Mike.

"She's also talking about kids."

"You mean having babies."

He hesitated. I think he knew that I was enjoying that conversation. "Yes. Babies."

"Told you so."

"I could use someone to talk to, Genie. Maybe some evening we could have dinner together? You know. Just dinner."

This wasn't the first time Mike had fished around about getting together. I wasn't sure how I felt about it. I had feelings for Mike but was still conflicted. After all, he was the one who had kicked me to the curb so he could start dating someone who had barely been born by the time he was graduating from high school.

I answered. "I'd like that, Mike. Once I'm done with this Whisper Room thing, we'll figure out when."

I cleaned up the detritus of my day, threw on some sweatpants and a tee and was just ready to hop into bed when my phone twittered, and I saw that the call was from Shana Neese.

"Shana?"

"Genie, our guy got a facial recognition hit on the girl in the blackmail tape."

I went quickly to my desk, picked up my pen, and sat down, ready to write down whatever Shana gave me. "Go."

"Her name really is Piper, Piper Edmonds. And she really is a nursing student at Norwalk Community College."

"Then, she's not fifteen."

"More like nineteen. But she could pass for much younger."

"How solid is this?"

"It's as solid as you can get. It's her. It's the girl in the video."

I opened my laptop and typed her name into the browser. Up came links to the girl's social media pages. Shana was right, Piper Edmonds was the same girl in the video. "Shana, how legal is the software your guy uses?"

"Well, let me put it to you nicely. It's none of your damned business." She'd said it with a chuckle.

I'd read about facial recognition software companies illegally reaping millions of bits of information from social media sites. Many of them are being sued. But obviously, whoever is helping the Friends of Lydia didn't much sweat the small stuff.

Shana continued, "I got a call from John tonight."

"Yeah?"

"He staked out the strip club in Danbury and saw Raoul Salazar come into the club and enter Matt Boca's office. Salazar is a lieutenant for the Juarez Cartel."

"So, Matt Boca is laundering Mexican drug money."

"Looks like it. But that's not our immediate concern. We're more interested in his human trafficking operation."

"Of course."

"John wants me to tell you that Raoul Salazar is a very bad guy. The Juarez Cartel was almost wiped out a number of years ago, but they're making a resurgence and that means they're being aggressive."

"How aggressive?"

"They're known for decapitating their enemies." There was moment of silence, then she added, "While they're still alive."

"Pleasant," I answered, sarcasm on my lips.

"John thinks you should have a gun."

I put a hand up to my forehead. "Connecticut has some pretty strict gun laws, Shana."

"Better to have one and ask for forgiveness than not have one and lose one's head."

"Tell John thanks, but no thanks."

Jesus, I'd just end up shooting myself in the foot...or worse.

Chapter Twenty-Six

I texted Stephanie because I thought she could use some good news, as thin as it was.

I know who the girl in the video is.

Deep down, I felt sorry for Stephanie. I know The Whisper Room was a company operating in a murky legal area. But up until the blackmailing started, no one was being hurt. Everyone came out a winner.

But did they?

It was possible that if Stephanie and Lorna recruited a girl with self-esteem issues, working as an escort could end up doing her more harm than good.

I received a text back.

Who is she? I want to talk to her. I want to find out who hired her. I want to know who ruined my life.

I sent her one more message.

Please be patient. I'll know more tomorrow. I promise, I'll call
    you.

The last thing I needed was for her or Lorna to try to track
down Piper Edmonds.

I spent a few more minutes studying the young woman's social
media pages. She had posted fewer photos than Mindy Getz and
Kristin Breese had, but there were still quite a few, mostly selfies
of her on the community college campus. There were several
photos of her working part-time as a barista in a coffee shop
called Cool Beans near the community college.

Interestingly, there weren't any photos of fabulous meals or
spectacular vacation getaways like Mindy and Kristin had posted.
And instead of saying that her occupation was in hospitality,
Piper's social media pages simply said she was a student.

Her wide-eyed innocent look amplified Piper's youthful
appearance. That, and she was barely five feet tall and couldn't
weigh much more than a hundred pounds.

I could see how she could pass for fifteen.

Under COMMENTS, I read that she was a night owl and loved
watching scary movies. I didn't see mention of a boyfriend.

The clock on my laptop told me that it was nearly eleven. Too
early for Piper Edmonds to be in bed? I found her cell phone
number and punched it in.

To my delight, the voice of a young woman asked, "Hello?"

"Is this Piper Edmonds?"

She was silent for a moment. "Who's this?"

I briefly deliberated about who I should be working for on
this call. The newspaper? Lodestar Analytics? Friends of Lydia?

"My name is Geneva Chase, and I'm working for a nonprofit
organization called the Friends of Lydia. We help women who
have been abused or sexually trafficked."

"Why are you calling me?"

"Do you know there's a video of you having sex with a man by the name of Elliot Carlson?"

Her voice was shaking when she answered. "Yes. Yes. I didn't know we were being filmed. I swear. I saw what happened to him. It was awful."

Then she broke down, and I heard her sobbing over the phone.

"Look, Piper, can I meet you somewhere?"

She didn't answer.

"Piper, I think you're in danger. I want to help you."

Through gasps and tears, she managed to squeak out, "Yes. Yes. Quick-Stop. On Liberty Square."

———

I threw on a pair of jeans, a black T-shirt, and sneakers, then quietly went down the hallway until I got to Caroline's room and peeked in. She was still awake but in bed, Tucker curled up at her feet. She was propped up on a pillow and reading a book.

"Whatcha reading?"

Caroline yawned. "*To Kill a Mockingbird.*"

"How do you like it? It's one of my favorites."

Tucker opened one eye, saw that it was me, then went back to sleep.

Caroline answered, "I like Scout. And Atticus reminds me a little of Daddy."

I could see why. Atticus was a single dad, like Kevin was, and a strong father figure. But I seriously doubted if Atticus Finch ever had a problem with addiction like Kevin had. "Hey, I've got to go out for a bit. Will you be okay?"

She rubbed her eyes. "It's a little late to be going out on a date with that John Stillwater guy, isn't it?"

Uh-oh. How much do you know, Caroline?

I gave her a weak smile. "This is work. I just tracked down someone I need to talk to."

"Is this about that escort service?"

She was at that age where she either didn't hear anything I said, or she heard absolutely everything I said. It was exhausting and scary at the same time.

"Yeah. I won't be too late. Promise."

As I started out her door, she shut off the light by her bed and I heard her say, "Don't forget to lock the door."

———

I backed the Lexus out of the driveway and onto Random Road, stepping on the gas and checking my rearview mirror.

Behind me a set of headlights came to life.

My heart skipped a beat.

Coincidence?

I glanced at the dash clock. A few minutes past eleven. We don't get much traffic in our neighborhood at this time of night.

I pulled onto East Avenue and took a right. Glancing up into the mirror, the vehicle behind me did the same thing.

Am I being followed?

If I stayed on East Avenue, it would take me right to the convenience store where I was supposed to meet Piper. In the mirror I saw the headlights stay about four car-lengths behind me, so I turned right at the next light onto Ballard Avenue.

I stared up into the mirror. The headlights kept going on East Avenue.

Just a little paranoid there, Genie?

For a moment, I recalled the old Woody Allen joke that goes, "Just because you're paranoid doesn't mean they aren't out to get you."

And then I remembered Shana Neese telling me, "You can't be *too* paranoid."

I swung around and turned again onto East Avenue. Liberty Square is a tiny strip center not far from the harbor in the seedier side of Sheffield. The surrounding neighborhood had a reputation as a haven for drug traffic, the occasional mugging, and a couple of sporadic drive-by shootings.

The strip center consisted of the Quick-Stop, a Dollar Store, Tom's BBQ, and Dolly's Beauty Salon. Everything at that hour was closed except the convenience store.

As I pulled into the nearly-empty parking lot, right in front of the well-lit Quick-Stop, I saw the tiny form of Piper Edmonds, golden hair tied back in a ponytail, dressed much the same way I was. She had on a baby-blue tee, jeans made fashionable by pre-worn holes in the legs and knees, and sneakers.

Piper was leaning on the counter, chatting with the man behind the counter. He could have been a linebacker for the Patriots. He was about forty, Black, tall, muscular, and very handsome.

I tucked my bag under the front seat, got out of my car, and locked the doors with my fob. Tiny bells rang when I pushed open the glass front door, and Piper and the man looked my way.

From the puffy redness around her blue eyes, I could tell that Piper had been crying. In a tiny voice, she asked, "Are you the woman who called me?"

I smiled at her. The word "waif" popped into my head. I held out my hand. "Genie Chase. You're Piper?"

She nodded her head slightly. Then she glanced up at the tall clerk. "This is my friend Mose. He's the owner."

He raised his chin slightly to acknowledge my presence. "Mosley."

"Like the mystery writer?"

"Yeah." He wasn't smiling.

I turned my attention back to Piper. "Is there someplace private where we can talk?"

Mose's voice was low and filled with gravel when he said, "Storeroom."

Wordlessly, she turned and started moving up an aisle, past boxes of cereal, toward the back of the store. I followed her until we came to doorway with a sign that said, "Employees Only." She pushed through it, and we entered a dimly lit room filled with cases of soda, soup, and toilet paper. A mop and a yellow bucket on wheels sat in a far corner.

When she turned around, Piper crossed her arms, and stared down at the floor. "Who are you again?"

"I work with an organization that helps girls in trouble."

"Am I in trouble?"

I didn't want to scare her, but I needed to be honest. "There are people looking for you."

She looked up into my face. "Who?"

I didn't answer that question. Instead, I asked my own. "Are you working as an escort?"

She glanced nervously around the small storeroom. "Not anymore."

"Who were you working for?"

She blinked her eyes for a moment in confusion. Then she answered, "I thought you knew. It's been all over the news. I was an escort for The Whisper Room."

Chapter Twenty-Seven

I'd completely trusted Stephanie Cumberland and Lorna Thorne and believed them when they told me they'd never seen the girl in the video before. And just before I left the house, when I'd texted Stephanie to tell her I'd tracked down the girl, she had seemed desperate to find out who she was.

Quite simply, it didn't make sense for The Whisper Room to put itself out of business.

No, Piper Edmonds had to be mistaken. Somehow, Matt Boca had to be involved in this.

"Tell me how you were recruited."

She bit her lower lip before she answered. "That girl, Kristin Breese? The girl they found in the water? She was a customer of mine at the coffee shop where I work."

So far, that made sense. Stephanie said they often recruited new escorts from referrals by their current escorts. "How well did you know Kristin?"

"Really, just through the coffee shop. Sometimes she'd be there when I took a break, and we'd talk. She knew I was having a hard time making ends meet only working part-time."

"She told you she was an escort?"

Piper slowly nodded.

"What did you think about that?"

She put her fist up to her lips, then answered. "I didn't know what to think. I always thought that being an escort was the same thing as being a hooker. Kristin didn't look like a hooker to me. She looked like me. She looked like a college student."

"What did she say to you?"

"She told me that while she was still in school, she was up to her ass in debt and working part-time at a Stop-n-Shop on the checkout line. Then a girl she knew introduced her to The Whisper Room. Now, she's got her degree, her college debt has been paid off, and she has a nice car and owns her own condo."

"And that sounded attractive to you."

"I needed the money, but I sure as hell didn't want to spread my legs for some guy ugly enough to make me gag. She told me she only slept with men when she wanted to. She was an escort, not a street whore. Kristin said that all the men treated her like a lady. They bought her nice dinners in fancy restaurants, took her to Broadway shows, and took her on exotic vacations." Piper stole a glance at me. "Yeah, it sounded damned attractive."

"So, Kristin got you started as an escort for The Whisper Room." I still had some doubts.

"She gave me a phone number to call first. When I did, I got a recording."

"What did it say?"

She shrugged. "That I'd reached the offices of The Whisper Room, the world's most exclusive dating service. Leave a name and a number and someone would call me back."

"Do you still have that number?"

She dug her phone out of her jeans pocket. "It's in my contact list."

"I'm going to need that number."

She scrolled through her contact list. "I'll give it to you, but it won't do you any good. When I saw that the news guy was being blackmailed and someone had leaked a video of me and him in bed, I called the number but it was disconnected."

"Was it a man's or woman's voice on the recording?"

"Man."

"So, someone called you back?"

"Almost immediately."

"A man?"

"Yes."

"Did he give you a name?"

"He said I could call him Ned. He said that he'd already gotten a phone call from Kristin letting him know I was interested in working for The Whisper Room. I asked him if he needed to meet me. He told me no. He said that Kristin vouched for me. That was enough for him, and I was hired."

"How did it work? When you went on a date?"

"He had me download the app. When I was called up for a date, I'd get a text message asking if I was available. If I hit the Yes button, then I'd get a text where I was meeting my date, his first name, what he looked like, and what he liked doing."

"You mean sexually?"

Piper nodded. "Mostly, these guys got off on being with a younger girl. So, I dressed the part. Short plaid skirt, white stockings, white top, and heels. Kind of like a Catholic schoolgirl."

"Did you have sex with all of them?"

Her voice was hesitant. "Yes."

"How were you paid?"

"Direct deposit straight into my checking account."

"Same hotel room every time?"

"Yes. Same room. At the Sheffield Inn."

"You had no clue someone was shooting video."

The young woman blushed a bright crimson. "God, no. Thank heavens that when they run the video on television, they blur me out."

I didn't tell Piper that on the video that was sent to Elliot Carlson's wife, her face was crystal clear. "How many dates did you go on?"

"Three, then I saw that video on TV. I won't go out on a date for The Whisper Room ever again."

"Do you recall the first names that you were given?"

She nodded again. "One was a guy by the name of Bill. I think he said he was some kind of big shot in the pharmaceutical business."

William Janik.

"You already know about Elliot. The news guy who shot himself."

Elliot Carlson.

"And a guy by the name of Theo."

Theo Andino, restaurateur?

"Was his last name Andino?"

"Never got a last name. He was a big guy. Kind of loud. I think he said he was some kind of chef or something. When I met him, he brought me a plate of grilled salmon and vegetables."

Theo said he hadn't been blackmailed.

Was he lying?

———

We walked slowly back into the convenience store until we got to the front counter. She turned to me. "What's going to happen now?"

I glanced at the big man behind the counter, who eyeballed me suspiciously. "Well, I want to find out who really hired you.

If it had been The Whisper Room, a woman would have reached out to you, not a man. They would have done a whole background check. They would have taken a professional photo and created a profile for you for their app."

"If it wasn't The Whisper Room, who was it?"

"That's what I plan to find out. In the meantime, you should lay low. Where do you live?"

"In the apartment house right next door. Am I in any danger?"

"I don't think so. But I think it's a good idea to stay out of sight."

Mose spoke up. "I can bring you groceries if you need them."

Piper smiled at him. "Thanks, Mose. But you know I'm only right next door."

Mose's size was imposing. But when he gazed at Piper, it was gentle, paternal.

"It may not be a bad thing for Mr. Mosely to check in on you."

She smiled again. "Okay, Genie Chase."

She gave Mose a tiny wave and then went out the door to the sound of the tinkling of bells.

"So, Mr. Mosely, how long have you known Piper?"

He gave me a small smile. "Since she moved in next door. That was a couple of months ago. She doesn't have a family. Grew up in the foster care system. I've been watching out for her." He pointed to a small television he had behind the counter. "I saw on TV where she fell in with a bad crowd."

Before I could answer, we both heard a woman's piercing scream.

Adrenaline hit my bloodstream, hard.

"Jesus," I sputtered, pushing open the door, rushing out into the parking lot.

Up the street, just out of the direct illumination of a street-light, an SUV was stopped at the curb, and I saw two people struggling. In the black shadows, a larger figure, a man, was trying to drag someone much smaller, a woman, into the vehicle.

Piper!

"Mose, call 911!"

Surprisingly fast, the big man was suddenly standing next to me holding a shotgun. He raised the barrel into the air and pulled the trigger. The muzzle flash lit up the night and the gunshot thundered, echoing up and down the street.

Just up the street, the struggling figures froze, solidified as if the two people had become concrete.

Mose started walking toward them, gun levelled. "Let her be," he hollered.

I followed him and saw that the attacker was wearing a black ski mask. Without a sound, he let Piper loose and leaped into the driver's seat of the SUV.

Get the license number.

I broke away from Mose's side at a dead run.

The attacker revved the engine, and the SUV tore off, but not before I saw that the license plate was covered with black plastic.

Piper's knees buckled, and she crumpled to the ground.

Mose and I got to her at the same time. He held out his hand and gently lifted her to her feet. "You, okay, girl?"

Her voice was shaking. "Son of a bitch tried to kidnap me."

I looked up at Mose, who held the shotgun in one hand and Piper's hand with the other. He exhaled and said, "I'd best get back to the store and put this under the counter. Not good if the police arrive and see a Black man in the street with a gun in his hand."

I asked him, "Why didn't you call 911?"

His face split into a grin. "They get called but they don't come down here too quick. Faster to handle it on our own."

Then he turned and walked briskly back to the convenience store.

I put my hand on Piper's shoulder, feeling her tremble. I told her, "Maybe you should stay with me."

Chapter Twenty-Eight

I should have called the cops. A crime had been committed. Attempted kidnapping. I should have called the cops.

I was rattled. Piper was rattled. We barely spoke on the ride to my house.

And when I got there, instead of calling the police, I called John Stillwater.

It was nearly midnight and Caroline, Piper, and I sat at the kitchen table, every light in the house was off. When my phone vibrated against the tabletop like an angry rattler, all three of us jumped. "John?"

"I just pulled up outside. I'm in your driveway."

"I'll come to the door." My eyes had adjusted to the ambient light coming through the windows from the street. I negotiated my way through the living room and unlocked the front door, cracking it just enough to see John standing on the porch. He was wearing the usual—jeans, sneakers, blue button-down shirt, and a black leather jacket. I had no doubt that he was carrying a gun under his jacket.

Without a word, he took one more look up and down the street, then came into the house. "Are you okay?" he whispered.

"I'm good. The girl has a case of nerves."

"For good reason." He studied me, and I knew that he could see that I did too. "Where is she?"

"In the kitchen with Caroline."

When I said that, his head jerked. That's when I realized that this would be the first time John would meet her.

I smiled. "Nervous?"

He took a breath. "A little."

"You should be," I chuckled.

I started to lead John into the kitchen, but he grabbed hold of my hand and pulled me close. He glanced at the kitchen doorway to make sure no one was peeking out at us, and then he leaned in and gave me a kiss, long and hard.

When we pulled apart, I put my hand on his chest. "I've missed that," I whispered.

"Me too."

"I wish we were together under different circumstances."

"And alone," he chuckled.

"Ready?"

He took another deep breath. "I guess."

I led John into the kitchen where the two young women sat in darkness at the table. John glanced around the kitchen, found the light switch, and turned it on. Both girls blinked and stared at him.

"Ladies, this is John Stillwater."

He looked first at one of them, then the other, clearly trying to discern which one was Caroline. I was pretty certain that to John, they both appeared to be fifteen years old.

Caroline clearly saw the confusion in his eyes. She stood up and studied him carefully. Then she cracked a crooked smile. "I'm Caroline Bell."

I gestured toward the other girl. "And this is Piper Edmonds." She spoke up. "Nice to meet you."

He sat down, and Caroline did the same. Then John turned to her. "Genie has told me so many nice things about you, Caroline. I'm going to want to get to know you better. But, unfortunately, tonight's not the night."

Then he turned and eyed Piper. "Are you hurt?"

She slowly shook her head. "No."

"Do you have any idea who was trying to force you into their car?"

Still shaking her head. "No."

She sighed. "Big, strong, ski mask. That's all I remember."

"Did he say anything?"

Piper frowned. "Yeah, he said to get into the car, bitch."

John glanced up at where I still was standing. He asked, "Did you get a look at the vehicle?"

"It was a black SUV. That's all I can tell you. I wasn't close enough to catch the make or the model, and there was black plastic covering the plate."

He nodded. "Okay. I'm staying here tonight to keep an eye on all of you. I don't think anyone would be stupid enough to try anything, but I'm not taking any chances."

Caroline immediately glanced up at me with a small grin playing across her lips. "Sleeping arrangements?"

I grimaced. "Caroline in her own room. Piper can stay in my room. I'll bunk on the couch." I looked at John. "Where are you sleeping?"

"I saw a chair in the living room. I'll pull that up where I can keep an eye on the street. I'll sleep tomorrow at the hotel."

———

I showed Piper up to my room and got her settled in. Then I stopped by Caroline's room, where she was in bed with Tucker, but still texting. "It's almost one, young lady. You've got school tomorrow."

She shook her head. "Tomorrow's Saturday."

I'd completely lost track of what day it was. "I'm sorry, baby."

"Look, with everything going on, we don't have to take me driving tomorrow."

I'd forgotten that as well. "Thanks. Hey, wait a minute, wasn't Kayla Daniels's party tonight?"

Caroline rolled her eyes. "Turns out her parents weren't home after all. They're in North Carolina visiting Mr. Daniels's sick father. Jessica found out and told her two moms. They called Mrs. Daniels down in Asheville. I heard she went ballistic on Kayla. And now Kayla's pissed off at Jessica."

"And just like that, the party was over before it started."

"I heard Kayla's boyfriend had raided her old man's liquor cabinet and everything. The party would have been off the hook."

"It's nice Jessica told her moms. If you'd known, would you have told me?"

She gave me a crooked grin. "Of course."

From her expression, I knew that she wouldn't have. "Right, 'night."

"I like him."

I'd almost closed the door. "What?"

"John. I like him."

I nodded. "Me too. 'Night."

When I went back downstairs, the lights were off again, and John had pulled a wingback chair up to the front window and was peering at the street through the curtains. I could see that his jacket was off and placed on the floor next to him. I'd been right about the gun. It was nestled in a black leather holster attached to his hip. "Thank you."

He glanced back at me. "For what?"

"Watching over us."

He rubbed his eyes. "Can't let anything happen to my lady and her daughter."

His lady?

It was the first time he'd put some kind of definition on our tenuous relationship.

John added, "Caroline seems nice."

"She is. Most the time. I hope the two of you get to know each other."

He changed subjects. "Any idea who tried to snatch Piper Edmonds?"

"I told you that two thugs in a black SUV told me to stay away from Matt Boca."

"You haven't been anywhere near that slimeball."

"But you have."

"They didn't know I was there."

"Don't be so sure."

He scowled at me. "You think this has something to do with them?"

"Could be. I thought I was being followed when I left here tonight to meet with Piper. I took a deliberate wrong turn, and they drove by on East Avenue. I thought I was being paranoid."

He turned back to studying the street. "I'll sweep your car tomorrow for a tracking device. Tell me how you think those two dead girls figure into this. They both worked for The Whisper Room, right?"

I sat down on the couch. "Yeah, they were escorts. If Boca's scaring off The Whisper Room's customers by blackmail, maybe he's trying to scare off their escorts, too. Although killing two of them, that seems extreme."

"Not too extreme for the cartel. How did they die?"

Mike Dillon had asked me to embargo the details so that if

anyone confessed to the killings, he could weed out the nutjobs. But this was business, and it was John Stillwater. "Suffocated. They had their hands tied behind them and a bag over their head."

He turned so that he could see me. "What else?"

"What do you mean?"

"Were they raped?"

"They found them in Long Island Sound. The medical examiner didn't find any evidence that they were sexually assaulted. But there is one detail that may or may not be pertinent."

"What's that?"

"Neither one of them was wearing panties."

"Anything else?"

"It's all I got."

He thought for a moment. "How was the bag tied around their necks?"

I blinked. "I don't know."

He stood up and stretched. "About five years ago when I was still in the NYPD, there were three murders, all young women, all blue-eyed blonds. Their bodies were found in the East River, hands tied behind them, bags over their heads, missing their panties. All three were prostitutes."

"They find the killer?"

"No, but here's something you can check out for me. The bags were specially made with a zip tie sewn into the opening so that once the bag is placed over someone's head, the tie could be locked in place around the neck of the victim with one pull. That would give the killer a few seconds to secure the victim's hands behind them, if they weren't already incapacitated."

"Where do you get a plastic bag like that?"

He shook his head. "I'm guessing it's a DIY job. One more thing."

"What's that?"

"There was almost a fourth murder. A young escort was directed to meet her john in a quiet place in Central Park. She said someone jumped her from behind, placed a bag over her head, secured it, and was scrambling to get her hands tied. While they struggled, he whispered, *tell me you love me.*"

I felt the hair on the back of my neck stand up. "Jesus. That's some weird kind of bullshit. She lived?"

"Lucky break. A late-night jogger came down the same path they were on. The bad guy ran away."

"Lucky girl. You think this is related somehow?"

"Don't know. Look, do you know how to handle a gun?"

"No."

"Want to learn?"

"No."

He grinned at me. "I told Shana that's what you'd say. What do you say to a knife?"

I chuckled. "I already own a knife. As a matter of fact, I have a whole kitchen full of them."

"Not like this." He pulled something shiny out of his pocket. "This is a Microtech combat knife. It's a favorite of law enforcement and the military." He hit a button and the blade came straight out of the front of the grip.

"A switchblade?"

"An OTF...out the front. It has a four-inch double-sided bayonet blade that will leave a triangular-shaped wound. That means if you stab someone and pull the blade out, the wound won't close back up." He pressed a button, and the blade slid back inside. Then he held it out to me.

"Really?"

"Yup."

I took it. "It's lighter than I expected."

"Only about five ounces. Try it."

I pushed the button. Almost faster than I could see it, the blade was suddenly there, gleaming in the illumination from the streetlight in front of my house. "Wow."

He smiled. "It's the same knife that Shana carries when she's working for the Friends of Lydia. Of course, she also carries a nine-millimeter Glock."

"Of course." I looked up from the knife. "Is she working the Matt Boca case?"

"You couldn't keep her away. She's the reason I can take the night off and stay here."

Chapter Twenty-Nine

I slept fitfully on the couch that night—even knowing that my guardian angel was across the room keeping an eye out for bad guys. Just before dawn, when he saw that I was stirring under my blanket, John asked if I'd be alright if he went to his hotel to shower, shave, and take a nap.

I grinned at him with sleepy eyes. "Get the hell out and get cleaned up. We'll be fine." With the advent of daylight came a new surge of courage.

I could see the fatigue on his face when he left, and I wondered if my friendship with him wasn't growing into something much more dangerous. My success rate with romantic relationships was downright dismal. I'd hate to do something that would screw things up between John and me.

And you know you will.

Still, my heart had raced last night when he called me his lady.

I snuck upstairs and into the bathroom to take a shower and put on some makeup. Then I crept into my room without awakening a snoring Piper, found a fresh pair of jeans and a sleeveless top. I grabbed my laptop and tiptoed back downstairs.

After making coffee and two slices of whole wheat toast, I sat down at the table and looked up everything I could find on Charles Odom, the man who knew both murder victims. I discovered that he grew up in Warwick, England, that his parents had been killed in a car accident when he was ten, and that he was raised by an unmarried aunt in London.

He went to college in America, attending Stanford University and studying computer programming. He went to work for Google, then Microsoft, and then Quantum Digital.

After that, I hit a dead end. It was like he purposely took himself off the grid. He had no social media presence whatsoever.

With the two young women still asleep, I took the opportunity to call Stephanie.

"Genie?"

"Hi. Hey, I need a favor."

"Just a minute." I heard a commotion in the background on Stephanie's end of the call—two voices, a man and a woman, sniping at each other. Stephanie must have put her hand over her cell phone because her words became muffled, but I was still able to hear her say, "Will you take it outside, please?"

Then she said, "I'm back. What's up?"

"I'm going to ask you the same question. What's going on over there?"

"Lorna and I are brainstorming ideas for our next business. Gary dropped by, and he got angry. He's arguing that we're throwing in the towel on The Whisper Room too fast. We're letting that sleaze bucket Matt Boca beat us."

"Lorna's not going along with her boyfriend?"

"Neither one of us sees a way forward at this point. The cops have access to all of our data. But Gary's really pushing it. This time of the morning, he's probably all hopped up on caffeine."

"Coffee addict?"

"Ugh. He'd inject it into an artery if he could. You said you need a favor?"

"Yeah, I need to talk to Ian Minor."

"What about?"

"There's a guy who lives in the same condo complex as Mindy Getz and Kristin Breeze. It turns out he also works for Quantum Digital. He's just somebody I'd like to know more about."

"I'll text you his personal cell. I'll also let him know you'll be calling."

"Awesome, thank you. Are Lorna and Gary going to be okay?"

"Trust me, Lorna can give as good as she gets."

I have no doubt.

"Did you find the girl in the video?"

I pictured Piper's face. "Yes, she told me that she'd been recruited by Kristin Breese."

"No." In that simple word, her voice registered both denial and betrayal.

"Kristin told her she'd be working for The Whisper Room. She gave the young lady a phone number to call. The girl got a recording with a man's voice claiming that she'd reached The Whisper Room and to leave her number. Then a man named Ned called her back and set her up to work as an escort. She had no idea she'd been filmed and used in a blackmail scheme until the Elliot Carlson story hit the news."

"Do you believe her?"

By way of an answer, I said, "We met in a convenience store. When she left, some guy tried to snatch her off the street."

"Matt Boca?"

"I don't know. Someone connected to the blackmail scheme. Someone who doesn't want her walking around talking to people."

"Like reporters?"

"Yeah, like reporters."

"But she has no idea who this Ned is?"

"Nope."

I heard her sigh. "Keep me posted, please."

While I waited for the text from Stephanie, I thought about Lorna and Gary arguing with each other. Gary's a pretty big guy, but I wouldn't want to get on the spooky side of Lorna Thorne.

For the hell of it, I did a search for Gary Racine. There was nothing on social media for him, but his business, Racine & Associates Detective Agency, had a website.

Gary Racine's agency specialized in investigations, security, background checks, and bail bonds. It was a simple single page site with positive reviews by individuals who offered only their first names and the first letter of their last names.

Meaning Mr. Racine most likely made them all up.

There was, however, a photograph of Gary Racine wearing a dark suit and red tie, in a darkened library, appearing very stern. Under the photo was the company's motto, "When you hire the Racine Agency, it means you're serious."

I could see why Lorna had feelings for him. He was a good-looking guy.

I closed the site when I heard two sets of footsteps coming down the stairs. They came into the kitchen almost at the same time. Caroline was wearing pajama bottoms and a pink T-shirt. Piper was wearing sweatpants and a sleeveless shirt I'd loaned her last night, in spite of the fact my clothes were too big on her tiny frame.

Both of them had the sleepy-eyed, witchy hair look of someone who had just rolled out of bed.

Caroline yawned. "Morning, Genie."

Piper followed suit. "Morning, Miss Chase."

I smiled at her. "Call me Genie. You ladies want some

breakfast? It's Saturday morning. I can whip up some scrambled eggs." I hoped we still had eggs in the house.

Caroline replied, "That sounds great. I'm starving."

Piper headed for the coffeepot. "I thought I smelled coffee."

I pointed up at one of the cabinet doors. "The cups are in the cupboard."

Caroline smiled at our guest. "Did you know that Piper graduated from West Sheffield High three years ago?"

Piper chuckled. "Barely. I wasn't very serious about school back then. I am now."

"Caroline, can you make some toast? Piper, I hope whole wheat is okay. It's all I've got."

She smiled and sat down at the table with her coffee. "It's all I eat. Is there something I can do to help?"

"Nope, now that it's light out, I'll drive you back to your place so you can pack a few things." I poured a little oil in the frying pan and turned up the heat.

"You don't mind if I stay here a couple of days?"

I stopped what I was doing and turned to look at her. "I insist." She was my single connection to whoever was blackmailing Whisper Room clients.

While she waited for the toaster to do its job, Caroline leaned against the counter. When she asked the question, it was from a place of curiosity and innocence. But I was absolutely horrified when she asked, "What's it like to be an escort?"

While I was appalled, Piper didn't seem to mind the question at all. She thought for a moment. "Well, it's not something I ever thought about until Kristin talked to me about it. My folks died when I was young, and I kind of grew up in foster homes. So, there's no family to help put me through school, and I want to be a nurse. I really want to help people."

When I heard that, my heart melted. I felt the urge to rush over and hug her.

But I didn't. I kept working on the eggs.

She took a sip of the hot coffee. "Tuition at the college isn't bad, but the books are really expensive, even the used ones. Plus, I have rent, and I'm saving up to buy a car, and I don't make much at the coffee shop."

She stopped talking.

And Caroline kept pushing. "Is it weird to have sex with a stranger?"

I shot her a look. "Caroline."

The young woman's face visibly reddened, but she answered anyway. "Yes. But it's like we're going out on a date. One of them took me out to a nice meal at an expensive restaurant. One of them brought me food from where he worked. They asked me about school and seemed to enjoy being in my company. And as far as going to bed with them, it was always my choice. I could have told them no."

"But you wouldn't get paid if you didn't."

"No. I wouldn't get paid."

I went back to cracking eggs and wondered if that was really the case with The Whisper Room. If one of the escorts backed out of the sex, would they not get paid at all?

Then I glanced back at Caroline. She was becoming a young woman, growing out of girlhood. Filling out in all the places she should. A beautiful teenager.

Please stay a virgin. At least until you're thirty.

———

Stephanie texted me Ian's number before we finished breakfast. I told the girls to keep eating, and I got up from the table to make the call in my room upstairs. When I got up there, I saw that Piper had neatly made the bed.

She might have grown up in the foster system, but someone taught her a thing or two about being a good guest.

Ian Minor answered on the second ring. "This is Ian."

"Ian, this is Geneva Chase. We met at Stephanie's house. You helped exorcise demons from my cell phone."

I could almost hear him smile. "And I was happy to do it. Stephanie texted me to let me know you'd be calling. How can I help you?"

"As you know, in the last week, the bodies of two of Stephanie's escorts were discovered in Long Island Sound. I'm just trying to tie a few threads together."

"Okay?"

"Coincidences always catch my attention. Both Mindy Getz and Kirstin Breese lived in the same condo complex as one of your employees. What can you tell me about Charles Odom?"

"Charlie? Well, I can tell you he's one of the best software engineers I have on staff. He's been with me for five or six years now."

"Married?"

"No, never married that I'm aware of."

"Does he date?"

Ian was silent for a moment. "He and I aren't really close enough that we'd talk about our personal lives."

"Do you think that Mr. Odom has ever been a client of The Whisper Room?"

"That's a question you should ask Stephanie. What's this about, Miss Chase? Do you suspect Charlie of something?"

Good question. What was I doing?

I sighed. "Mr. Odom lives in the same condo complex and knew both of the young ladies who were murdered."

"My guess is that when you live in one of those condo complexes, pretty much everyone knows everyone else, don't you think?"

I'd try one more angle. "Financially, does Mr. Odom do well?"

"Oh, yes. Mr. Odom does very well."

"The condo complex he lives in is in a very nice neighborhood, but it seems to me that he could afford a much larger place."

"I'm sure he could. But Charlie is very careful with his money. He's always been concerned with having enough for when he retires. And who knows? Maybe he enjoys the company of his neighbors."

Like Mindy Getz and Kristin Breese?

Chapter Thirty

My next call was to Mike Dillon.

"Genie?"

"Hey, Mike. Any progress on the two homicides?"

"Your friends at The Whisper Room are insisting it's Matt Boca. They claim he's the one who's been blackmailing their clients. They also think he's the one who killed the two girls."

"What do you think?"

"Well, if Stephanie Cumberland is right, and Boca is in bed with a Mexican cartel, it could be possible, I suppose. But right now, there's zero evidence tying Matthew Boca to any of this."

"So, we're back to the escort service's clients."

"They all have alibis. Mostly."

That made me think of Theo Andino. I knew that he was one of three clients who had sex with Piper Edmonds. Was he lying about being blackmailed?

He said that after he closed Firefly on the night of Mindy Getz's murder, he went home. He didn't have a corroborating witness.

And I knew that he was one of the last clients to be with Kristin Breese before she was killed.

I drifted over to the window of my bedroom and looked down at our tiny backyard. Tucker was scrambling around in the grass while the two young women sat at the picnic table basking in the sunshine. "Mike, the plastic bags that were tied around the girls' necks, they weren't your typical shopping bags you get from Stop-n-Shop, were they?"

He held his tongue for a moment, then asked, "Why?"

"Did they have a plastic zip tie embedded around the opening, like the drawstring on a garbage bag?"

"What do you know, Genie?"

"Remember John Stillwater? He says about five years ago, when he was still a cop in New York, there were three murders, all prostitutes killed the same way Mindy Getz and Kristin Breese were killed."

I knew Mike clung to an animosity when it came to John. He suspected I had a big-girl crush on John, and I think he might be slightly jealous. So, there was a hint of sarcasm in his voice when he said, "That's what John Stillwater recalls, huh?"

"Don't be bitchy, Mike."

"I'll check into it."

I was about to say goodbye, but Mike interrupted. "Hey, there was a disturbance last night at Liberty Square. The resident of one of the apartments overlooking the street called 911 to report an attempted kidnapping and a gunshot. She also described someone who was on the scene that sounds an awful lot like you."

I couldn't very well tell Mike that I was harboring Piper Edmonds, the lady in the blackmail videos. So, I didn't. "That neighborhood scares me, Mike. You won't catch me down there after dark."

"Right." More sarcasm. "Stay safe, Genie."

I'd only put on the minimum amount of makeup that morning, so I finished the job, brushed my hair again, and went back downstairs, patting the side of my jeans where I could feel the flat metal hasp of the OTF knife in my pocket. Then I headed out to the backyard, where I heard both girls giggling.

"What's so funny?"

Caroline and Piper clasped their hands over their mouths and mumbled, "Nothing."

Sex talk?

It had to be sex talk.

I focused on Piper. "Let's head out to your place and get you a few things to tide you over while you stay here."

Then I glanced over at Caroline who was blushing a deep scarlet.

Yup, sex talk.

———

Piper's studio apartment could best be described as spartan. Bed pushed up against the wall, small desk and chair, a kitchenette. Instead of a table, there was a bar with two stools where one could eat meals. Nothing hung from the walls but there were plush, stuffed bears on her bed. They were the only decorations she seemed to possess.

She didn't have a television but owned a laptop, and she told me that it was better than a TV. The Quick-Stop next door had Wi-Fi, and Mose had given her the password. She packed up her computer and threw some clothes and cosmetics into an overnight bag.

Looking around her place, it made me sad to think she had to prostitute herself to pay the rent. I asked, "Do you stay in touch with any of your foster parents?"

The expression on her face turned sad. "No, they never seemed interested in hearing about how I'm doing."

That made me sad as well.

Our next stop was the Cool Beans Coffee and Sandwich Café to let them know she wouldn't be working her shift for a couple of days. I stood in the doorway while Piper talked to the manager. He looked mildly pissed off, but when she told him that she'd been attacked, he glanced up at me and his face relaxed a bit.

He probably thought that if his employee was involved in some kind of domestic spat, then the last thing he needed was for it to spill out into the coffee shop.

I surveyed the coffee shop clientele. In addition to drinking their coffee, they were either looking at their cell phones or had an open laptop in front of them. A young man in a polo shirt and shorts sat with his back to me so I could see what was playing on his computer. It was the blackmail video that had gone viral.

Thank God all of the news programs on TV had obscured Piper's face. Seeing yourself, naked, having sex, was the kind of thing that drove Elliot Carlson to suicide.

I can't imagine how it would emotionally scar someone as young as Piper Edmonds.

While I was there, I ordered a latte. Waiting, I noticed how familiar the logo seemed to me. I'd seen it somewhere before.

Two coffee beans, anthropomorphized with arms and legs, smiling, jumping into a steaming cup of coffee, hand in hand, tiny red hearts in the air around them.

Deja-vu? Whatever, it was cute as hell.

Chapter Thirty-One

I made a calculated decision to drop off Piper at our house and let the two young ladies fend for themselves. I was gambling that whoever had tried to snatch her off the street the night before didn't know she was staying at my house.

And if they did, they wouldn't be stupid enough to try something in broad daylight.

I gave them both instructions. "Don't leave the house under any circumstances, okay? And if someone comes to the door, don't answer it. If you see or hear anything that seems out of place, call me right away."

They both nodded, wide-eyed.

"And if you're really spooked, call 911. Now, do you both have enough to stay busy?" I was a little worried that Caroline would pepper Piper with more questions about being a sex worker.

Piper was the first to answer. "I have homework."

Caroline chimed in, "Eww, it's Saturday."

I asked, "Is there a law against doing your homework on Saturday?"

She rolled her eyes, but then brightened up when she said, "Hey, we can watch Netflix."

I sighed and nodded.

Then, just to get under my skin, Caroline added, "And if we get bored with that, we can talk about what it's like to have sex with strangers some more."

I felt my face redden while the two of them howled in giggles and laughter.

Against my better judgment, I left and drove to Stamford and Theo Andino's restaurant. It was not quite ten thirty, and the front door was unlocked. I immediately spotted the owner seated at the bar, wearing his chef's jacket and his signature leather cap. He was studying an iPad and holding a cell phone against his ear.

He noticed me and waved me in. I got within a few feet when he disconnected his call and turned to get a better look at me. He wasn't smiling when he asked, "How can I help you, Miss Reporter?"

"Why did you lie to me about being blackmailed?"

He glanced up at the ceiling and then back at me. "Do you think I want the fucking newspaper to print that Chef Theodor Andino, owner of a dozen restaurants, including this one, uses an escort service?" He leaned forward, clearly angry. "I used The Whisper Room once." He held up a finger, as if to punctuate his statement. "Once."

"Look, we both know you were a regular customer of Mindy Getz. As a matter of fact, everyone who was blackmailed was a regular customer of Mindy Getz."

He appeared momentarily mollified. "Oh."

"Plus, you were one of the last clients to see Kristin Breese alive."

"Now Kristin is dead too?"

Evidently, Theo didn't keep up with local news. I said, "The girl in the sex tape was recruited by Kristin Breese, who was murdered the same way Mindy was."

The color in his ruddy face went pale. "Dear God." He held up his hands. "Surely you don't think I had anything to do with those two poor women?"

"Have the police talked with you yet?"

I saw anger creep back onto his face. "Yes. I'll never forgive whoever owns The Whisper Room for giving them my name."

"They didn't have much of a choice, Chef."

Still angry, he asked, "Was Kristin in with the blackmailer?"

"It looks that way."

"How about Mindy?"

"They were friends. That's all I know."

"Why would someone kill them?"

"I'm not sure. Maybe because they were loose ends in the blackmail thing. Anyway, I'm still trying to find out who blackmailed you."

He grunted, "Don't need your help."

"What's that mean?"

"It means I'll take care of it myself. I have friends who specialize in this sort of work."

"What sort of work?"

He stared at me and sneered. "Why don't you just leave now, Miss Reporter? You're not welcome here anymore."

"Why don't you tell me what you're talking about?"

For the first time since I'd entered the restaurant that day, he smiled. It wasn't reassuring. His grin was scary. "I know who the girl in the video is."

When he said it, the hair on the back of my neck stood on end. "Oh?"

"Lives down by the convenience store at Liberty Square. Works at a coffee shop called Cool Beans."

He knew about Piper Edmonds!

"How do you know this?"

He held up his cell phone. "I got an anonymous tip. Didn't leave a name. Told me who the girl in the video is. Told me her name. Told me everything about her."

"When?"

"About an hour ago."

I asked, "Man or a woman?"

"What?"

"The anonymous caller. Was it a male or a female?"

He shook his head slightly. "Why?"

"It's important."

Theo shrugged his shoulders. "Man."

"So, what are you planning to do?"

"My friends are going to ask this girl some questions. They know how to get information. I want to know who blackmailed me. I want to know who I have to squeeze to get my money back."

"How much did they get from you?"

"A hundred grand."

The same amount that they got from William Janik. "That must have hurt."

"It's going to keep me from opening another restaurant I had planned in Darien next year. But I'll get my money back. Once my friend has the girl, she'll tell him who's behind this. She'll tell him anything he wants to know."

I felt a distinct chill. "She doesn't know."

"She just didn't tell you. My friend knows how to get information."

Whoever his friend was, they were going to hurt her.

And Caroline?

I quickly thought it through. Unless I'd been followed home last night, it was unlikely that anyone knew Piper was at my house.

Unless they tracked my damn phone.

I jumped when my cell phone buzzed in my bag. I rummaged until I found it.

Caroline was calling!

My hands shaking, I answered. "Caroline?"

Her voice was small and uneven. "There's someone at the front door and they won't go away."

I quickly walked away from Theo, out of earshot, rushing for the front door. "Call 911, now."

Before I opened the front door, I punched in Mike Dillon's private number. "Genie?"

"Mike, you've got to send someone to my house, now! Someone's trying to break in. Caroline's there…alone…with a friend."

"On it."

Then I turned back to look at Theo. "Who are these friends of yours?"

He gave me an evil smile. "People who helped finance my restaurants. People who don't want to see their investments put in danger. People you don't want to know, Miss Reporter."

"Call them off, now!"

He just smiled.

"Bastard!" I shouted and ran out the door.

———

I'd gambled that nobody would be stupid enough to try something in broad daylight.

I was wrong.

I broke every speed law between Stamford and Sheffield, drove through stop signs, ignored red lights. But I got there just as Mike was pulling up in a police cruiser. Another squad car was already in the driveway, and an officer was on my front steps.

I parked at the curb and ran across my tiny lawn. When I got to the top of the steps leading to my front door, I shouted at the cop, "Are they okay?"

I recognized her. Officer Faulkner waved and said as I passed her by, "They're fine, Miss Chase."

The two young women were both seated on the couch, arms around each other. Officer Jodie Gerber was seated in my wing-back chair, notebook in her hand. When she saw me, she got out of the chair and stood up. She acknowledged my presence with a head nod. "Miss Chase."

Staring at Caroline and Piper, I asked, "Everyone okay?"

They responded in unison. "Yes."

Mike Dillon came through the front door, taking off his police cap. He glanced at Officer Gerber. "Did you get everything you need?"

"I did. The ladies were very helpful."

Mike said, "Genie, I'm going outside to have a word with Officer Gerber. I'll be right back."

Once the two of them had stepped out of the room, I went to the couch, sat down next to Caroline, and hugged her tight. At that moment, I wondered how I could have possibly left the two of them alone. How stupid was I to bring Piper Edmonds into our home?

I took a breath and lifted my face from the top of her head. "Tell me what happened."

Caroline answered, her voice low and measured. "We were upstairs playing a video game when I heard a car pull up in the driveway. It's a nice day and the window's open, so when we heard car doors opening and closing, we went to see who it was."

Piper spoke up, "We saw two guys get out of a black cargo van. There was a magnetic sign on the side that said it was from Gold Coast Power and Gas."

"I looked it up on my phone," Caroline offered. "I couldn't find any company by that name."

At least Theo's "friends" weren't very bright.

Piper continued. "They were dressed in T-shirts with the same logo as the van, jeans, and work boots. They both were all tatted up."

"Tatted up?"

She pointed to her neck and arms. "Tattoos."

Caroline looked up at me. "They started pounding on the front door. They shouted that they needed to check our house for a gas leak. They said it was an emergency. They needed to come in right now."

Piper said, "While we were peeking out of the upstairs window, we saw them say something to each other, then one of them stepped off the front steps and went around to the back of the house."

"That's when Piper called 911, and I called you."

I sighed. "You did the right thing."

I noticed that Tucker was lying across Piper's right foot. She reached down and gave him a pat on the head. "This little guy was barking his head off the entire time."

Caroline said, "We really panicked when we heard someone trying to open the sliding glass door in the kitchen."

My heart started pounding again. "What happened?"

Caroline shrugged. "They heard the first police siren."

Piper smiled. "Those two rat bastards couldn't get out of here fast enough."

Caroline grinned at me. "Oh, we did get photos of the two of them and their van."

Theo's "friends," as scary as he made them out to be, were dumber than a bag of rocks.

Chapter Thirty-Two

When Mike came back into the house, he stared at Caroline and Piper. "You two okay?"

They both nodded and replied in unison, "Yes."

"You did the right thing by calling 911. And you did a good job with your statements to Officer Gerber. The photos you took of the perps and their van will help us find out who they are." Then he fixed me in his sight but continued talking to Caroline and Piper. "Do you mind if I speak with Genie privately?"

I think they were relieved to be away from us because, without another word, they both got up off the couch and trotted upstairs, followed closely by Tucker.

Mike sat down in the wingback chair previously occupied by Officer Gerber. He placed his hat on his knee, took a breath, then asked, "What the hell is going on, Genie?"

I did my best to put on my innocent face. "What do you mean?"

He pointed toward the ceiling. "That young lady with Caroline? She's the woman in the blackmail video. She told Officer Gerber her name is Piper Edmonds. What's she doing here? And who were those men who tried to break into your house in broad daylight?"

I smiled at him. "Oh, that."

He didn't smile back. "Yeah, that."

"Well, you know I'm doing a gig for the *Post*. I'm just trying to find out who's blackmailing The Whisper Room clients."

He sat back. Disbelief written all over his face. "Oh, this has gone way beyond doing a news story."

I leaned forward. "Look, blackmail was committed not once, but three times. One man killed himself over it."

Mike still looked doubtful.

I added, "I'm not sure, but whoever is behind the blackmail might also be responsible for the deaths of Mindy Getz and Kristin Breese."

He blinked as he peered at me. "Just this morning, you were trying to convince me that those two women might have died at the hands of a serial killer."

"I'm not taking anything off the table."

"Let start with Piper. Who is she, how did you find her, and why is she here?"

Reluctantly, I started. "She's a nursing student at Norwalk Community College. She was recruited to be an escort by one of the dead women, Kristin Breese. Piper was then contacted by phone by a man named Ned who claimed he was from The Whisper Room. Then she had 'dates' with three men." I used my fingers to form air quotes when I said the word dates. "All three dates ended up in the same hotel room at the Sheffield Inn, and all three were filmed and blackmailed. Piper claims she didn't know anything about it. The first time she heard about it was when it was all over the news with Elliot Carlson."

"How did you find her?"

"Facial recognition software."

He shook his head slightly. "Are you that tech savvy?"

I chuckled. "No, but someone in the Friends of Lydia is."

Mike rubbed his eyes. "Oh, great. The Friends of Lydia. Are they mixed up in this?"

"They're looking into Matt Boca's operation. The rumor is he's trafficking minors."

"And you still think that Matt Boca is behind the blackmail?"

"Who else would benefit? He's already won. The Whisper Room is history. His escort service can swoop in and scoop up their clients."

"Maybe it would be helpful if you quit calling them escort services and called them what they are—prostitution rings, online brothels."

I refused to argue with him because part of me thought the same way.

Mike asked, "So why is Piper Edmonds here?"

"When I met her last night, someone tried to snatch her off the street."

"At the Liberty Square Quick-Stop. So, you were there. Who fired the weapon?"

I shook my head, not about to give up the man named Mosely. "It all happened so fast. I didn't see who pulled the trigger."

I could see the anger and frustration in his face. "You want to know the real reason I broke up with you? You can't be honest with me."

That stopped me cold. All I could do is sit on the couch and stare at him. "What?"

"I'd never be able to trust you. I'd never know when you were telling me the truth, and when you were playing me."

For a moment, I felt a knot in my throat. I'd always thought it was because I had commitment issues. "My job...your job... there's always going to be a wall between us."

Mike raised his hand and shook his head. "I'm sorry. This isn't the time or place. Who do you think was stupid enough to come here in broad daylight and try to break into your house?"

I was still a little stunned from his outburst but was determined to move forward. "Theodor Andino, the owner of the Firefly restaurant and a dozen more, was one of the men who was blackmailed. Mr. Andino is pretty pissed off about losing a hundred thousand dollars. He wants his money back."

"These dopes work for him?"

"He told me he has friends who take care of this kind of thing. He sent them to interrogate Piper. They think she knows who the blackmailer is."

"You're sure she doesn't?"

"Yes."

"I'll ask the Stamford PD to have a talk with Mr. Andino."

"One more thing about Chef Andino. He was a regular client of Mindy Getz and was one of the last clients to see Kristin Breese alive."

"We may have to bring him down to the station for questioning." Mike got up out of his chair. "So, now what are you going to do? It's obvious you can't keep Miss Edmonds safe. And by extension, Caroline and yourself."

"What do you suggest?"

"Let me take her into protective custody."

I shook my head. "No can do. How about you have Officer Gerber keep an eye on us?"

He glanced at the front door. "Great. More overtime." He sighed. "I'll keep a cop parked out on the street."

"Thank you."

"But you got to let them use your bathroom when they need to."

I smiled. "Small price to pay."

"And I'm going to want to spend some time talking with Piper Edmonds. I know you're good, but maybe I can poke at her memory to get some clue who this mysterious guy named Ned is."

"You're not going to arrest her for solicitation?" I knew that he had a copy of the video, same as me.

"There's really no evidence that money changed hands, is there?"

Just when I get pissed off at Mike, he goes and does something nice.

———

While Mike quietly interviewed Piper in the living room, I went upstairs and checked on Caroline. She was sitting at her desk, typing on her laptop, fingers flying. From the texts that scrolled up her screen in multiple colors, I could tell she was chatting with multiple individuals simultaneously.

"Who ya' talking to?"

She stopped for a moment, turned in her desk chair, picked up her glass of iced tea, and took a sip. "Some kids from school. Telling them about those two guys who tried to break into the house."

"And Piper?"

"They all think she's cool as hell."

Caroline had obviously recovered from the sheer terror of two strangers looking to do her harm. She had moved on to the novelty of it all and was thrilled to be able to share with her friends.

And be the center of attention?

"I was just checking to make sure you really are okay."

She frowned. Pointing to her screen, which continued to scroll even without her adding to the conversation, she said, "Everyone thinks this is the coolest house in Sheffield."

"Yeah, that's what I was hoping for."

She turned back and without missing a beat, her fingers were a blur again.

I went to my bedroom. It was nearly one in the afternoon. Wondering if John had caught up on any sleep, I called his number.

He answered on the first ring. "Hey, Genie."

"Get any sleep?"

"Got a few hours. I took a shower, shaved, and I'm good to go. You doing okay?"

That's when I told him what had happened, the meeting with Theo, the two men in the van at my front and back door, the cops, and now Mike was talking with Piper.

"Jesus, Genie. Do you need me to come to the house?"

"Mike's going to have a police cruiser parked outside. Where are you and Shana on your Matt Boca investigation?"

"We've confirmed that Boca has a safe house for girls he traffics in from Mexico and Central America. He even traffics girls he finds here in the U.S. Mostly runaways. Shana and some other of our associates are staking out the place. We think he keeps the women here for a couple of months, then ships them out to a new location and gets a fresh shipment in. Shana thinks that a change of inventory is coming soon."

A chilling description of human beings. Inventory.

"When that happens, we'll step in."

I didn't ask what that meant. I was with John and Shana once when they liberated a half dozen women who'd been smuggled into the country and trafficked for sex. The Friends of Lydia doesn't play by the rules. Once they've been "liberated," the women are taken to Hartford and given new identities and an opportunity to assimilate into a life that doesn't mean being a sex slave.

And by sidestepping the authorities, the Friends of Lydia assure the women that they won't be sent back to the hell they escaped from in the first place. Is it legal?

Of course not.

Do the F.O.L. care?

Of course not.

Chapter Thirty-Three

There's no central database available for unsolved crimes. At least, not a good one. I'm talking about the kind of database that I could access and would do all the work for me.

So I spent the next three hours combing the internet for murders using the search words *women, prostitutes, escorts, body in water, asphyxiation, plastic bag.* I read through dozens of news accounts and found the sickening truth. That prostitutes and escorts are the favorite targets for serial killers.

The list was long and gruesome. The Eastbound Strangler, near Atlantic City, New Jersey, killed four sex workers. The murders were never solved.

The Long Island Serial Killer left behind the bodies of eight women, one man, and a child. All of the women were prostitutes. The killer has never been caught.

The Denver Prostitute Killer murdered at least seventeen women, all sex workers. There have been multiple suspects, but the murders were never officially solved.

Between 1970 and 2009, twenty-two percent of confirmed serial killer victims were known prostitutes. Over the last ten years, that's climbed to forty-three percent.

Gary Ridgeway, the convicted Green River Killer, murdered forty-eight women. He said that he killed prostitutes because "they were easy to pick up" and "they wouldn't be reported missing right away, maybe even never."

No wonder the vetting system that The Whisper Room had in place made the escorts feel safe.

Until it didn't.

I stepped away from my desk for a moment and gazed out my bedroom window overlooking the back lawn. I smiled at the golden forsythia and sunshine-colored daffodils growing next to the chain-link fence separating our property from the neighbor's. When Kevin, Caroline's father, was alive, he'd been a contractor. The backyard was his storage area.

After he died, I cleared out the lumber, sawhorses, and piles of gravel and put down some flowers and grass seed. The flowers were kind of hit or miss, but the grass had taken and was now about two weeks overdue for a trim. I knew I could do it myself or hire the kid down the street.

I gave Caroline an allowance. Maybe I could coerce her into cutting the lawn.

I thought about her and Piper Edmonds. They looked the same age, but Piper was a few literal years and a figurative lifetime older.

True, Caroline had lived through the deaths of both her mother and father.

But Piper's parents were dead as well, and she'd grown up in the foster system, shuttled from family to family, household to household. According to her Facebook page, she even lived for a while in a tent behind the Costco until she finished high school and got a job, saving up enough money to rent the tiny studio apartment on Liberty Square.

Someone had used her. She'd been recruited by Kristin Breese to be an escort but not for the same service that Kristin worked for. She was specifically recruited for blackmail.

And then someone killed Kristin.

I went back to my computer and spent the next two hours scanning news stories of unsolved murders of prostitutes, their corpses dumped into bodies of water. I discovered that five years ago in March, three women were killed within a month of each other in New York. The same three women John Stillwater had told me about.

Then, in chronological order, four years ago in June, there were two bodies discovered in Lake Michigan not far from Chicago; three years ago in August, two more bodies found floating in San Francisco Bay; and more recently, two years ago in September, four women were found in Lake Pontchartrain near New Orleans.

Which brings us to the two women, Mindy Getz and Kristin Breese, discovered in Long Island Sound. That brought it up to a total of thirteen women. And those were just the ones I could find.

How many more were there?

I still had some work to do to reach out to the various law enforcement agencies to see if the method of killing was the same as the two escorts here in Connecticut. I glanced at the time on my screen. Not quite four o'clock.

Time to hit the phone.

———

I finished up at shortly after six. I already knew that the killings in New York matched the ones here. But I was able to confirm that the murders in Chicago and New Orleans were also the same.

I couldn't get anyone in San Francisco to give me confirmation about their deaths.

Quite finished with death, I ordered dinner and went downstairs. Not surprisingly, Caroline and Piper were at the table with their laptops open. As I walked in, Caroline looked up at me. "What's for dinner?"

"Pizza. Oh, and a salad. Got to have something healthy, for God's sake."

Piper smiled. "Thank you again for letting me stay here, Genie."

I smiled back. "How was your talk with Mike Dillon?"

She scrunched up her face. "He seemed nice enough. He told me he wasn't interested at all in what I've done in the past. He wanted to find out who recruited me."

"Did you tell him anything more than you told me?"

She slowly shook her head. "I told him what I told you. It's all I know."

Caroline perked up. "Hey, are you around tomorrow?"

I suddenly recalled that it was the weekend, and I'd promised to take Caroline driving. I gave her an exaggerated sad face. "I'm not sure. I'm right in the middle of something."

She pouted. "But it's Sunday."

"Yes, I know. I'm sorry."

Piper reached out and put her hand on Caroline's arm. Then she looked up at me again. "How about if I got Mose to give her a driving session?"

I pictured the man at the convenience store who was about the same size and shape as a refrigerator, the same guy who fired a gun into the air to scare off Piper's attacker. A stranger in the same car as my little girl? "I don't know."

Piper grinned. "He closes the store on Sundays, and you know we'll be safe with Mose around."

"How well do you know Mose?"

"I've known him since before I moved into the neighborhood. He looks out for me. You know, I think he kind of adopted me."

"Tell me more."

"He's married, has two daughters of his own, ten and twelve, and he owns the Quick-Stop."

I still wasn't convinced.

"I'm going to need my car tomorrow," I stated.

"He's got an Audi. It's only three years old."

I glanced at Piper and then at Caroline. "I don't really know Mose."

Piper offered, "He taught me to drive. When I was homeless, he used to give me food to eat. He's the one who loaned me the money for a deposit on my apartment. He's kind of been the father I never had."

I was running out of objections. "If I'm not available tomorrow and Mose is, I guess it's okay."

Carolina stood up, squealed in delight, and gave me a hug. All the while, I was studying Piper, who was busy texting Mose.

Lordy, girl, you honestly don't look any older than Caroline.

Chapter Thirty-Four

While I ate my salad, I watched Caroline and Piper attack the pizza like two starving wolf cubs. Marveling at how much food two tiny ladies could pack away, I jumped when John buzzed my cell phone.

Before I could say anything, he interrupted. "Genie, we need you tonight."

The tone of his voice made my nerves jangle. "What's going on?"

"We got a tip that the cartel is bringing new girls to the safe house tonight to exchange them for girls who have been working for Boca for the last couple of months."

I thought about the term John had used the night before. *Swapping out the inventory.*

"What are you planning to do?"

"If everything goes according to plan, we're going to rescue all of the women. The six going in and the six going out."

Caroline and Piper kept on eating, ignoring me. I stood up and walked into the living room so there was no chance they'd hear my end of the conversation. I asked, "How are you going to do that?"

"We can't go into the safe house when they're making the exchange. Too many armed soldiers in one place. So, we divide and conquer. Either stop the van on the way in or on the way out. We think they'll be less attentive on the way out."

"How about the girls left behind in the safe house?"

"Shana will get inside with an associate, incapacitate the two overseers, and take the women out."

I paced back and forth across the living room rug. "Holy shit, John. This sounds risky as hell. Why not just call the cops? Let them handle it."

"If we do that, there's always the chance the girls will be sent back to whatever hell hole they originally escaped from."

"Have the Friends of Lydia ever done something like this before?"

His voice sounded slightly bemused, as if I was asking a ridiculous question. "This is a little ambitious, even for us."

I took a deep breath and then asked, "What can I do?"

John's voice was deadly serious. "We think we can do this over the course of about ten minutes, quietly. If it goes south, we need to know what Matt Boca and his handler, Ernest Ruiz, are doing. We'd like you to stake out the strip club while this goes down."

I surprised myself when I exhaled. I'd been worried I was going to have to hold someone at gunpoint.

I reached into my pocket and felt the reassuring solidity of the knife John had given me. I was glad I had it but was pretty sure it would be useless in the kind of operation John was detailing.

"Stake out the strip club. I can do that. When?"

"How long will it take you to drive to Danbury?"

I glanced at my watch. "About thirty minutes."

"The sooner the better, Genie. We're not exactly sure when the van from Jersey will arrive."

I glanced through the kitchen doorway where Caroline and

Piper were whispering to each other around bites of pizza. Just
a few minutes ago, knowing there was a cop watching our house,
the most frightening thing to me was letting a man named Mose
teach my Caroline how to drive.

Now I was worried that my two dear friends, John Stillwater
and Shana Neese, might not survive the night.

———

I sat in the darkened parking lot of an auto repair shop directly
across the street from Panache. As I bit into a cold slice of pizza,
I studied the square, one-story, windowless cinder-block building that professed to be an upscale gentleman's club. A dozen cars
were parked in its lot, most of them expensive late-model vehicles.

From my vantage point, when the front door of the strip club
opened, I could see the bulky form of the bouncer standing in
the lobby, welcoming and appraising the guests. Chewing a
mouthful of crust and tomato sauce, I picked up my binoculars
from the passenger seat and got a better look. The parking area
of the club was well illuminated and a pink-and-blue neon sign
with the Panache logo hung over the main doorway. Other than
that, there wasn't much to see.

Seeing no movement, I put the binoculars back down and
considered the risky plan to liberate a dozen women who were
being trafficked for sex. While I'd driven north to Danbury, I'd
called John to get clarification about what they were planning
to do.

He said they'd watch the vehicle disguised as a church van
roll up to the safe house and let the women get out. Then the
armed cartel gang members will load the women who had been
working for the last few months as Boca's escorts and strippers
into the van.

About half a mile away, before the van got to Route 7, a disabled vehicle will be blocking the road. The driver of the vehicle, a woman, will flag down the van.

"What if they don't stop?" I asked.

"I don't want to sound sexist, but this particular operative is drop-dead gorgeous."

Prettier than me?

John continued. "They'll stop. We're betting that at least one of the two men will get out and see if he can lend a hand. If that doesn't happen, our operative is bilingual, and she'll ask one of the thugs to take a look under the hood."

"So, you'll split them up. Divide and conquer, isn't that how you put it?"

"Exactly. Then, we'll have another vehicle, one of ours, pull up behind the church van. An associate and I, both heavily armed, will get out, flank both sides of the van while the woman pulls a gun on the bad guy who came to help her."

"We'll pull the other bad guy out of the van, tie up both thugs, take their cell phones, and leave them at the side of the road. Our female operative will get into the van and drive off with the six women, followed by us, one in the vehicle that had been behind the van, and one in the car that was supposed to be disabled."

"I don't know, John. This sounds a little thin. What part do you play?"

"I'll be the driver of the car that pulls up behind the van."

What could go wrong?

For one, I thought, the bad guys for sure will have their own weapons. If they panic, there's going to be a gun battle, and someone's going to die.

Please don't let it be John.

———

About twenty minutes later, when the door of the strip club opened, I picked up my binoculars again. Putting them to my eyes, I saw that Matt Boca and his handler, Ernest Ruiz, were heading for Matt's Maserati.

I wondered if he'd bought it at Cumberland Motorsports.

There would be a certain irony to that.

As it roared out of the parking lot, I followed at a discreet distance, pleased that if I lost the car, I already knew where it was headed. John had been watching the club and the owner for a couple of days, and he told me that the two men always left to have dinner at the Barbary Black Angus Steakhouse at about eight thirty every night. They would be there for about an hour, then they'd head back to the strip club, staying there until last call.

As I pulled into the parking lot, they were just entering the restaurant. The steakhouse looked relatively new and modern, despite the attempt to shoot for an old-time appearance inside. Once I entered, I saw the walls were wooden planks, and covered in old product signs and logos for familiar products—Pepsi-Cola, Budweiser, Ford Motor Co., Oldsmobile, Mobil gas, Old Crow Bourbon. Just like the walls, the floor, the chairs, the tables, and the booths were also wood. A lot of trees died for the Barbary Black Angus Steakhouse.

I spotted Matt and Ernest sitting in a booth in the back of the dining room. Discreetly, I took a seat at the bar, farthest away, but from where I could keep an eye on them.

"What can I get for you?" The bartender was a tall, young man with ginger-colored hair and wide brown eyes.

His question threw me. I knew that to avoid suspicion, I should have a drink in front of me. "Absolut and tonic. And a glass of soda with lime, please."

On the other side of the steakhouse, I watched as their server, a woman in her early twenties, carried over two drinks to the strip club owners, who ordered their meals without opening their menus. Matt crooked his finger, the server leaned over, and he whispered something into her ear. She laughed, stood up straight, and swatted him on the shoulder.

Matt Boca, the flirt.

The bartender brought my vodka and glass of sparkling water and left them in front of me. I didn't touch the glass with the alcohol but took a sip of the soda and lime.

Then I glanced at my phone. John had just texted me. Where are u?

I texted back. Steakhouse.

You have eyes on them?

Yes.

My heart raced with his next text. Church van left safe house. We're on.

I glanced up at Boca and Ruiz, who were engaged in conversation, sipping their cocktails. I took a drink of my soda and tried to control my anxiety.

Slow your breathing, relax your body, concentrate on the sparkling water in front of you.

I knew John's part of this audacious and very dangerous plan, but he'd also told me what Shana would be doing. Much like the clumsy attempt to break into my house earlier that day, she'll pull up in a van marked with a Connecticut Natural Gas logo. She'll also have the same logo on hoodies she and an associate will be wearing. Attached to her belt will be a device she'll claim can sniff out a gas leak. It had a technical look to it, but the device was bogus.

I was with her when she used that ruse to get into another

house to rescue trafficked women last fall. It had ended badly for the man who had been guarding them. But before it had, he'd gotten his hands on me.

I rubbed my shoulder where the bad guy had thrown me into a wall.

Things can go south really fast.

John told me that Shana wasn't going to be alone. She'd be accompanied by her martial arts instructor, Uri Tal, retired Israeli Special Forces. I'd watched him and Shana spar in her special workout room. When they moved, it was almost in a supernatural blur of fist, elbows, knees, and feet.

Uri and Shana had even shown me some rudimentary self-defense moves. One of which had saved my life back in February.

I jerked when my phone chimed again. John's text read: Shana's in. I'm in place, waiting for the church van to arrive on scene.

When I put the phone back on the top of the bar, my hands were shaking.

I glanced over at the two men in the booth. Their plates were just being served by the perky, young waitress. They smiled up at her, and then they tore into their steaks.

I looked at the time on my phone as the minutes crawled by.

John had said they'd be in and out in ten minutes.

The seconds ticked by as slowly as hours.

Five minutes.

I took a drink of my soda, stole another glance at Boca and Ruiz. Eating and talking at the same time.

Eight minutes.

I tried to steady my nerves by studying some of the other patrons of the restaurant. None of them seemed interesting to me.

Ten minutes.

"Can I bring you a menu?" asked the bartender.

My stomach was roiling with nervous tension. "No, thank you."

He eyeballed my tumbler of vodka. He could see that it was untouched. "Is everything okay with your drink?"

I replied, "Yes, thank you."

Twelve minutes.

I could feel my hands sweating. I checked the screen on my phone for the twentieth time. Nothing.

Thirteen minutes.

My phone chimed.

I read the text. We have both sets of women. Everyone safe. Status?

At that moment, I looked up and saw that Ruiz was on the phone. Suddenly, they both burst out of the booth, Boca throwing money on the table.

I put my head down and punched in a return message. They know. Stay safe.

I jumped when I heard his voice, close to my ear.

"Geneva Chase." I could feel his breath on the back of my neck. I glanced back to see Boca leaning in and glaring at me. "I told you to stay out of my business."

I attempted an expression of confusion. "I'm just grabbing a drink before I head home. Running into you is an unfortunate coincidence."

I'd tried to sound snarky, but it didn't work. I worried that the nervous quiver in my voice betrayed me.

He stood up straight. His eyes narrowed. "I hope for your sake, this is just a coincidence."

When the two of them rushed out the front door, I exhaled in relief, both for me and the brave people from the Friends of Lydia who had just extracted a dozen women from sexual slavery.

But Boca and Ruiz had both seen me.

I'd been made, and it wouldn't take long for them to realize that I had something to do with the disappearance of twelve of their sex slaves.

Chapter Thirty-Five

Driving home from Danbury, I called John. "Are you okay?"

"Yeah, we're all on our way to Hartford."

"Everyone is safe, though?"

"We're fine. Shana tells me that she and Uri had to rough up the two bad guys at the safe house."

"Boo-hoo. Hey, there's a slight glitch."

"Talk to me."

"Boca and Ruiz made me at the steakhouse." Just recalling his breath on the back of my neck made my skin crawl.

"What happened?"

"They were in a hurry, so basically he acknowledged that I was there, and it had better be a coincidence, otherwise it would be unfortunate. I think that was the gist of it."

"Okay, look, I'll turn around and head back to Sheffield."

"John, as much as I love seeing you, we still have the police protection outside in the street."

"Okay," he said reluctantly. "Once we've got the women safe, I'll head straight back."

"Don't. The cop is still watching the house. Do what you need to do in Hartford."

We disconnected, and I focused on driving to Sheffield. It wasn't until I got home, made sure the young ladies were properly put to bed, and I was in my sweats sitting on the couch in the living room, that I realized how much danger I might have put myself in.

Maybe put all of us in.

Before curling up under a blanket on the couch, I quietly padded over to the window and was reassured by the presence of a police cruiser. While I'd been in Danbury, a new cop had shown up and was now watching our house. Fresh eyes, clear head.

Every time I started to fall asleep, Matt Boca's face showed up, just behind me, whispering the words, "Unfortunate coincidence, Geneva Chase. Unfortunate coincidence."

Then what John had told me about the serial killer in New York popped into my consciousness. After sliding the plastic bag over his victim's head, the killer had whispered, "Tell me you love me."

The next morning was a Sunday and no real reason to roll off the couch early, other than the gray murky daylight slithering past the blinds in the living room window. I got up and peeked outside. Steel-colored clouds blocked out most of the mid-April sun.

I made a pot of coffee, poured two cups, put on my slippers and ratty old robe, and took the second cup out to Officer McKenzie, who had kept an eye on us through the night.

Then I tiptoed up the stairs and into my bedroom, where Piper was still asleep. I found my running clothes, went into the bathroom, and changed. Then I went for an exhilarating run down to the harbor, along the waterfront, and back, feeling much better than I had over the last twenty-four hours.

Not having any real direction for the rest of the day, I thought I might join the ladies and Mose on their driving excursion.

That plan didn't last long.

When I got back to the house, the girls were up, and Piper was making scrambled eggs. Wet with perspiration, I came into the kitchen, and she chirped, "Morning, Genie. Want some eggs?"

"Sure, let me shower first. I'll be down in a few minutes."

When I got out of the shower, I put on a minimal amount of makeup and threw on jeans and a loose-fitting top. Then I noticed that my phone had multiple phone calls from the same number—Stephanie Cumberland.

I called her, and she answered on the first ring. "Genie."

"Hey, Stephanie, what's up?"

"It's all over the news. I'm surprised you haven't heard."

"What?"

"There was a double homicide last night in Danbury." It sounded as she were reading a news story. Most likely from a website. "The owners of the gentleman's club called Panache were found murdered there. Matt Boca, thirty, and Ernest Ruiz, thirty-five, both of Danbury, were found with their hands bound behind their backs and each had received two gunshots to the back of the head. The police say there is evidence they might have been tortured before they were killed."

"Holy crap," I whispered.

Stephanie sounded giddy. "Sounds like they pissed off the wrong people."

Unintended circumstances from last night's raid on the cartel's safe house?

"I think I know why they were killed."

"Save it and tell us later this afternoon. I know this sounds macabre, but we're going to toast his demise. Come join us for cocktails and munchies. Gary's bringing his famous crab dip."

Gary Racine was a man of many talents. Owner of a detective agency specializing in background checks, security, and bail bonds. Wooer of the Amazonian Lorna Thorne. And now, he's got famous crab dip.

Racine.

There was something about his last name that nagged at me. Like having a tune in your head, an earworm, but not knowing its name. There was something about Gary's name that I should know but was just out of reach.

"Can you come, Genie?"

"What time?"

"I'm thinking first bottle of champagne uncorked at noon," she laughed.

I felt a twinge of guilt about not being around when Mose gave Caroline a driving lesson. But the thought of Caroline in my cute little Lexus made my stomach clench.

And I'd already told her I'd most likely be out most of the day.

"I'll be there."

Then I sat down at my desk and opened my reporter's notebook. Before I went to The Whisper Room postmortem soiree, I thought about stopping by to talk with Charles Odom. I punched up Ian Minor's private number. "Geneva Chase?"

"Good morning, Ian. I'm sorry to bother you on a Sunday, but I wonder if you can do me a favor?"

He chuckled. "You're like me, Geneva. Never take a day off."

"Creative minds are always cranking."

"What can I do for you?"

"If I text you a series of dates and locations, can you have someone check to see if Charles Odom was there or near there at the same time?"

There was silence for a moment. "This is the second time you've asked me about Charlie. Is there a problem?"

"Just looking for patterns."

"Patterns for what?"

It was my turn to be silent. I decided to go for broke. "You know the two women who worked for Stephanie and were found dead?"

Ian answered, "Yeah. Steph thinks Matt Boca had something to do with it. That was some news about him, by the way, wasn't it?"

"Scary stuff. Look, Ian, I'm not so sure Boca was behind the murders. I think that maybe it could be a serial killer."

"You can't suspect Charlie."

I stared at the dates and locations and the number of women killed. "I'm fishing, Ian. Just that."

He sighed. "Okay. Give me the dates and locations. I'll try to get to it later this afternoon, after the thing at Stephanie's house. Gary makes a mean crab dip."

I smiled. "So, I hear. See you there."

I disconnected and took a sip of my coffee. Then I heard the front doorbell.

By the time I got downstairs, Caroline had answered the door and I saw Officer McKenzie standing on the stoop. Caroline glanced back at me. "Can Mose come in?"

As I got behind Caroline, the cop said, "The guy in the Audi says his name is Mosely Jones and you're expecting him."

Just then Piper came into the living room. "Mose is here?"

I grinned at the officer. "It's okay. Please let him come in."

The young cop went out to where Mose was sitting, waiting in his car parked at the curb. When he got out, I wondered for a moment how in the hell he was able to fold himself up to get into the car in the first place.

I'd almost forgotten how big Mosely Jones was. Well over six feet and solid, like a boxer, wide in the shoulders, head shaved, serious expression on his face. He was dressed in a maroon shirt, buttoned at the throat and wrists, black slacks, gleaming black shoes, and a black bow tie.

Coming up the sidewalk, he never cracked a smile until he saw Piper standing with us. When he got to the top step, he stopped. Then he glanced at me and then Caroline. "Morning, Miss Chase. You must be Caroline."

"Yes, sir."

His grin grew wider. "Call me Mose."

I waved him inside. "Please, come in. We're having breakfast. Can we get you some eggs? Coffee?"

"Coffee, yes. I've already had breakfast. Knowing I was going to give Miss Caroline a driving lesson this morning, I went to an early church service with my family. Then I dropped them off at the house and came straight here."

It seemed like Mose practically filled the kitchen when we moved in there. Tucker took to him right away, tail wagging, looking for attention. He's a good judge of character.

While we sat at the table, I ate a slice of toast, and the others drank coffee and juice, and we made small talk. Mose told us that he bought the Quick-Stop on Liberty Square about ten years ago, as well as a house in South Sheffield right after. Then as he sipped his coffee, Mose asked Caroline a question. "So, Caroline, have you ever driven a car before?"

She blushed, then answered sheepishly, "Back when Genie owned her old Sebring, I used to take the car around the block while she was asleep."

I felt my face get hot as I flushed red. I was sure that when she said sleep, she meant when I was passed out in my bed after a night of too many vodka tonics.

I glanced at her, only slightly shocked and annoyed. "Really?"

She held up her hand. "To my credit, I haven't done the same with the Lexus."

I sighed. "Good."

She added, "Yet."

Chapter Thirty-Six

I had a little time to kill before being fashionably late for Stephanie's victory party. While I drove, I considered how strange it was to be celebrating the death of a foe, especially since we hadn't proved that Matt Boca and the cartel actually had anything to do with blackmailing three Whisper Room clients and driving the company out of business, let alone killing two of Stephanie's escorts.

Before I even got to the Merritt Parkway, John called.

"Hey, John. Everything good?"

"The women are in a safe house run by one of the Friends."

"Awesome."

"I saw the news this morning about the murders of Matt Boca and Ernest Ruiz."

I followed a Volvo SUV and merged into traffic. "Do you think they were killed because of what the Friends of Lydia did last night?"

"Maybe. I have an informant who told me the strip club was laundering cartel money. But there's a rumor that Boca and Ruiz were skimming some of it for themselves."

"They were stealing from the cartel?"

"That's what my informant said."

Then I was struck by a strange thought. "Is your informant a stripper?"

"It's someone on the inside."

I laughed. "On the inside of what?"

"You protect your sources. I protect mine."

As I drove, I considered that if John and I ever had sex again, he was going to have to be tested for STDs first. "Cops said that they were probably tortured before they were executed. Do you think they ratted me out?"

"I think the men the cartel sent were after the money those boys stole. Give me a couple of days and I'll find out for sure. In the meantime, watch your back. If you see anything that seems out of place, call me."

I was still thinking of John making time with a stripper when I pulled into the parking lot of Charles Odom's condo complex. I parked in the guest space and involuntarily glanced at the condo that was owned by Mindy Getz and then at the one owned by Kristin Breese. I sighed. Both townhouses waited for their inhabitants in vain.

They were never coming back.

I walked up the sidewalk, past the tiny front lawn and flowers, and up the steps to Charles's front door. I pressed the bell while glancing at the sky. The clouds were threatening rain. I hoped that any kind of storm would hold off until after Caroline's driving lesson.

While I waited for the door to open, I noticed the curtain in the front window twitch, as if someone was stealing a look. When the door opened, Charles poked his head out and studied the entire expanse of parking lot. Then he focused on me. "Can I help you?"

Didn't he recognize me?

"I've been here a couple of times…"

Before I could finish, he interrupted. "Yes, yes, I know who you are. The lady from that research firm."

"Geneva Chase."

"Can I help you?"

He was dressed in jeans, slippers, a short-sleeved shirt over which he wore a sweater vest. "I just wanted to check in and see if you might remember anything more about Mindy and Kristin. Something that you might not have told me when I was here last."

He touched his fingers to his lips as he considered my presence at his front door. "Do you want to come in?"

Into the house of a potential serial killer? I don't think so.

I shook my head. "I'm on my way to see someone else. I really can't stay. I thought I'd just stop by." I noticed how nervous he seemed. "Are you expecting someone?"

"I'm sorry. It's just that the police have been here several times now. I suffer from anxiety attacks."

Of course. The fact that he knew both of the victims hadn't been lost on the Sheffield Police Department. I'm sure they've been out to talk with Stephanie's father and the off-again on-again boyfriend who details cars as well.

He put up his hands, palms out, as if to metaphysically push me away. "I don't really want the neighbors to see me talking with a woman on my front steps. There is already way too much gossip going on in this neighborhood. So, either come in, or go away."

I wasn't sure what I was looking for. The two other times I'd been there, he was friendly and self-assured. Today, he was twitchy and nervous.

Then I was struck with the notion that if he really was a serial killer, picking two victims in his own condo complex would be incredibly stupid. It would invite police scrutiny.

But didn't some serial killers enjoy outwitting the police?

Mike had said that by not puncturing the bodies and knowing that they would float, the killer was probably hoping the bodies would be found.

I was accomplishing nothing. "Mr. Odom, I'm very sorry to bother you."

As I turned, he whispered, "Wait, Miss Chase."

Suddenly he remembered my name?

"One more thing."

"What's that, Mr. Odom."

The look of confusion on his face vanished and anger clouded his face. "Ian Minor told me you've been asking questions about me."

"When?"

"Day or so ago. Have I done something to offend you?"

"No, of course not."

"Have I not always been helpful and courteous to you?"

"Yes, you have."

"Then please, Miss Chase, leave me the hell alone."

I shrugged. "Just trying to cover all the bases, Mr. Odom. Please don't take it personally."

As I walked to my car, I could feel his eyes boring into the back of my skull. Opening the driver's side door, I glanced back. He was still in the doorway, looking much more relaxed, but still staring at me.

Mood swings? Never a good sign.

Chapter Thirty-Seven

Before I got out of the car at Stephanie's townhouse complex, rain began to pelt the windshield. I pulled my phone out of my bag and punched in Caroline's number.

"Hey, Genie."

"I hope you're not driving and talking to me on the phone."

She chuckled. "We finished about twenty minutes ago. Mose has already left."

I suddenly felt relaxed, not realizing the tension I'd been feeling over a stranger teaching my girl how to drive. "How did it go?"

"We went out to the Industrial Park like you said. You're right, it's pretty empty on a Sunday. Mose was really patient, and I'm feeling pretty confident that when I take driver's ed, I'll have at least a little experience under my belt."

Remembering what she'd said about taking rides in my old Sebring without me knowing it, I said, "Apparently, you have more experience than I thought."

I could almost hear her smile over the phone. "When will you be home?"

Glancing at my watch, I answered, "Not long. I'm just going to poke my head in here and say hello. I'm not going to stay."

"Drive carefully."

Knowing she was home safe and sound gave me such a sense of relief that I actually looked forward to spending some time with this group, toasting the demise of Mr. Matthew Boca.

When Lorna let me into the townhome, everyone was already there and sitting in the living room, flutes of champagne in hand. Charcuterie trays were set out as were plates of pita points and a bowl of Gary Racine's famous crab dip.

Stephanie and Lorna were both wearing shorts and sleeveless tops. Gary was in blue jeans and a green-and-yellow tropical shirt. Ian had on a black T-shirt and black jeans. Everyone was wearing a smile.

Lorna asked, "Can I pour you some champagne? Maybe something a little harder? We have most everything. Gin, vodka, scotch."

I smiled and literally ached for a tumbler of vodka and tonic.

I just held up my hand and said, "Water and maybe a little ice."

When Lorna went off to the kitchen, I sat down on the couch next to Ian.

He pointed to his phone that was resting on the top of the coffee table. "Charles Odom texted me just now. He said you stopped off at his place again."

I shrugged. "Like I told you before, I'm fishing."

He gave me a sly smile. "What would you do if you found out Charlie really was a serial killer?"

Gary heard the last portion of Ian's question. "Did you say something about a serial killer?"

Ian's question struck me as being odd. "What do you mean? I'd go to the police."

"You wouldn't try to get an exclusive interview?"

That stopped me in my tracks. Would I go immediately to the cops? Or was Ian right? Would I try to get an exclusive?

"Being a journalist doesn't mean I'm stupid."

Lorna came back with my glass of water. "What are we talking about?"

Stephanie was grinning as she held her glass of champagne. Her eyes were slightly glassy. "Ian just asked Genie if she'd do an exclusive interview with someone if she knew he was a serial killer."

Lorna clapped her hands together. "Oh, this sound like a fun game." Then she picked up a pita point, dredged it in the crab dip, and popped it into her mouth. "Gary, this is so good."

He held up his champagne glass. "All for you, my Matty Walker."

Ian glanced at him. "Who's Matty Walker?"

Lorna sat down, sipped her champagne, and answered, "Kathleen Turner's character in the movie *Body Heat*."

Ian studied Lorna and squinted. "Yeah, I see that."

Something nagged at me again, but I wasn't quite done with Ian's line of questioning. "Why did you ask me about interviewing a serial killer?"

Now he focused on me. "Because it seems you enjoy putting yourself in harm's way. Like when you went up to Danbury and interviewed Matt Boca in his strip club a few days ago."

"That didn't feel dangerous to me."

"How about last night? You and Boca were in the same restaurant at the same time."

That surprised me. Suddenly the whole room was staring at me as I wondered how he knew that. "What?"

Ian's lips were pressed together in a thin smile as he paused for effect. Then he explained, "When I heard the news this morning, I got curious about why Boca might have been executed. For the hell of it, I traced his phone. And yours. You were both in the same place at the same time. A steakhouse. Did you have dinner together?"

"Why did you trace my phone?"

He waved his hand in the air. "You always seem to be in the center of things, don't you?"

"How did you trace my phone?"

"Both you and Matt Boca downloaded The Whisper Room app."

I wanted to smack myself on the forehead for being so stupid. "In answer to your question, Ian, I was watching Boca and Ernest Ruiz from across the dining room."

"Why?"

"This won't make newspapers, but a dozen women that the Juarez Cartel had been trafficking were rescued last night. I was sent to keep an eye on Boca and his cartel handler until the raid was over."

Lorna asked, "Who? Who sent you to watch Boca?"

I took a sip of my water, then answered. "There's a group of individuals who prefer to keep their identities a secret. They're dedicated to saving women who are being trafficked for sex."

Gary guffawed like he'd already had a little too much to drink. "Keep their identities secret. Like superheroes?"

Lorna frowned at him.

Stephanie studied me. "Are you part of this group?"

I blinked. "The company I freelance for sometimes does pro bono work for them."

Ian tapped at the coffee table. "Were you able to prove that Boca was behind the blackmail?"

Gary said, a little too loudly, "Of course that son of a bitch was the blackmailer."

I was suddenly struck by the way he resembled a young William Hurt from *Body Heat.*

Body Heat.

It was at a showing of *Body Heat* where Lorna and Gary Racine had met.

I forgot about Ian and turned my attention to Stephanie. "How did Kristin Breese come to work for you?"

She shook her head in the sudden change of conversational direction. "Gary recruited her."

I stared at Gary. "How did you know her?"

Gary sipped his champagne. "Before she came to work here, she got busted for solicitation. I was her bail bondsman. I convinced her that working for The Whisper Room was a hell of a lot safer than turning tricks on her own."

Both Stephanie and Lorna winced when Gary said that. They had always preferred to think of their girls as going out on "dates." Not turning tricks.

I was thinking hard. "The young woman in the blackmail videos was recruited by Kristin Breese. After her initial contact, she was to call someone called Ned."

I picked a pita point off the tray on the coffee table and dredged it in the crab dip. "This man, Ned, set her up with an app that would mimic The Whisper Room. Ned was also the one who fitted out a room at the Sheffield Inn with cameras to video your clients. There were three of them—Elliot Carlson, William Janik, and Theodor Andino. Janik and Andino paid the blackmail money. As we all know, Carlson did not."

Ian shook his head. "Does any of this have to do with Matt Boca?"

"Not in the least. When one of these three clients chose an escort, the blackmailer sent the young lady in the video instead. Then specifically set them up with a room fitted out with cameras."

Stephanie stared at me. "So, if this Ned guy isn't Boca, who is he?"

I took a bite of the pita and dip. It was delicious.

Lorna leaned forward in her chair. "Go on, Geneva."

While I spoke, I focused my eyes on Gary. "The blackmailer wanted to exercise maximum pressure on his victims, so he recruited a woman who both needed the money and looked much younger than she actually is. Someone who could pass for fifteen. Someone he knew. Someone he knew because he gets coffee there every day. Someone who happens to be a barista at the Cool Beans Café."

Lorna's mouth opened as she stared at a dumbfounded Gary Racine. She got up out of her chair and went to the kitchen trash can. She opened the top and reached in, extracting a recycled paper coffee cup with the whimsical Cool Beans logo. She brought it back into the living room.

I finished chewing and fixed Gary with my eyes again. "You picked the name Ned because that's the name of the William Hurt character in *Body Heat*. Ned Racine."

With a mild stammer, Gary said, "I…I don't know what the hell you're talking about."

"Gary couldn't directly contact the barista because she already knew him. He's a regular at the coffee shop. So, he paid Kristin to do it. I didn't know the connection between Gary and Kristin until just now. Delicious crab dip, by the way."

He snarled at me. "You're out of your freaking mind."

"When he heard that I'd found the girl in the video, he tracked me through The Whisper Room app on my phone and tried to kidnap her off the street. And then when that failed, he called Theo Andino and told him where he could find the girl."

Lorna blinked as she started to understand what I was talking about. She stepped up to where her boyfriend stood. "Is this true?"

Gary stood up and pointed at me. "She's hallucinating. I've been as invested in this business as you both were."

Lorna threw the empty cup at Gary, bouncing it off his chest. She shouted, "You put us out of business."

A few drops of coffee remaining in the 'cup splashed onto Gary's tropical shirt. While he wiped it off with a napkin, he argued, "This is insane." He gestured toward me. "She doesn't know what the hell she's talking about."

Then Stephanie stood up, her face crimson with rage. "Why? Why?"

Gary licked his lips, glancing first at Lorna, then Stephanie, then at me.

Still seated, Ian looked up at Lorna. "Did he have access to the system?"

Her anger growing, Lorna never took her eyes off her boyfriend. "Yes, he had access to the system. He said he wanted to monitor it for hackers."

I went further. "Did you kill Kristin Breese and Mindy Getz?"

Gary held his hands up in front of him as if to ward off an evil spirit. "Why would I have done that?"

"Kristin could have tied you to the blackmail scheme."

Lorna asked, "Then why would he have killed Mindy?"

I took a breath. "I don't know. Kristin and Mindy were friends. Maybe you thought Kristin told Mindy about everything."

Gary shook his head. "This is crazy. Crazy."

Stephanie was clenching and unclenching her fists. "Why, Gary? Why? You were like fucking family."

Sensing he was trapped, Gary looked at Lorna and replied in a voice that was barely a whisper. "I did it for us, Lorna."

She snarled, "What?"

"Don't you see? It was a way to make a lot of money fast."

"You put us out of business."

Gary stared wide-eyed at Stephanie. "You'd still be in business if it hadn't been for that goddamned TV news asshole. If he'd paid up, everything would still be good." Then he stared at me. "And you. You're to blame."

Now I was standing. "It was stupid to send the video out to the news media, Gary. You should have just let Carlson slide. You'd still be blackmailing Whisper Room clients because no one would have been the wiser."

Gary suddenly flipped the coffee table in front of him into the air, pita points, crab dip, and champagne flying across the room. "Bitch!"

In a heartbeat, he was on top of me, pushing me back down onto the couch. One hand was around my throat, the other clutched at my hair.

All three of them—Stephanie, Lorna, and Ian—were pulling Gary up and off me. I could just see Lorna pummeling the side of his head with her fist.

Stumbling back to his feet, he shook them off and pulled a handgun from his belt hidden under the tropical shirt. He shouted, "Everybody just stop."

We all did just that, frozen in place, staring at the gun as if it was a murderous predator that had just jumped into the room.

Still prone on the couch from where he'd tried to choke me, I slowly slid myself up into a sitting position. "What now, Gary?"

He pointed the gun at me.

I tried to keep my breathing measured, trying not to let him see how terrified I was. I kept my eyes locked on his.

"Now, I walk out of here. We all go on with our lives."

Stephanie suddenly had her phone in her hand. "Screw you. I'm calling the police."

Gary turned and pointed the gun at Stephanie. "Don't."

"Too late."

She held up her phone, and we could hear the voice on the other end. "911, what's your emergency?"

I stood up on unsteady legs. "Even if she doesn't answer, the cops will trace the call and will be here in a few minutes."

"Goddamn it," he shouted, rushing for the door.

Stephanie spoke quickly into her phone as Gary disappeared into the rain. Lorna went slowly across the living room and stared out the open doorway.

The man she loved had betrayed her, had used her.

Ian stood next to me and surveyed the food that was splattered all over the floor. He sighed. "I guess the party's over." Then he folded his arms. "Do you really think that Gary killed those two girls?"

I picked up my glass of water and noticed that my hand was shaking. The confrontation with Lorna's ex-boyfriend had rattled me. I took a sip and put the glass back down on the end table. "I don't know. I know he's capable of blackmail. And he tried to snatch the girl on the video off the street two nights ago. So, he's capable of attempted kidnapping. We just saw that he's violent."

Ian gave me a shy grin. "Look, I obviously underestimated you. I'll head home and look up Charles Odom's travel schedule over the last five years. I'll call you when I have something. Why don't you come by my house when I do? I'll text you my address."

Saying his goodbyes, Ian left, and I took my notebook out of my bag. Then I wrote down the dates and cities where the sex workers had been murdered and gave it to Lorna and Stephanie.

"Search your memories and see if you can recall Gary telling you if he'd ever been to these cities before. Someone targeted and killed sex workers in those locations on those dates. Maybe you can remember Gary saying he'd been there."

Lorna shook her head, "I still can't believe that son of a bitch used me like he did. Goddamn him to hell."

Stephanie stared at the notebook paper with the dates and places on it. "We'll try to recall what he told us. But now I'm not sure there's anything he's said that we can believe."

I shrugged. "Just do the best you can."

If I hadn't wanted a drink when I walked in, I sure as hell wanted one now.

Chapter Thirty-Eight

I drove to Westport, but instead of going directly to Ian's place, I took a detour down Compo Road until it took me to the beach. I slid my car into a parking spot and shut the engine off.

Because it was gray, overcast, and raining, my car was the only one in the lot. From where I was parked, I had the entire vista of Long Island Sound in front of me. I watched as droplets thumped against the windshield while I thought about what had transpired at Stephanie Cumberland's.

The blackmailer had been there all along.

Did Gary Racine hatch the blackmailing scheme and then target Lorna Thorne? Or had he come up with the plot after he met her?

And did he kill Mindy Getz and Kristin Breese?

I held my hands out in front of me. They'd stopped shaking.

When I left Stephanie's place, I wanted a drink. It used to be my method of self-medicating when I was afraid or anxious or insecure.

Hell, it was just something to make me numb.

I took a couple of cleansing deep breaths, reached over to the passenger side of the car, and rummaged around in my bag until

I found my phone. That's when I noticed that I'd gotten a text from Nathaniel Rubin. He was asking me to call him.

On a Sunday?

I punched in his number.

He answered on the third ring. "Geneva."

"You asked me to call you. On a Sunday? I'm off the clock."

"We're never off the clock. Hey, I got a phone call from a very angry Charles Odom."

I watched a powerboat skid across the black surface of the sound. I wondered if the boater had been fishing and got caught by the rain. "What did Mr. Odom have to say?"

"He said you're harassing him, and if it continues, he's going to sue us."

I sighed. "He might be a serial killer, Nathaniel."

That shut him up.

"What makes you think that?"

"There's at least a half dozen young women, all sex workers, all fitting a certain profile, that have been killed in four different cities over the last five years. They were all killed the same way. I have someone checking if Mr. Odom was in those cities at the same time the women were murdered."

"What led you to Mr. Odom in the first place?"

"The two women the cops fished out of Long Island Sound were killed in the same exact way as the others. Charles Odom knew them both and lives in the same condo complex they lived in."

As I gazed through the rain to the flat surface of the water, Nathaniel observed, "Not a good idea to kill in your own backyard, is it?"

"It's not a good idea to kill at all, Nathaniel." I watched as another car slid into a parking spot on the other end of the beach.

"Anyway, I thought you'd better know that you've kicked a hornets' nest."

"Not the first time."

"Before I let you go, good work on the Friends of Lydia project."

Even though nobody could see me, I shrugged. "All I did was keep an eye on a couple of slimeballs."

"We rescued a dozen young ladies and put a trafficking operation out of business. You're the reason we started looking at Matt Boca in the first place."

Thinking about how Matt and Ernest had met their end, I observed, "Not much of a retirement plan when you're working for a cartel, is there?"

"It pretty much always ends the same, Genie."

I watched as the car that had just parked, backed up and drove slowly my way.

"Thanks, Nathaniel. I was glad to do my part."

The car moved closer to where I sat.

My phone beeped. "Nathaniel, I have another call coming in. Enjoy the rest of your weekend."

I disconnected and then saw that the incoming call was from Ian Minor.

"Genie, you were right about Charles being in those cities at the same time as those women were killed."

"Well, how about that?"

The car was directly behind me.

Did it stop?

I was suddenly gripped with fear.

Ian said, "Look, come over to my place. I've sent you the address. I'll print out everything you'll need to continue your investigation. Who would have guessed that Charles Odom might be a serial killer?"

"Do you know what kind of car Mr. Odom drives?"

The car behind me began to roll forward again, accelerating.

"Some kind of SUV, I think. Why do you ask?"

The car behind me was a Range Rover.

I watched as the vehicle exited the parking lot and disappeared in the mist and the rain. "No reason. Just getting a case of the nerves."

"Genie, while you're here, I'll remove The Whisper Room app from your phone. If I can track you, Charles can too."

I noticed that Ian had stopped calling him Charlie. Ian was taking this seriously.

Chapter Thirty-Nine

When Stephanie had told me that Ian was the founder and CEO of Quantum Digital and that he did well for himself, I had no idea just how well. Before I left the beach, I looked up his address on my phone.

I saw that the property was currently worth over four million dollars, that the house boasted five bedrooms, four baths, a library, a study, an in-ground pool, and a guesthouse. With a white brick exterior, the two-story house sat back away from the road, fronted with enough trees and landscaping that it was completely hidden from the highway.

The rain was falling harder, so when I parked my car in the circular driveway and ran up the sidewalk, I pulled the collar of my windbreaker over my head. Before I got up the stone steps and could ring the bell, Ian had the door open and was waving me inside.

As I went past him, I noticed that he was studying the long driveway behind me.

Making sure that Charles Odom hadn't followed me?

The vaulted ceiling and the floor-to-ceiling windows on the other side of the living room were the first features that caught my eye. Because every time I'd seen Ian, he was dressed primarily in black, I'd thought his house would be dark as well.

It was just the opposite. Almost everything in his home was white or a shade of white. The walls, the couches, the armchairs, the fireplace, the carpet—all white. Large canvases of modern art graced the walls and were welcome splashes of color.

"Can I take your jacket?"

He graciously helped me slide out of it. "Thank you. What a beautiful home."

"Thank you, I'll give you a tour."

"I would think with everything so white, you'd have a problem keeping everything clean."

Ian hung up my windbreaker in a closet and then glanced around the spacious living area. "Well, it's just me, and I have a lady who comes in and cleans for me a couple of times a week."

"Do you have family?"

"My father died when I was young, and Mom passed away about six years ago."

I reached back into my memory and recalled that Lorna had told me that after his father passed away, his mother had driven Ian to work hard in school, to strive for success so that he wouldn't have to demean himself the way she had to just to eke out an existence.

"No brothers or sisters?"

He offered me a shy smile and a shrug that I thought was adorable. "Just me. Come, let me show you around."

I'd come to Ian's house for verification that Charles Odom had been in the cities at the same time as the young sex workers had been killed, but curiosity got the better of me. What did this very wealthy young man's house look like? "Sure, love to see it."

He started with the kitchen. White brick walls, gleaming stainless-steel appliances, white cupboards, kitchen table and chairs all wood and stained a light-blond color. "Do you cook, Ian?"

He chuckled. "I rarely use the kitchen. Sometimes if I'm entertaining a client or holding a brainstorming session with my staff, I have a caterer who comes in and prepares the food. Other than that, I mostly have takeout delivered."

Not much of a cook myself, I responded, "I understand that."

"Can I offer you anything? I have juice and soda in the refrigerator. I've already observed that you don't drink alcohol."

I smiled. "No, thank you."

He fixed me with his dark eyes, his eyebrows knotted, his face serious. "Do you think it's possible someone like Charles can fool everyone for so many years?"

"Charles seems mild-mannered and likable. It wasn't until I talked to him this last time that I saw a flash of anger. Yeah, someone like Charles could fool people for years. Jeffrey Dahmer killed seventeen men over the course of thirteen years. No one suspected him and, in my opinion, he looked like a psychopath."

Ian nodded thoughtfully. "And nobody suspected Ted Bundy for a long time."

"From what I've read, he appeared to be mild-mannered and pretty normal."

"And he killed, what? Over thirty women?"

"I can't recall. That sounds right. So, Charles Odom? Yeah, nothing out of the ordinary stands out about him."

"Follow me." He led me into a sunroom that overlooked his backyard and swimming pool. Rain was pockmarking the surface of the water in the pool. The way the trees, bushes, and shrubbery were planted, the patio and pool were completely private. "This is beautiful, Ian."

"I like to come out here and sit sometimes. It's so relaxing."

"Can I ask you a question?"

He gave me a quizzical expression. "Of course."

"Why aren't you and Stephanie together?"

He offered me that shy grin again. "We are together. Sort of." He glanced out at his flower garden and thought for a moment. "We're both so much alike. Driven to succeed. Me with the company. Stephanie with The Whisper Room. I guess we've never allowed ourselves time to get tied down to another human being."

Then he glanced at me and shrugged. "I feel bad about the way Steph's company ended. Kind of tragic."

It was an interesting perception on the collapse of an escort service, albeit a high-end escort service.

I asked him, "Why did you take time out of your obviously busy schedule to help her? I'm sure you could have assigned someone from your company to do what you were doing."

He pushed his hands endearingly into his pockets. "We grew up together in Greenwich. That can be difficult enough, but Stephanie and I had some things in common. Things that made us different from the other kids. Her mother is from Thailand, and mine is from Syria. That alone made us outsiders."

But I knew there was something else. Would he tell me? "Was there something else?"

He took his hands out of his pockets and folded his arms against his chest. "Did someone tell you about her mother and my mother?"

"That once they were both sex workers?"

He winced, as if my words had caused him some pain.

I continued. "Yet, knowing that, you helped Stephanie put together an escort service."

"After leaving Syria, my mother had been forced into prostitution. While in Thailand, Steph's mom had been sold into prostitution by her own family. Neither of them had a choice. Stephanie and I didn't want to see anybody forced into doing sex work against their will. If they really wanted to earn a living that way, we wanted it to be safe."

"Thank you for being so open."

"Come on, I'll show you the library."

Being the tech guy that Ian was, I was mildly surprised that he would have a library. After all, we lived in the twenty-first century. Everything is on the internet.

But, yes, there were books in Ian's library. Hundreds of them. But in addition, there were vintage arcade games. There was Pac-Man, Centipede, Asteroids, and a half dozen pinball machines. I had a hunch that Ian didn't do a lot of reading in his library.

"Very cool, Ian. I'll bet my daughter and her friends would have a ball in here."

He grinned. "Maybe we'll have to invite them over sometime." Then he turned to me, and his face took on a serious expression. "Do you remember when I asked you if you'd do an exclusive with Charles if it turned out he was a serial killer?"

I felt a tiny chill. "Yes."

"I think I'd better tell you."

"What?"

"I've been tracking his phone. He's been following you ever since you left his condo complex this morning."

Chapter Forty

I turned cold with fear. "Are we in any danger?"

He glanced back at the living area and the front door. "I wouldn't think so. I have a state-of-the-art security system."

"No way a smart, tech-savvy guy like Charles Odom could circumvent it?"

He sighed. "Nothing is absolute, is it? Why don't we see where Charles is right now? He might have seen you drive up here and then gone back home."

"If he suspects I'm on to him, he might already be packing. He's a smart guy. If he disappears, there's no telling how many more women he'll kill. If he's who I think he is, we'll need to let the cops know as soon as possible."

Ian's face registered disappointment. "No exclusive interview?"

I forced a smile. "I'm not tangling with someone who may have already killed thirteen women."

He brightened and grinned back. "Then let's go up to my office, and we'll see where he is now."

We left the sunroom, padded through his living room, then climbed the white carpeted steps. We got to a short hallway, walked past two bedrooms, and then he opened a door to his inner sanctum.

His office was much like how I had imagined his house to be. It was dark. Heavy curtains over the windows blocked out the dim light from the storm outside. The walls were paneled with dark wood and devoid of artwork or photographs. The desk was pushed up against the wall farthest from the doorway.

"This is different," I murmured.

I saw there were three large computer monitors on his desk along with a wireless keyboard and mouse. The room was illuminated by a single brass lamp sitting on his desk. Along with his workspace, there were two cloth couches, one on either side of the room.

"When I'm working, I don't like distractions. I think better when the room is dark and quiet."

"I understand. Where is Charles Odom?"

He moved across the room, sat down at his computer, and pulled up a map, leaning in to get a better view. Then he twisted around so he could look at me and said, "According to this, he's sitting at the end of my driveway."

I got another chill. "Do you have any security cameras?"

"Not where he's parked."

"But he's not moving this way? He's just parked?"

"According to this. But Charles is not stupid. I'm tracking his phone. Not Charles. If he wanted to throw me off the scent, he could leave his phone in the car. I'd have no way of knowing where he was unless he crossed in front of one of my cameras."

I could see on another monitor that the screen was set up like a grid, camera shots around the exterior of Ian's house. I couldn't see any movement at all.

I took stock of the situation and recalled why I was there. "Look, you said you had verification that Charles Odom was in the same cities at the same time those women were all killed."

Ian shook his head. "All sex workers. So tragic. I took a look at our HR records, and sure enough, Charles was in New York, Chicago, San Francisco, and New Orleans on the exact dates those women were murdered. Quantum Digital bought the first-class airfare and hotel rooms. Somehow, I feel complicit. Like I might have had something to do with their deaths."

Seeing the sad expression on his face, I touched him on his forearm. "You had no way of knowing."

He straightened himself back up. "But we can certainly do something now." He sat down at his desk, facing away from me and punched up the travel records he'd talked about. Then he hit the Print button. "I'm going to go get the hard copies. The printer is in the storeroom next to my office." He gestured toward the only chair in the room, his desk chair. "Make yourself comfortable. I'll be right back."

I put my bag down on the floor and sat down in his incredibly comfortable ergonomic chair. I noticed there were no other items on his desk other than the monitors, mouse, and keyboard.

Ian must be incredibly disciplined.

I studied the computer screen with the exterior camera shots. It was difficult to see what was happening in the shadows because of the gray, blowing curtains of rain, but I didn't detect any movement.

How am I going to get past Odom when I leave here?

Maybe the best thing to do would be for me to call Mike Dillon. Tell him that I have evidence that Charles Odom is the serial killer. Get him to escort me off the property and make an arrest.

Or at least open an investigation.

I turned my attention to the screen with Charles Odom's travel records. All the cities corresponded to the dates that those women had been killed.

The third monitor had been asleep but suddenly blinked to

life. It took me a moment to register what I was seeing on the screen. But when I did, I was thoroughly confused. It was a large, color photo of Caroline and Piper, sitting on a picnic table in our backyard.

From the height, I guessed it must have been taken from a drone with a telephoto lens.

But there was no mistake, it was a high-definition photo of the two girls. Who would do such a thing? Had Odom hacked into Ian's computer?

I turned back to the travel records and took a closer look. I leaned in and stared at them. Then I realized what I was staring at.

They weren't Odom's travel records at all.

They're Ian's!

I never heard him come back into the room behind me.

Heavy gauge plastic suddenly was over my head, vision obscured, something tight pulled around my throat!

Fingers scrabbling, I pulled at it. A plastic zip tie was already locked tight around my neck.

Panic stricken, I stood up, struggling for air.

I dug my fingers into the skin on my throat, trying to get under the zip tie.

Need to get air!

From behind, Ian grabbed my left wrist, and I felt another plastic band capture it. Then he tried to grab my right hand to tie them together behind me.

Breathing hard, using too much air still in the bag.

I struggled to keep him from tying my right wrist, kept moving away from his grasp.

No!

Ian's voice was right behind me. "You know, those two girls are exactly my type."

Horrified.

Caroline and Piper. When he's finished with me, he means to kill them.

He struggled to get my right arm in his control.

I pushed my right hand into my jeans pocket, hoping that would make it harder for him to get at my wrist.

Running out of air.

My terror was complete when I heard him whisper, "Come on, Genie, relax. It's okay. Tell me you love me."

No air.

Right hand in my pocket, fingers numb from fear—I felt it.

John's knife.

I yanked my hand out of my pocket. Ian grabbed at it, successfully, yanking it backwards.

I hit the button, praying the blade was out.

Still in his grasp, I used his own strength to reach out behind me, stabbing whatever I could find.

Ian yelped like a dog that had been kicked.

He let go of my wrist and I stabbed blindly at where I thought he was.

Ian whimpered, "Jesus, God, what did you do?"

Suddenly, he released my left wrist.

I turned, expecting to see Ian behind me through the opaque plastic covering.

He's not there.

My vision was fading. I carefully held the plastic surface of the bag away from my face and poked a hole into it. Then sawed a larger opening.

I still can't get a decent breath of air.

The zip tie around my throat.

I was losing consciousness.

I needed to cut the tie. I collapsed to my knees, snaked the blade of the knife between my neck and the plastic zip tie. Then, working fast, I sawed at the tough plastic strip.

When it fell away, I fell forward onto the carpeting, gasping.

It took a few moments for my eyes to begin to clear, and I realized that I was lying in something wet and sticky. I held my hand up in front of my eyes in the dim illumination of that dark room.

Blood.

I glanced around the floor where I lay. Blood, lots of blood.

I got to my knees. There was blood almost everywhere on the carpet.

Looking down, it was on my shirt and jeans from where I'd been lying in it.

Struggling to my feet, legs weak from shock and terror, I stumbled out of Ian's office into the hallway. The lighting was better, and I could clearly see the crimson against the white carpeting, leading to the stairs. Not just droplets, but trails of it on the floor and against the white walls.

Still clutching the knife, I walked to the steps and cautiously descended, amazed at the amount of blood on the carpet.

When I got to the first floor, I saw him. He was sitting on his white couch, naked from the waist up, his black T-shirt balled up and held against his inner thigh.

His eyes were half open, his face and chest were sickly pale. The couch and rug around him were soaked in blood. When he saw me, he offered a weak smile. "You managed to get my femoral artery."

Standing at the bottom of the steps, swaying from side to side, feeling faint, I almost mumbled, "I'm sorry."

But I didn't.

He said in a voice almost too weak to hear, "Called 911. I'm afraid I'll be dead by the time they get here."

I studied him with both fear and sorrow. I asked, "Would you really have gone after Caroline and Piper?"

He blinked, with a half grin on his lips. "Oh, yes."

Then his eyes lost focus, he exhaled, and he was dead.

Chapter Forty-One

No, Charles Odom hadn't been following me. It was part of the trap that Ian had created. Mr. Odom was a soft-spoken, introverted, software engineer. The fact that he and the two murder victims lived in the same condominium complex was just a coincidence.

The Whisper Room app was Ian's baby, so he could move around in it without anyone knowing. For him, choosing Mindy and Kristin to go out on a "date" was child's play. And, true to form, the two girls were petite, blue-eyed blonds. They were Ian's type.

All the women he killed were his type.

I keep thinking of the chill I felt when I saw the photo on the computer screen in that dark room of his. Caroline and Piper sitting on the picnic table in our backyard.

They were both his type!

For two weeks after my near-death experience in Westport, I stayed close to home. Shana helped me through it, helping me to move on through meditation and exercise. She even stopped by once for tea. It was so civilized.

I had no real desire to go anywhere until John Stillwater asked me to join him for dinner. I suggested Bricks. We could have dinner at someplace much fancier, but I wanted a quiet place where we could talk and relax.

He had the veal Parmesan, and I picked at a Caesar salad with blackened chicken.

John poured some Sam Adams from the bottle into a mug that sat in front of him and smiled at me. "So, how was Caroline's birthday party?"

"Her sweet sixteen sleepover? Five girls, one bedroom, no sleep for anyone."

He chuckled. "Anyone sneak in any booze?"

"Who knows? The next morning, I thought I smelled cannabis."

John shrugged. "Teenagers." He snapped his fingers. "Hey, was that girl Piper Edmonds there?"

I smiled. "No, she's back at her tiny apartment, taking classes. I've talked to her and Mr. Mosely Jones, and she seems to be doing okay. She got a better-paying job as the part-time receptionist for an accounting firm."

"No more escorting for her?"

I cringed a little. "No, I think that's behind her."

He took a bite of his veal, chewed, then asked, "Speaking of escorting, what's going on with those two women who owned The Whisper Room?"

"They're starting a boutique distillery in Darien. They're calling it Gin & Things. It was what they had originally wanted to do when they were business majors in college."

"Sounds legal."

"It is. Stephanie's father is even helping to bankroll it. I'm not sure if that's a good idea or not."

John shrugged. "Maybe it'll bring them closer together."

"Mixing family and business? I don't know. Hey, how are those women you rescued from Matt Boca and the cartel?"

He took a swallow of his beer. "The ones who wanted to go back home are back home. The ones who wanted to stay, we've found places for and given new identities."

"Not going through a long and arduous immigration process?"

"We would have helped them if they wanted to do it that way. Not one of them did. Too much of a risk in being sent back to a bad situation." He tapped the top of the table with his fingertips. "I haven't been keeping up with the news. What happened to the blackmail guy?"

I took my fork and speared a tomato. "Gary Racine? He was arrested for blackmail, attempted kidnapping, and solicitation for prostitution. The judge took it all seriously and slapped him with a two million–dollar bond. Apparently, all of Mr. Racine's bail bond connections have dried up because he's still in jail awaiting trial."

John's eyebrows knitted together as he thought. "Help me out here. When Elliot Carlson didn't pay his blackmail demands, Racine sent the video to his wife and every news outlet in a tri-state area. Is he also the one who told Elliot he had evidence that he had killed Mindy Getz?"

I laughed. "Gary Racine is as dumb as the William Hurt character in *Body Heat.*"

In the movie, the protagonist, Ned Racine, falls in love with a married woman, Matty Walker, who persuades him to kill her husband so she can inherit his fortune and they can be together. Ultimately, she runs off to an exotic island, wealthy, and he ends up in prison.

I explained, "Since he's not giving me a jailhouse interview, some of this I have to guess at. He realized he'd made a mistake when he'd released the sex video, essentially torpedoing his girlfriend's successful escort service. Gary hoped to discredit Elliot in the press with accusations that he killed Mindy Getz. All he really did was push Elliot to commit suicide."

Sometimes when I close my eyes at night, I can still see Elliot Carlson, sitting on the floor, with his brains dripping down the wall.

I continued. "Then, when he heard that I'd found Piper, the girl in the video, he panicked and tried to kidnap her off the street. When that didn't work, he called Theo Andino and hoped he'd eliminate the girl altogether."

John shook his head. "He thought that the owner of a dozen successful restaurants would make a woman disappear?"

"Andino doesn't make it a secret that he knows people in low places. It turns out Andino was talking about a developer who invested in his eateries. The developer knew some thugs who sell him grass and blow and who'll do odd jobs for the right price."

"The two jokers who tried to break into your house in broad daylight."

"Yup. My guess is they must have been high."

He took another swallow of beer. "Anybody arrested for that?"

"Nope. The cops have other pressing issues."

"Theo Andino skates?"

"Yup."

There had been a subject we'd avoided. But John came at it head on. "Are you getting any counseling?"

"Why?"

"Your encounter with Ian Minor. I read the police report. You were almost killed."

For a week, I'd had nightmares, bad dreams where Ian Minor puts a bag over my head, and I scramble, searching in my pocket for the knife.

And it's not there.

"I've spent some time talking with Shana. She's been helping me through it."

"Oh?"

"Exercise and meditation. She's had Uri Tal working with me."

"Self-defense?"

"He's a good teacher."

"Is it helping?"

"The nightmares have stopped."

There was an awkward silence, and I thought about what Mike Dillon had told me when they searched Ian's mansion. They'd found photos of all the women he'd killed. In total, there had been twenty-two.

And the collection of trophies. He'd kept their panties, displaying them in glass cases in a large room in his basement.

John whispered, "You're lucky to be alive."

"Only because of the knife you gave me." I patted my leg and felt the hasp. I'd never go anywhere again without it.

He gazed at me from across the table. "So, you picked this place because it doesn't get a huge crowd and it's quiet. Is there something you want to talk about?"

I reached out and took his hand. "Yeah, before you get another assignment from Nathaniel and I don't hear from you for a month or two, I wanted to see if you'd like to stop by and have dinner with Caroline and me. Maybe get to know each other a little better."

He reached up, pushed a lock of hair away from his glasses, and grinned. "Yeah, I'd like that. I guess the cat's out of the bag about you and me?"

"I told her. She turned sixteen, and I think it's time that she knows that you and I are occasionally intimate."

He raised his eyebrows. "Like maybe tonight?"

"As long as you don't say something stupid."

John laughed again. "I'll do my best. What did Caroline say when you told her you and I sleep together every now and then?"

I rolled my eyes. "She said that she'd already known and that it was no big deal."

"Huh." Then something suddenly occurred to him. "She's not sexually active, is she?"

"Lord, I hope not. But something I'm sure of, she's already nagging me for her own freaking car."

He flashed me a big grin. "Maybe Shana will give you a deal on that Mustang of hers."

"Didn't I just tell you not to say something stupid?"

ABOUT THE AUTHOR

Thomas Kies lives and writes on a barrier island on the coast of North Carolina with his wife, Cindy, and Annie, their shih tzu. He has had a long career working for newspapers and magazines, primarily in New England and New York, and is currently working on his next novel.

Allie Miller Photography